BURNED QUEEN

TO DEFEAT HER ENEMIES, SHE MUST JOIN THEM.

ELLIE EMBER

Juniperus Press
Copyright © 2025 Ellie Ember

Paperback: ISBN 979-8-9898701-1-0
Kindle: ASIN B0D7WD4JFK

First paperback edition February 2025.
Second cover edition July 2026.

Cover and interior design by Ellie Ember.
No AI was used in the creation of this book.

BURNED QUEEN

Also by Ellie Ember

Paper Castles

To those who bear the weight of the world,
and to those who help shoulder the burden.

Author's Note

Thank you for picking up *Burned Queen*! Please note this book contains the following content, which may be triggering to some: aftermath of torture, alcohol abuse in a POV character, bombings and mass shootings, death of loved ones, drugging, grief, kidnapping, loss of limb use in a POV character, references to abuse of a POV character, self-harm imagery, terminal illness, violence and death (both in self-defense and otherwise), and mentions of vomiting.

If you have any questions about the content warnings, please feel free to email me at ellieemberwrites@gmail.com.

PART I
THE QUEEN

ONE
ALEXANDRIA

The jagged outline of Genea's capital broke through the horizon, glinting against the grey sea like a set of sharp teeth.

Alexandria clutched the ship's railing, her nerve-damaged arm held stiff by the sling around her shoulder. She had prepared for her meeting with Natania ever since the foreign queen sent her an invitation four months ago. Through the harsh winter, she had warmed her weary muscles in daily sparring sessions with Leianna and maneuvered Kevelda's politics with the Dais and the mayors. Yet even braving a tour of her own country–meeting the sometimes wary, sometimes hopeful gazes of citizens too long forgotten–could not hold a candle to navigating the city that scraped the sky before her.

Her people had fought their conflict with Genea for decades. Now, those who had been drafted were under Natania's power in Thaertos. The ministers seemed oblivious to Mendoza's suggestion that they were not fighting on the island but were being forced to serve their enemy somehow. If she ever wanted answers, she needed to negotiate with Natania, whatever the risks may be.

This could all be a trap.

That truth settled deep in her bones, winding her muscles taut. She bounced on the balls of her feet, tapping her heeled shoes against the deck. A thick black coat made sweat soak her blouse despite the harsh wind whipping her cheeks. She could almost empathize with Minister Greer's plight, with the man keeping his head in a bucket to avoid spilling his guts on the deck.

It wasn't seasickness that plagued her, however. Fear gnawed at her stomach. She blew out a long breath, fighting to keep herself steady. Even this far from shore, she knew the massive buildings would tower over anything she had seen in Kevelda. Her heart thumped against her sternum, making it hard for her to breathe. She squeezed her eyes shut. *Focus, Alexandria.*

If she did not play her cards correctly, she would lose any chance to find out what happened to Phillip after he was drafted. Worse, she might not make it out of the enemy kingdom alive.

But she did not have any cards, did she?

Leianna sidled up to the railing, her head on a swivel as she surveyed the landscape. As Captain of the Queen's Guard, Leianna had become her closest friend–if she used the phrase lightly, of course. In the five months since her husband's execution, the woman had not opened up about her feelings, though Alexandria hoped at times she would.

She had kept secrets from Leianna, too, so she supposed she could not judge her for holding her thoughts near to her chest. The closing sentence from Evangeline's letter flashed behind her eyes.

We can win this war, but only if we work together.

"Are you ready?" Leianna asked, her voice garbled by the wind.

Alexandria shook her head. "No, but it has to be done."

"You've handled the Dais well over the past few months. I can't imagine Queen Natania could be much worse."

She hummed a noncommittal noise, attempting to ignore the bitter taste that flooded her mouth at mention of the Dais.

In her first four months as queen, they had interrogated her about her relationship with Isaac and bombarded her with decisions about the Draft. Not knowing that the former queen was, in fact, alive, well, and apparently in possession of the means to send messages, the Minister of Justice—Erna Wagner—had recommended that Isaac be executed for Evangeline's assassination, since his father could no longer face punishment himself. Alexandria vetoed that proposal as soon as it hit the floor.

She shook away the memory of Isaac walking away from her for the last time. Closed the door in her mind and locked it, just as she had that day in the palace. The day he left. The day she ordered him to go. She would not imagine him standing by her side now. She would not imagine him as her guard, as her–

Her fingers ached as she flexed them.

Now was not the time to dwell on a past she could not change. Unfortunately, the future that lay before her might end as soon as it had begun.

If this was a trap, she had no choice but to walk into it, palm raised. Prime Minister Scottsdöttir–Vada, as she preferred to be called–and Minister Agate had assured her that she was making the right choice by answering the call to Dane. She trusted those two more than the others, but she doubted their judgment now that she stood before the glittering city.

She pressed her hand against her hip to keep it from shaking. Adrenaline coursed through her limbs, a hot fire in her veins.

It's just like one of the queen's galas, she lied to herself. It was not very convincing.

The ship navigated into port, mooring next to a massive military vessel double its length. Multiple ships formed rows along the shore, and despite their differing sizes and equipment, all of them towered above the patrol vessel that brought Kevelda's last hope.

Alexandria's stomach dropped. Was Natania just trying to show off, or was Genea's entire fleet like this?

When the only movement she felt was the waves rocking the boat, she turned away from the railing. She squared her shoulders and held her chin high as she walked toward the boat's captain, who was setting the gangway onto the dock.

Leianna gripped her shoulder. "Wait," she said.

Alexandria tensed, holding her breath.

A swarm of soldiers dressed in Genean silver rounded the corner. They headed straight for the boat, guns drawn. Alexandria threw her hand into the air in a sign of peace. The soldiers either did not notice or did not care.

"State your purpose," the soldier at the front of the pack ordered as they boarded the boat. Three stripes wrapped around the arm of his uniform, the same white color as his buzzed hair. His badge read *Lange*.

Alexandria stepped forward, arm still raised. "I am Queen Alexandria of Kevelda, and I request an audience with Queen Natania." Though she steeled her voice, she could still hear it shake. She hoped none of the soldiers could tell.

Out of nowhere, Lange laughed, a patronizing, irritating sound. The rest of his team joined in a cacophony that took Alexandria aback. Leianna lowered her hand to her gun.

"Her Majesty does not follow the beck and call of other leaders, especially those she is at war with. In fact, I should have you detained."

Alexandria clenched her teeth before responding. "I received an invitation to come when the ice thawed. Do you wish to defy your queen?"

The man stared at her for far too long. Alexandria did not back down. She met his glare with an even sharper one. A twinge of doubt crept into her mind, but she fought hard not to let it show.

If Natania had set her up, she doubted that the soldiers would be completely clueless. The queen would have told them to immediately imprison her or kill her on the spot. This was just a misunderstanding. It had to be.

The war is already lost. What else could she possibly want to take from me?

Lange turned to the woman next to him. Two stripes were sewn onto her silver uniform. "Hold them. I'll be back in a minute."

He spared one last glare at Alexandria before walking the gangway back onto the pier.

The soldiers turned their guns to Alexandria, Leianna, and the rest of her Guard. Minister Greer had not emerged from the depths of the ship. *Better for him,* she thought. One less person to be caught in the crossfire if Natania changed her mind.

Ten soldiers surrounded the six of them. Even if they could reach for their weapons, they were outnumbered. Alexandria cursed herself for thinking this was a good idea. Desperation never led to a positive outcome, and she had been far too desperate to end the war, to keep her friends safe. She vowed not to let her personal history cloud her judgment again.

Lange returned with thinly veiled surprise drawing his eyebrows upward. "Come with me, Queen Alexandria. Alone."

Leianna shifted closer to her side. "No," Alexandria said. "Captain Olivier will come with me."

"That is not what Her Majesty requested." He squared his shoulders and locked eyes with her again.

Alexandria exhaled slowly as she glanced at Leianna. The woman's eyes narrowed before relaxing into an unreadable expression.

"Okay," Alexandria agreed, forcing a civil smile. Desperation, once again. She had nothing to bargain with.

The soldiers did not notice that Leianna slipped an extra dagger into Alexandria's coat as they led her into the city.

She caught a glimpse of towering metal and glass buildings before a soldier gestured for her to enter a black van. The tinted windows made it impossible for her to see where Lange was taking her. Her skin prickled as she thought of what might happen next.

Either she was going to meet the enemy queen, or she was going to end up in a shallow grave. Both outcomes sent a chill down her spine.

After a couple of minutes, the van stilled. Lange opened her door and pulled her out by the wrist. Alexandria wrenched her hand away and straightened her back as she stood. He would not see her stumble.

The van had stopped in a concrete structure that smelled of old fuel. She had the distinct feeling of being underground. No fresh air.

"Peterson, Wilkes, take her to Her Majesty's office," he ordered without breaking eye contact.

Two soldiers emerged from around the car. One of them—Peterson, by the name on his badge—nodded at her before leading the way to an elevator. Alexandria followed, the other soldier trailing behind her. She softly patted her coat pocket as the doors closed, checking to see if the dagger still rested there.

Her ears popped as they ascended. The elevator shaft transformed into glass, allowing her to observe the capital.

Across the courtyard that separated the tower from the rest of the city, a crowded cluster of buildings clawed at the clouds. They became a kind of parasite, shifting and spreading beyond her field of view as the elevator granted her a higher perspective. Their reflective metal siding created kaleidoscopic images of the streets below, of crystal fountains and perfect squares of grass. Alexandria had never seen anything like it.

She had believed that Regia was the height of luxury, but its white plaster buildings seemed centuries older than the glass oasis that surrounded her. They likely were, since most of Kevelda's architecture had existed before the Fall. Genea had not just survived the devastation but grew out of it.

Alexandria became more convinced with every passing second that this meeting was no peace offering at all.

She inhaled sharply as the elevator doors opened. The room was spacious, with giant windows for walls. If the slight reflection of her and the soldiers did not trail across the glass, Alexandria might have thought there was nothing keeping her from tumbling off the side of the building.

The woman in the middle of the room made her pause. She reclined behind a hardwood desk, glancing up at Alexandria as the three entered.

Everything about the woman was cold, from her ash brown hair to her pale skin. Her eyes flashed a sharp blue. As she stood, her tall frame moved like water, a graceful flowing walk gained from years of practice. Where Evangeline was elegant in the way of a soldier trained for battle, Natania was a queen trained for conquest.

Six years ago, Natania became the Queen of Genea after her father's death. Alexandria didn't know if he died of natural causes, but she supposed it did not matter now. Vada had informed her that Natania was seventeen at the time of her coronation, or at least when she had sent her first war communication. She was two years older than Alexandria, and while she did not expect to be friends with the woman, she hoped that the queen's age would make her more inclined to a partnership.

"Queen Natania," Alexandria began, clearing her throat to make her voice stronger. Natania's eyes pierced right through her facade.

"You will call her 'Your Majesty,'" Wilkes snarled, sending a jolt through Alexandria's body.

Will I? Though the other queen had all the power in the room, Alexandria would not forget the title she now possessed.

"She will do no such thing," Natania responded, waving Wilkes's comment off. "We're equals. You may leave us."

The two soldiers nodded, returning to the elevator. Once they disappeared behind the metal door, the queen sidled up to Alexandria, shaking her hand. "You may call me Natania."

"Alexandria," she responded, moving alongside the queen as she returned to her desk.

"You're here for peace." Natania did not intend it as a question.

"Yes, I am."

"I have a solution for you, then. Join the Genean Coalition."

Alexandria stiffened. "No," she said without a thought. She would not give up her power so easily, not when she could finally use it for good. The Dais had warned her about this possibility. Kevelda's former allies, Victori and Duarmme, had joined Genea years ago and lost their ability to make the best choices for their people.

Natania shook her head. "Mendoza would have been much easier to deal with."

"Mendoza is dead," Alexandria snapped.

The queen laughed sharply before narrowing her eyes. "And who do you think made that happen?"

TWO
ALEXANDRIA

Alexandria snapped her teeth together to keep her jaw from dropping.

"Why would you kill him? What could you possibly gain?" she asked. Her hands clenched under the desk.

"He failed. I don't tolerate failure." Natania swept her eyes across Alexandria's face, taking in every emotion hiding underneath the surface. "You have more questions, I know."

She bit the inside of her cheek. Mendoza had failed Natania, which meant that he had been working *for* her. It shocked Alexandria for a moment before she remembered how vile Mendoza was, and then it did not surprise her at all. He had aimed to kill Alexandria and take the throne for himself, but it went deeper than that. He knew the war was over. That could leave one solution.

"Mendoza was going to surrender Kevelda to the Coalition."

"Took you long enough." Natania's sarcasm did not contain any hint of humor, only a cutting chill.

"You promised him something in return, didn't you? A position in your government maybe, though I can't imagine he had much to negotiate with."

"I promised him comfort and the ears of my advisors. He knew Kevelda had no chance of winning if my forces decided to strike."

"I don't accept," Alexandria gritted out.

"I didn't offer. Within the Genean Coalition, you will retain your title. Kevelda will be autonomous."

"But you'll take and take and take until we wish we weren't. Until my people beg for you to provide for us."

"The Coalition will require some investment, yes. I require the same of all members."

"I don't accept," Alexandria repeated. "I will not allow you to take resources from my people."

"You believe Kevelda provides more than it actually can. Truthfully, your kingdom is in shambles. Your farms and greenhouses don't produce enough food for the people in your borders. You have less technological capabilities than what Genea took underground a hundred years ago. Your people are weak and untrained, even the soldiers you send to fight mine. You have nothing to give that I cannot take."

The declaration twisted a dagger in her stomach. She ran her tongue along the inside of her teeth, training her expression into neutrality. "Then what do you want?"

"Why do you think we've been fighting over Thaertos all these years?"

Alexandria did not care. She wanted to scream at Natania to just give her a straight answer. "Tell me."

Natania leaned forward onto her elbows, her eyes piercing down to Alexandria's core. "When the Old World tore itself apart, the countries that survived thought the threat was over, that the weapons they used were impossible to recreate. Genea found the key to creating them again in Thaertos. The mineral just had to be mined."

"And you want people to mine it," Alexandria said. *Slaves for Natania's activities in Thaertos,* she recalled Mendoza saying. Her lungs fought to take in oxygen. "The world ended the last time countries had this power, and you want to create it again."

"Don't look at me like I'm the villain, Alexandria, when all I'm doing is keeping my people safe. It is in the best interest of the Coalition to control these resources before someone else can develop them."

"You cannot expect my people to help you."

"They already are. Most of your soldiers have been captured and sent to the mines. We already have the first of the bombs developed."

Alexandria's heart stopped. Her mouth went dry, any response lost amongst the turmoil in her mind.

"I pity you," Natania continued. "You never could have won, and you can't win now. Yet, I watched you fight in that throne room. I appreciate your mettle. So, I'll give you one last chance. Join us."

Kevelda had no options. She would have to give in to the Genean Coalition, no matter what it required. Her people would hate her, blame her for the decision she made, but it was really no choice at all. If Evangeline knew Natania was going to ask this of her, Alexandria had no idea how the former queen would want her to respond. It didn't matter, not now.

"What will you demand of us?"

A smile spread slowly across Natania's face. "All of your workers in Thaertos will serve in the mines on a rotation. When they are not mining, they may return home to Kevelda. More people may be required to serve at any time, and it will be your responsibility to select them for me."

Though the arrangement was not ideal, it seemed too good to be true. Her people would be forced to work for Genea, but at least they would be able to see their families. "Why not force all of them to continue?"

"Exposure to the mineral has side effects. Rotating shifts will make the workers last longer."

Nausea settled like a weight in Alexandria's stomach. She would not simply be signing her people up to work for the enemy. They would die. Tears threatened to spill over her eyelids as she thought of Phillip, of the pain he might have endured while he wasted away.

"I won't let my people suffer."

"Before you give your final answer," Natania replied, "perhaps she can convince you."

The queen pressed a button on a device at the corner of her desk and called for Peterson. Before Alexandria had a chance to wonder what she meant, the elevator doors opened.

Amira stumbled out, her hands held behind her by the two soldiers who had led her to the queen's office. Alexandria knocked over her chair as she rose.

"You're the one that took her," Alexandria spat at Natania. She could not decide whether to lunge at the queen or rush to her friend's side. Her legs carried her over to Amira before she considered for another second.

"Did they hurt you?" Alexandria asked, brushing her friend's hair behind her ear. She glared at the soldiers. They did not bother to meet her gaze.

Amira didn't appear injured, but the glassy look in her eyes hinted at the horrors Natania put her through. Her golden-brown hair had a muted hue, even more than it did in the winters without much sun. Her skin, too, held a pallor that made her look sick.

Had they kept her underground this whole time? *She's been here for five months.*

"They made me work for them," Amira whispered. "I had to do it. They threatened Sam."

Everyone in the room could hear them, but Alexandria did not care. Fire tore at her chest at the thought of Amira being imprisoned. "What did they make you do?"

"I built the device that killed Mendoza." Her voice cracked. "I couldn't let them hurt him. I'm so sorry."

Alexandria's muscles strained to keep her still, to prevent her from doing something rash. "It's not your fault," she said, turning back to Natania. "It's hers."

"Amira has been a wonderful asset to us, and I have no doubt she will continue to be, with the developments in Thaertos." Natania walked toward them, her silky gait incongruent with the threat lining her words.

"I won't let you force her into building your weapons."

"It seems you've forgotten that you cannot stop me. I have treated her well, but I will only keep doing so if you give me a reason to. You either agree to my terms, or your kingdom will fall. Choose wisely."

The people of Kevelda would blame Alexandria either way. They would suffer in Thaertos's mines, or they would die at Genea's hands. Only four months since she had taken the throne, and now she would lose her kingdom. It might still be hers, but in name alone. Everything she had, she would be forced to give it to Natania. To the Genean Coalition.

She met Amira's eyes, chest aching at the guilt she found there. Her best friend, who had already sacrificed so much for her family, had worked with Genea to save them.

Alexandria would tear this kingdom down for what its queen had done to her friends. She would take it apart wall by wall, shatter its glass windows and crystal fountains. All the buildings may be made of metal, but she would find a way to burn them down, until they were nothing more than paper set ablaze.

She would only play Natania's game until she found a way to win.

Alexandria wrapped her arm around Amira's shoulders. The soldiers tensed at her movement, but they allowed it.

"I'll come back for you," she whispered, "I promise. I'll keep Sam safe, and I will get you out of here."

Amira shook her head against Alexandria's neck. "Don't let her use me against you. If you have to decide between me and Kevelda, choose your people."

"*You* are my people." A single tear slid down her cheek. She loathed that the guards were watching. When she pulled away, her fury drove her to face Natania once more. "How many people, and for how long?"

"Eight hundred workers on a six-month rotation."

"I'll give you four hundred for two months." Even if she handed more people over in the end, spending less time in Thaertos per shift might save them. She let that hope take root in the ruins of her dream that they might all escape unscathed.

Natania's eyebrow quirked. "That much movement with such short turnover is a security risk. I assume you know that."

Her jaw tightened. She clutched the fabric of her coat. "I don't care about your security and what I might do with it. If given the choice to keep my people healthier longer, I'll take it."

"Six hundred for three months. Choose them however you desire. You will send them without weapons. My officers will handle the rest."

The sight of Amira's distressed appearance reminded her what was at stake. If simply working on the weapons could do that to her friend, she did not want to imagine the destruction they could bring if used on her people.

"I'll take your deal," she said with as much strength as she could muster.

"Alexandria—" Amira began to protest, but the soldiers pulled her back into the elevator before she could finish. Her green eyes flashed with panic, arms twisting against their grip. "Don't take me back down there, please!"

Alexandria ran to the doors as they closed and slammed her fist against them. "No!" she screamed. "Bring her back!"

She rested her forehead against the metal. Regret flooded her as she realized the weakness she had shown. Natania knew just where to twist the knife.

The enemy queen's presence shifted the air behind her. "The Genean Coalition will be honored to welcome Kevelda as a member." Her tone implied anything but that.

Ice filled Alexandria's veins. "Have them bring Minister Greer and I'll sign your treaty."

Green still colored the contours of her Foreign Affairs minister's face when he emerged from the elevator some time later. The lines between his white brows deepened as she explained the arrangement they had made in his absence. He could not fight it, same as she.

Both of them scrawled their signatures onto the two copies. One for Natania to showcase to her court, and one for Alexandria to read to the Dais. Her ministers' reactions would chip away at her resolve, but she would hold fast. It was her only choice.

Five months ago, Mendoza had named her the heir. Four months ago, she sat on the throne. And yet, until that very moment, she had not known the full weight of her crown, not truly.

With the spilling of ink, she had either saved her people or damned them.

THREE
ALEXANDRIA

Leianna sent a sharp elbow into Alexandria's side.

She set her teeth against the burst of pain and tried sweeping her captain's leg out, but Leianna blocked it, sending Alexandria sprawling to the packed earth. The sliver of sunshine peeking over the palace walls warmed her face as she lay on the grass. When she didn't rise, Leianna crouched next to her.

"Too much?" she asked.

Alexandria coughed. "Training with my best agent is supposed to teach me something." Despite her bruised pride—it hadn't been wholly intact since she signed Natania's treaty two months ago—she took her captain's outstretched hand. Dirt and grass stains splattered her old denim, but she didn't bother to try wiping them away, knowing her back must look much more disastrous.

"You've made progress." Leianna shot a glance to Prior and Lawton, the other on-duty agents of the Queen's Guard, that she pretended not to see.

Lawton stepped forward and handed Alexandria's dagger back to her. "I agree," he said.

"You're duty-bound to tell me that." The blade weighed at her waist when she slid it back into its sheath. "What do you think, Prior?"

Prior, as per usual, shifted uneasily at her direct attention. He was younger than Lawton, who appeared to be in his forties, but by how much, Alexandria couldn't tell. None of her guards were new to this; Leianna made sure to select experienced agents for her team. Still, failing to protect her would be as good as treason, and she understood his desire to put as much professional distance between them as possible.

The last time an agent got too close, it might have saved her life, but thinking of him also kept her awake at night.

Prior responded, but she didn't perceive his answer from so deep in her own head, so she simply nodded and turned back to Leianna. "Let's go again."

They went a couple more rounds, Alexandria failing to gain any real advantage each time, yet Leianna was a shockingly patient teacher. She pointed out adjustments to her stance and showed her how to defend herself with one arm.

Six months ago, when she first lost use of her right arm, these sparring lessons had been demoralizing. Her body was no longer the one she had grown to know. It still felt that way at times, like the woman staring back at her in the mirror was a stranger, scars marring her once-smooth skin. Now, she was more equipped to fight, but the mental battle would trouble her for far longer.

Defeating Natania was her priority. Everything else could wait, shoved into the depths of her mind, resurfacing only when the tide of war turned in her favor.

That resolution chipped when Beckett, another of her guards, appeared in the courtyard with a message from Vada. The ship carrying the workers home from Thaertos had just been spotted. And with that crack in her resolve, a sliver of hope bled through.

Phillip.

Alexandria searched for him in the faces of every person who disembarked the ship. They staggered down the gangway, listless and lifeless, as if rising from one grave only to walk into another. Some had Phillip's blonde hair, others had his blue eyes, but none had his smile. She still remembered that smile, bright enough to bring light to the darkest of rooms, just as she would always remember the way he kissed her the last time she saw him.

Try as she might, she could not stop that memory from evoking another one, one she wanted to forget more than anything else: the dream of Isaac taking Phillip's place, pressing his lips against hers. The vision that had carried her through her hypothermic daze, held upright by a man who used a different name. *Carter.*

She shook her head, focusing on the stream of workers instead of the two people she could not have.

No, she thought, *there's still hope for Phillip. He has to be here.*

Some of the workers had bandages wrapping their limbs, while others had scars and bruises on their faces. Their cheeks were hollow, eyes vacant.

Alexandria had tried to bring them home earlier, but after joining the Genean Coalition, there were still logistics to be sorted. The terms of their treaty had to be fleshed out, and she had needed to make the announcement to her citizens. That speech had been met with cries of indignance, shouts of anger, calls for her abdication.

Today, the workers who saw her only took her in with that distant expression. She was just as much a phantom to them as a savior. Their freedom had been given by her hand, but Natania was pulling the strings.

Or maybe they didn't know a thing about what had happened in Kevelda, and Alexandria was overthinking the way they looked—or didn't look—at her.

She tried to shake the hands of those who were not injured. Though she had gotten used to shaking with her left hand since her ascension, it felt awkward at times, ghosts of muscle memory tripping her up. Here and there, a worker would smile in response to her reaching out. Polite, but not real.

A woman who appeared much younger than the eighteen years required for the Draft nearly toppled over as she tripped onto the dock. Alexandria caught her arm, the guard next to her lunging forward in tandem. Whether he did so to help the woman or protect her from an invisible threat, she did not know.

It had taken three months after the Campaign for her to bear being close to anyone. If she heard a noise behind her or felt someone coming up to her side, she immediately dropped her hand to her knife. Instinct still made her do so, but the panic that rose in her chest at their approach had dwindled over time. Perhaps it had just become a part of her, seeping into her muscles and bones.

"Are you alright?" Alexandria asked, threading her arm under the woman's shoulders.

Her straw-colored hair blew between her cracked lips, but the woman seemed too weak to move it. The yellow strands paled her complexion beyond what Alexandria thought possible.

"I will be," the woman said, "now that I'm home."

Until you're sent back. It would be a few months, ideally a year, until the rotation pulled her in again. All these workers would return to the mines. That was the deal.

The wind grazed Alexandria's skin as if Natania herself was breathing down her neck.

She turned to her guard, a new appointee whose name she could not remember. "Take her to the medic."

Despite the general public not knowing the mineral would ravage their bodies, she had asked the Minister of Health, Ben Sawyer, to set up clinics to keep the workers healthy as long as possible. The trembling woman on her arm showed her how futile that effort was.

"Really, I'm fine," the woman murmured.

The guard flicked his eyes between her and Alexandria. "I can't leave my post. Captain Olivier's orders."

"Is Leianna the queen now? I hadn't heard that news. How exciting." She raised her eyebrows until the guard took the woman by the hand and led her away.

His compliance made her feel like a stranger in her own skin. She detested using her position to get anything, but that was how the world worked now. And she needed a lot of things.

Phillip, she told herself, as she pictured Isaac's face. She let herself wonder, for the blink of an eye, where her Protector and her friend had been those past six months. If Natania was holding Amira hostage, then his and James's investigation was far off course. The alternative struck her like a blow to the chest.

No, she rationalized, *Natania would use them against me if she could.*

As the last few workers trailed out, she hugged and greeted and smiled at the group that had gathered. They waited for their families, eyes finally sparking with hope and longing. Some had come back to find loved ones gone, lost to sorrow or hunger—or simple old age, that elusive creature. All of them ached for home.

None of them were Phillip. There was no home for Alexandria to go back to.

After she spoke a few words of gratitude and encouragement to the workers, grief tugging at her heart like an old friend, her guards whisked her back to her armored vehicle.

Alexandria did not realize how tight her lungs had been until she slumped against the seat. She shook out the adrenaline buzzing through her arm.

The sun drew orange lines in the sky as it began its descent into night. She would return to the palace, review all the memoranda that had made their way onto her desk during her absence, and then retire to her bedroom without speaking to anyone unless absolutely necessary. That was how she had spent most of her nights since ascending, but especially now that she had sold out her country, people who wished to talk to her were scarce.

Leianna understood that Alexandria did what she had to do, but the woman was not one to make small talk. Alexandria didn't realize how much she missed pointless conversations. Now, everything was life or death. Deciding which lives to put at risk for their three-month work mandates in Thaertos. Meeting with the mayors, who resented her power, though she really had none. Keeping her people happy, or at least content enough not to try to kill her.

She scanned the waterline, praying that another boat would somehow arrive, and that it would be carrying a familiar face.

A vehicle pulled up next to them as they waited at an intersection. She caught a glimpse of the driver's face before a bright light exploded.

Her head slammed into the window. Ringing filled her ears. Muffed voices broke through, but the warm trickle up her temple distracted her. She brought her hand to her face, and when she pulled it away, red stained her skin.

It was then that she realized she was hanging upside down. Blood rushed to her head, the pressure building in her temples as she sat there. She fumbled with the seatbelt. Without it holding her to the seat, she dropped onto the roof, catching herself with her elbow just in time to keep her neck from breaking.

She flipped herself upright, ripping her dress on shattered glass. The sleeve slipped down her moving arm. The old wound in her shoulder burned, new ones sending lances of pain through her limbs as she clambered out of the broken window.

"Your Majesty!" someone shouted. She ignored them. The smoke made it impossible to discern which direction she was crawling in. Crackling and popping sounded next to her. Her instincts forced her away from it.

A noise like a gunshot spliced through the cotton that filled her head. Heat singed her skin. She looked back to find the armored vehicle on fire.

The question of what had happened lingered in the back of her mind, but she had to keep going. She dragged herself across the glass and gravel. Pieces punctured her skin. Her teeth ached as she gritted them, and she lurched forward, pulling herself to the side of the street.

A callused hand gripped her arm. She recoiled before realizing it was Leianna.

The captain dragged her to her feet and supported her as they stumbled through an alley. Leianna spoke into the radio attached to her shoulder. Harsh static greeted her. "No one's in range. Where are they?"

Alexandria opened her mouth but found her tongue too heavy to move. She spit blood onto the ground. It dribbled onto the white cotton of her dress, stark against the soot and ash that marred it.

After a few blocks, she was finally able to speak. "Did the new guard make it out?"

Leianna shook her head. They staggered the rest of the way to the tunnel that led to the medical wing.

"Get inside. I have to go back and find the others."

"I'll come with you." A rattling cough joined her bold proclamation.

"You make my job impossible."

Before Alexandria could protest again, Leianna shoved her into the dim corridor and slammed the door shut behind her.

~

The next morning, after having been kept up all night by the palace doctor, who had wanted to monitor her injuries, Alexandria limped into the throne room.

All six Dais ministers sat around the table in the center, waiting for her to take the seat nearest the throne. She squinted against the colored light from the stained-glass windows as she made her way across the floor.

Leianna entered through the main doors. Alexandria sighed in relief. At least she wouldn't have to explain everything that had happened yesterday.

"Do you have a report for us?" Alexandria asked.

Leianna bowed slightly, making eye contact with each of the ministers before answering. "I don't have all the details yet, but this appears to be an attack by a group of subversives."

"Which ones?"

"Ones who do not look fondly upon your leadership."

Again, I ask, "Which ones?" Alexandria thought. She spoke aloud, "Do you have any more information about this group?"

"The driver of the vehicle set off an explosive device when he stopped next to you. He is, unfortunately, not alive to give us any more information."

Realization sent a spear through her heart. Not only did a group of people want her dead, but they desired it so much that they would kill themselves to take her down.

With her silence, Leianna continued, "However, we did apprehend a woman running away from the explosion who was seen speaking with the driver beforehand. We will be interrogating her shortly."

Alexandria nodded. "Work with Minister Wagner to set up an investigation task force. And keep me updated on the woman. I would like to see her once you're finished."

"I don't–" Leianna stopped mid-sentence, as if realizing they were still surrounded by the ministers, and she should not argue with her queen.

Alexandria wished she would just finish her thought—Leianna never hesitated to question her otherwise—but she would have to talk to her captain afterwards.

"I will arrange that," Leianna said.

"Thank you, Captain Olivier."

Leianna barely escaped before multiple ministers attempted to speak at once. Alexandria pointed at Minister Wagner and the rest of them quieted. Her head throbbed at the reedy sound of the woman's voice.

"Minister Agate and I believe that it is in the best interest of Kevelda that you cancel the upcoming Coalition gala," the woman said.

Vada answered before Alexandria could come up with a response. "You know how fragile our relationship with Genea is. That is an impossible ask, no matter the safety concerns. Especially with what we now know of Mendoza's death. Queen Natania is watching our every move."

Alexandria had told the Dais that the enemy queen was behind the former Prime Minister's death; after weighing the decision her entire journey back to Regia, she knew that they needed all the motivation they could get to agree to the treaty. Her people, on the other hand, still thought Mendoza had died of injuries obtained while challenging her, and that he had planned Queen Evangeline's assassination. While Alexandria had provided Kevelda with a half-truth, given that Leianna *had* stabbed the man multiple times, reality was much more terrifying.

Genean spies could be anywhere—Leianna had scoured the throne room for listening devices, and she only allowed vetted Queen's Guard members to stand outside the doors, but they could not be entirely sure of their privacy. Alexandria tried to remember that, burying her true feelings about Natania as best she could.

"I second that," she said, grateful that Vada was on her side. Though she believed at first that the Prime Minister had disliked her, she quickly understood that the woman wanted the best for Kevelda. She just had to convince Vada that *she* was the best for Kevelda.

"This is not our event to cancel. Natania is the one in charge of gathering everyone here. I'm simply opening the doors to our new *allies*." The word was bitter on her tongue.

Minister Agate chimed in. "In the interest of your safety, Your Majesty, please reconsider."

"Thank you for your concern," she responded, without her usual sarcasm, "but once again, this event is important for us. We have to show Genea that we are on its side."

"But are we?" Minister Greer asked. He folded his hands on the table.

"You of all people should know that we must be, if we don't want to be destroyed. Those bombs will not only kill our people but will make our land uninhabitable. We cannot recover from a fight against them."

"At this rate, our people will destroy themselves before Genea has the chance," Minister Wagner retorted.

"It is your job to make sure that doesn't happen, minister." Pain slammed like a battering ram into her skull. "This is my final answer. We *are* hosting the Coalition gala, and I will not be convinced otherwise. If you do not understand why this is necessary, then I will make sure to replace you with someone who does."

The ministers stared back at her in silence. She did not realize how loudly she had been speaking until remnants of her voice echoed from the walls. Her teeth clenched as she rose from the table, joints stiff and muscles tight.

"We're done for the day. You're dismissed."

FOUR

ISAAC

Of the last hundred and seventy-nine days, not one had gone by that Isaac didn't think about Alexandria.

He turned on the rusted faucet in the corner of his room and splashed icy water onto his face. The chill seeped into his bones. It jolted him awake, even though he had hardly slept for the past few months. Years, really.

One month into his and James's search for Amira, Evangeline's rebels had found them and brought them to the abandoned hotel they used as a base. They decided to stay with the group to see if the former queen knew anything about Amira's whereabouts. And then, before he realized it, he had gotten sucked back into Evangeline's plans.

Alexandria wouldn't let him come back, even if he did find Amira. Not with all the secrets he had kept from her. The utter betrayal on her face after she found out he was Mendoza's son haunted him. He had to fix it, even if she never knew.

Someone knocked on the door. He opened it to find Reagan standing there. The young girl was the first person they had sought after leaving the palace—Isaac's suggestion, though James begrudgingly agreed, not wanting to waste any time. She had been holed up in the shack he and Alexandria had stumbled across during the Campaign, almost like she had been waiting for them to come back for her. He could not bear the thought of leaving her there, and once she told him that her twin brother had died, a combination of starvation and sickness, he was even more grateful they found her when they did.

"The General wants you," she said. After recovering from her malnourishment, the girl looked older than she had in the forest. She eventually told Isaac she was fourteen.

Still too young for what she's had to endure.

"Tell the *General* I'll be down in a second." He regretted the sarcasm in his voice after he spoke. Reagan wasn't the person he was angry at. There was no one he could be mad at but himself. Evangeline, or the General, as the rebels called her, wasn't dead, even though he had carried the guilt of killing her during the Campaign. Sometimes he wished she actually *had* died so that all his lies and shame hadn't been for nothing. "Thank you for letting me know."

The girl smiled back at him. She looked like a little soldier in her all-black outfit, her auburn hair set in two plaits down her back. He was proud of how quickly she had gotten to work in the organization–until he remembered who they were working for, and the very complicated history he had with the woman.

As he walked down the hall, walls lined with ripped wallpaper and carpets plastered with decades-old stains, he wondered what Evangeline could possibly want to talk to him about. Ever since the attack on Alexandria's vehicle, he'd been itching to leave the group and make sure she was okay. Evangeline was smart for not telling him about it in advance. His allegiance to Alexandria kept him there, solely to keep an eye on the former queen's movements.

When Alexandria had announced that Kevelda would join the Genean Coalition, the number of people in their organization soared. It was like Evangeline had known that Alexandria would be forced into a position that would turn her people against her, and she had laid the infrastructure to take the throne again, if only from the shadows. He couldn't imagine what she was playing at.

At first, the rebels were a small militia preparing to undermine Genea one way or the other. Evangeline had been secretive about her plans, not even hinting anything to him, while the soldiers trained for an undefined mission. Now, despite their highest goal being to take down Natania, they had Alexandria in their sights.

"Mendoza," Evangeline said as he entered the suite that served as her office.

He bristled at the use of his last name. That was what they did here.

The abandoned hotel made for an interesting hideout. A torn mattress had been set on its side against the wall, the table pulled into the center of the room. Once he spotted the three other rebels, he knew why Evangeline had used his surname, instead of his first name like she did in private.

"General." He saluted without much care, his mind occupied by Alexandria's wellbeing.

Evangeline's eyebrow twitched. She'd noticed his inattention. His shoulders stiffened and he stared forward.

She pulled out a chair and motioned for everyone to do the same. He folded his hands to keep from tapping his fingers on the table. Evangeline needed him to be the loyal agent he always had been, no hesitation, no wavering.

He was Carter today.

"I've gathered you here because I have reason to believe I can trust you. Is that correct?"

They all nodded, not making eye contact with one another. This was their chance to prove that they deserved to be in her inner circle. He knew how deadly that ambition could be.

"Good," she continued. "I am putting you in charge of a mission. The three other kingdoms of the Genean Coalition will be gathering in the palace next week. You will do whatever it takes to kill Natania in the throne room."

"The palace will be heavily guarded, even more than usual. They'll kill us if we attack her, let alone if we even get in," the woman to his left argued.

"Take out as many guards as you have to, anyone who stands in your way."

Isaac's fingers tightened around each other. "Even our own?"

"You've done worse, Mendoza."

The words bit into his skin, gnawing at his chest. They knocked the wind out of him in their truthfulness. He had executed every one of her political opponents, at her and his father's request. Most were innocent. Some had served her. This would be no different.

"What about Alexandria?" the man across from him asked. His face revealed nothing of his thoughts. Isaac hoped he looked the same, even as his paralyzed lungs fought for breath.

"Do what you must." Her eyes bore into Isaac's. "Is that clear?"

He told his muscles to nod, but he couldn't tell if they listened. She knew exactly what she was doing, forcing him to prove his loyalty, to finally decide between the two queens.

Evangeline, the one who had cared for him even when his father didn't. Who had taken him in, given him duties he would excel at. Who had trained him to be the perfect soldier.

Alexandria, who, for the first time in a decade, had showed him that he didn't have to be.

With each passing day, it grew harder for him to choose the devil he had known for so long.

Scuffling noises alerted him to the rest of the soldiers' dismissal. He pushed up from the table, stopping short when

Evangeline held up a hand. He sat back in the chair, his eyes downcast as her shape shadowed the grain of the wood. With a sharp-nailed finger, she raised his chin, directing him to look up at her.

"What has she done to you?" she asked. It wasn't anger that laced her words, but something like sadness. Nostalgia. Disappointment.

He tried to break eye contact but couldn't. "I don't know what you mean."

"I know you. I was one of the first to see you after you were born. I have spent years protecting you, guiding you. Never once have you questioned me. You always knew that what we *want* to do and what we *have* to do are often different." She brought her face level with his. "You would do anything to bring Natania down, wouldn't you?"

His head said, *no, not anything*, but the signals crossed on their way to his mouth. "Yes."

"Remember who you're doing this for." With those words, she departed, leaving him with nothing but his spinning thoughts and the echo of the door clicking shut.

The sun had risen by the time he could move. He had to do something, stop this plan before it began. But with three other soldiers on the mission, any move he made would send alarms straight to Evangeline. If he couldn't stop them from attacking the gala, he would have to do the next best thing: get Alexandria out of there.

He started down the hall with one thought in his mind. His plan could fail and get him killed. Evangeline did not tolerate disloyalty, and while he hoped she cared enough about him to spare him, he could not take the chance. Especially with Reagan still at her mercy.

Before he could dissuade himself, he was at James's door. In the past five months, James had secured the trust of many of the rebels, hoping to find clues about Amira. He wasn't much of a fighter, but he channeled his anger into their training. When they weren't working, Isaac watched as James joked with the other soldiers, reminiscing about parallel adolescent memories they all shared, mugs of beer in hand. Isaac was still separate from them, Evangeline's favorite, and even if he wasn't, he couldn't relate to their trysts and tales.

He and James had decided to not be seen talking to one another, lest the group catch onto their search for information. He sometimes wondered if Evangeline had won James over, even after all his talk about not trusting anyone from the capital, but Isaac had no one else to rely on when it came to keeping Alexandria safe.

After surveying the hallway, he knocked softly. His muscles twitched as he waited. *Hurry up, James.*

James had no sense of self-preservation. He opened the door wide, wiping crust out of his eye. Pieces of his red hair straggled across his face. "Hello?"

"Good morning to you, too," Isaac said, pushing inside. He pressed the door shut. "I need to talk to you."

"It couldn't wait until after breakfast?"

He tracked the height of the sun through the half-cracked blinds. "You missed breakfast. Shocker."

"I'm still not used to this whole military schedule."

"You're going to have to get used to it, because I might not be here to help you."

Those words woke James up. "What? If you found a lead on Amira, I'm coming with you."

"No, I didn't." He calculated the risk of his next sentence, though he supposed coming there held enough danger on its own. "I need to know whose side you're on."

James's brows furrowed. Isaac watched the wheels spin in his mind. He was calculating, too. From what James could tell, Isaac was a loyal soldier. He would have to lay his cards down.

"Are you here to serve Evangeline?" Isaac asked.

"I would never serve Evangeline," James whispered harshly. "I'm here to find Amira, and you said this is our only lead."

He had long accepted that the rebels likely weren't involved in Amira's kidnapping. James didn't need to know that.

"Then I sure hope you're a good actor. I'm going to do something that will probably get me killed. Whether Evangeline executes me or I die before then, you have to convince her you're on her side. Undermine her from within. Do whatever it takes to keep her from hurting Alexandria. Can you do that?"

"Of course." James shrugged on his jacket and swiped his hair in place. "What is it you plan on doing?"

"It's better if you don't know."

"Is she planning another attack on Alexandria? Are you going to stop it?" When he didn't answer, James grabbed his shoulder. "Let me help. She's my family."

"You can help by staying alive and putting yourself at Evangeline's side."

"They've already almost killed her once, and even if you succeed, they'll try again."

"We'll have to keep stopping her, then." He crossed his arms. James was right; it would never end, not unless they did something more drastic. They had to be careful. Any move would have to come from within Evangeline's ranks. "How well do you know the other soldiers?"

"I can gauge a few of them, their motivations for being here." A sly smile crept onto his face. "You want me to turn them?"

Isaac matched his expression, despite the doubt seeping into his mind. "Let's build an army of our own."

FIVE

ALEXANDRIA

A sharp pain stabbed Alexandria's chest as she stared at the wooden door shielding her from the throne room. Her head still ached from the attack a week prior, though the dim light streaming through the windows no longer bothered her. She prayed that her guests' voices mingling together wouldn't give her a migraine. To survive the Coalition gala, she would need a clear mind.

The imprisoned rebel had given them no information about who arranged the attack, whether they were organized or acted alone. Her agents did their best to secure the palace, but the unknown weighed in her stomach. She would not be the only casualty if that night went awry.

Leianna opened the door from the other side and signaled to the agent currently watching Alexandria's back. "It's secure."

She stifled a gasp at the size of the crowd. Her lungs would not expand even if she hadn't been wearing a stiffly structured dress, the boning of which currently poked into her bust. Leianna had to help her into it, a duty that she surely did not expect with her promotion. Alexandria promised to ask the former queen why she insisted on stocking her wardrobe with torture devices when she spoke to her next.

If she ever did. Evangeline had not sent another message since Alexandria's visit to Genea, and she had no clue how to find the woman. She thought about sending her guards to look for her, but something stopped her. It was best if Evangeline's survival stayed quiet. Otherwise, the kingdom would descend into chaos. As if it hadn't done that already.

"Your only concern is entertaining them," Leianna said. "We'll take care of the rest."

Alexandria pushed out a breath as she stepped forward into the throne room. "You know me. I'm excellent at entertaining."

She plastered on a closed-lipped smile and shook hands with ambassadors, ministers, mayors, and spouses. The Dais mingled as well, their first interactions with representatives from Duarmme and Victori in decades. The former Genean queen, Natania's mother, had visited a few times, a false symbol that they were progressing toward peace despite the ever-rising tension. Alexandria would set the tone for how Kevelda handled its allies, and whether or not it even had them.

Her eyes drifted over the crowd, subconsciously searching for her mother amongst the tables and chairs that had been set up evenly along the length of the hall. In all the years she had attended events like this, she could always find Anastasia talking to the other mayors. A brief twinge of panic twisted her stomach at the thought of her parents. She hoped they had listened to her warning and gone to the cabin.

When she noticed Marlowe talking to the Mayor of Lyrica, she hustled in the other direction. The girl had helped her during the Ascension, but only because she thought she would be on the winning side. And Alexandria was far from the victor when it came to Natania.

A tall man with steel-grey hair and a soft expression approached her. The gilded crown upon his head startled Alexandria out of her practiced formalities. She inclined her head slightly, not too much to imply deference, but enough to give respect to his title. Having foregone her sling, she took the initiative of putting out her left hand, hoping his gaze wouldn't linger on the jagged scar marring her right arm.

"It's a pleasure to meet you," he said. "I'm Argon, King of Victori." His accent made his words thick, the syllables raising at the ends of his words. They all spoke Genean to one another, as the language was universal before the Fall. It still remained on many signs in Regia and Kureya, and Keveldans spoke a mixture of traditional and foreign words in their daily conversations. In her quest for allies, Alexandria was grateful for that.

"The pleasure is all mine." Her heart pounded as she spoke the words. "How are you liking Kevelda?"

King Argon laughed. "It's much colder than we're used to. Tell me, is the garden by the sea still around? My wife loved those little blue flowers. Though I suppose it has been thirty years since our last visit, so I would not be surprised if they were gone."

Alexandria took his wistful expression to mean that his wife had passed away. "I will be sure to ask around and have someone take you there."

A middle-aged man came up beside him, a red sash crossing his military uniform, gold medals adorning it. Argon rested his hand on the man's shoulder before introducing him as his son, Prince Louis. The prince bowed before taking Alexandria's outstretched hand and pressing his lips against it. "Nice to meet you, Your Majesty."

"And you as well, Your Highness." She could handle Prince Louis. Though the mayors did not have the same power as the king, she had been dealing with their children her entire life.

"Louis will be taking over for me in a few years, so I hope to include him in our new friendship," Argon said.

Alexandria plastered a smile onto her face. "Of course. I look forward to welcoming all of your family into our new alliance." She quickly added, "In the Genean Coalition."

That's the real reason why everyone's here. At the thought of the Coalition, she glanced around the room, looking for Natania.

As if on cue, the throne room doors opened. Two guards flanked Natania as she strode down the center of the hall. Her eyes bored into Alexandria as she made her way over. Natania looked between her and Argon with a smile Alexandria thought far too warm for her character.

Another woman stood by her side, and as they approached, the rest of the room disappeared. *Amira.* Alexandria's smile broadened, genuine at the sight of her friend. She looked better than she had two months ago, her skin almost reaching its usual golden brown under the chandeliers' light, but working on the weapons still had an impact. Her eyes looked bruised, deep purples and blues painting the circles underneath.

"Argon, Alexandria," Natania said as she took their hands, "and Prince Louis, great to see you. I'm glad you all have met. I cannot begin to express how excited I am for our burgeoning relationship with Kevelda."

Amira said nothing, her lips drawn into a thin line, but when their eyes met, her face flashed with urgency. They would need to find a way to talk.

When Natania caught her gaze again, Alexandria's mouth moved into a tight smile. A similar expression settled on Argon's face.

"Neither can I," Alexandria responded. Bitterness permeated her false sincerity, and she pressed her lips back into a placating grin, hoping no one noticed.

Fortunately, another man came up to introduce himself before she had to speak again. He wore no crown and no medals, just a simple, starched, dark-grey uniform. A gold insignia was embroidered near his shoulder. His face had not yet been marked by age, though his narrowed eyes and furrowed brows hardened his appearance.

Natania introduced him as the Premier of Duarmme, and to Alexandria's shock, she inclined her head slightly. She had not seen the queen show deference to anyone, not even Argon. Alexandria followed her action.

The man did not say anything, only shaking Alexandria's hand, until two other men came up to them. Their appearances were similar, the same pale skin and icy blonde hair, but one was a teenager at most. She soon found out that the older man was the Southern Councilchair, who oversaw the southern region of Duarmme. The boy was his son, Jude.

Alexandria wished she had the chance to meet these people before the gala, but her concussion had kept her in the palace for the past few days. She fought to remember their names and positions as her head spun.

Eventually, she moved to the platform, where the throne stood high above the crowd. She clinked a fork against her wine glass. It was filled with water; Alexandria had enough history with alcohol to let herself slip now, and the palace doctor would not look favorably upon her drinking while she was still recovering from the attack.

"Hello, everyone," she said, forcing confidence into her voice as she recited her practiced speech. "Welcome to Kevelda. I am grateful for all who have gathered here today to celebrate our new alliance. As you know, it has been decades since Kevelda last opened itself up to relations with other countries. It is my hope that this will bring a new era of peace, both to our kingdom, and to the world that remains. Now, it is my *honor* to introduce Queen Natania of Genea." She cleared her throat to avoid rolling her eyes. "The woman who has made it possible for us to gather here tonight."

Natania joined Alexandria on the platform. Her soldiers watched from below, their heads on a swivel. Alexandria began to descend the steps before Natania took her hand–the one she couldn't move or pull away with. "I am so proud of Queen Alexandria's decision to put her predecessors' misgivings behind her. This will be a beneficial partnership for us all."

Alexandria clenched her teeth and straightened her back. She smiled out at the audience, even as blood rushed to her face. Tears stung the corners of her eyes, but she blinked them away before anyone could notice. It was bad enough that she had to sacrifice her people for the Coalition. Now, she couldn't even fight against the queen's grip as she made it seem like this deal was Alexandria's idea all along.

"I have been informed of a recent attack on Alexandria, carried out by a group from within Kevelda's borders," Natania continued. "As the Coalition, we cannot stand for this. Genea will dedicate its resources to investigating this attack at Kevelda's request."

Kevelda has not requested anything from you. Alexandria held her tongue and kept listening.

Natania raised Alexandria's hand in her own. "We stand together. An attack on Kevelda is an attack on us all."

When Natania decided she was no longer necessary, she dropped Alexandria's arm, leaving it to fall limply back to her side. The old wound twinged. She descended the platform, avoiding eye contact with the crowd as Natania kept speaking.

Her muscles twitched as she forced the fake smile to stay in place. She positioned herself at the edge of the crowd, where she could see Natania, but no one could see her face. She hardly listened to Natania's speech. The dress suffocated her. Her people were deteriorating in Thaertos's mines at that very moment, and Alexandria felt like she was underground with them.

Images of those workers spun around her mind until something Natania said made her snap to attention.

"We have another cause for celebration. I am happy to announce that I will be getting married in a few months."

Alexandria clenched her jaw to keep it from hanging open. *Married?* Even if the queen was not as coldhearted as she appeared, the announcement had to have some ulterior motive. Her head ached as she laid out all of the puzzle pieces, muffling the rest of the queen's speech.

A hand gripped her arm and jolted her out of her thoughts. She inhaled sharply, turning to face Leianna, whose tightened jaw set her on guard.

"Someone's here to see you," she whispered. "Slip away quietly."

Alexandria's eyes darted between the queen on the platform and the woman next to her. She followed Leianna to the door that led up to her quarters, hoping no one observed her exit. Leianna stationed herself next to it as Alexandria entered the stairwell.

Silence greeted her as the door sealed shut, encasing her in near darkness. The walls blocked out Natania's voice. Her pulse pounded against her bodice, compressing her lungs even further. Lightness clouded her head by the time she reached the top of the stairs. Panting, she opened the door and gasped at who she saw standing there.

"Isaac?" she all but shouted. She stepped forward, but the fuzziness in her mind cleared enough for her to remember their history.

I can't say that I trust you. I can only say that I forgive you.

It had been six months since he left, since she said goodbye to him in this room. Not that she had been counting.

His mouth turned up in a smirk. "Miss me?"

Alexandria fought to forget what his real smile looked like, the one that set a dimple into his cheek.

"Yes. I did." She tried to lie, but her tongue wouldn't form the words. They both stood there for a moment, frozen, assessing each other. "Where's James?"

Isaac took another step closer. "He's okay. Not ready to come back yet, not until we've found Amira."

"I know where she is. He can come home."

"Can I?"

Alexandria chewed on her lip. She broke their eye contact, training her gaze on the wall behind him. "No. Things are too complicated right now."

"Which 'things?' The Genean Coalition, or me?" The space between them was slowly closing with each deliberate step he took.

"All of them." She shook her head. "We're not talking about this now. Why are you here?"

His eyes widened as if coming out of a trance. "You need to come with me."

"Why?"

"I can't explain right now. Please, just listen to me." He took her hand in his, and she immediately pulled it away.

"No. As far as I'm concerned, Natania is wondering why her favorite little ally isn't listening to her speech. Give me a reason or I'm going back in there."

Her biting tone hid her true meaning: *You need to leave before you get hurt, Isaac.*

Muffled gunshots cut off his next words. Fire rose in her chest, spreading into her limbs. She palmed the knife that had been hidden underneath her skirt and rushed to the door.

"Wait!" Isaac shouted, but Alexandria was already taking the stairs two at a time. "You can't fight them."

"I'm assuming you know who *they* are." A second round of gunshots made her falter. Her foot caught on the step, and she nearly went sprawling to the ground before Isaac grabbed her arm. "You told them how to get in, didn't you?"

He caught her stare with a fierceness that startled her. "No, I didn't. I wouldn't betray you like that."

"Tell me, then. How did you know to get me out of there?"

"I couldn't stop them, but I could protect you. I made a choice."

The world appeared to her through a spinning, red wave, crashing against her skull. "You chose wrong. If anyone survives this, I'll have a target on my back. Next time you decide to be an accessory to treason, tell me in advance so I can make sure no one else dies."

Before he could say another word, Alexandria opened the door and stepped into the warzone.

SIX
ALEXANDRIA

*B*lood does *have a smell.*

The scent of rusted metal filled Alexandria's nose as she looked out over the ravaged throne room. She gripped her blade, inching along the bullet-ridden wall. Shattered glass and splintered wood cradled a dozen bodies, crimson pools slowly overtaking the shards. In the carnage, guests in gowns and suits had met the same fate as guards from all kingdoms. Dread unfurled deep in her stomach. A small voice pleaded for her to return to the stairwell.

As she crept up to the closest woman, her body went cold. The blood coating the woman's cheek dyed her brown hair black. Matching eyes, unseeing, stared at the chandelier. A silent scream built in Alexandria's chest, tearing at her ribs. *Amira.*

Her knees cracked against the floor. With trembling fingers, she brushed the sticky strands aside, finding an unfamiliar face. Someone else had lost a person they loved. She felt sick at her relief.

She turned her eyes away from the corpses. If she could not see them, she might keep her hope that they would soon awaken, that breath still filled their lungs.

Only four people remained–living ones, at least. They huddled in the center of the room, and if not for their cries, she might have thought they were the attackers. Jude, the Councilchair's son, wept over his father's body. The Premier stood and stared at the dead leader. Alexandria choked as she saw Prince Louis lying lifeless on the black tile, blood spilling beneath him. Argon held Jude's shaking shoulders, even as he whispered, "My son. I've lost both my sons."

A guard wearing Victori's colors drew his gun as she stepped toward Argon. She held her hand in the air.

"What happened?" she asked. The words stuck in her dry throat.

The guard's voice was gruff, panicked. "You would know. Where were you when they attacked?"

"I was loosening my dress." Even though her feelings about Isaac were complicated at the moment, she would not let anyone know he had been in the palace, not until she understood how he was involved.

Her lungs tightened as the guard moved closer. Argon barked at order at him in Victorin. The guard hesitated, then holstered his gun. She crouched next to the king, whispering apologies she knew meant nothing to him.

Another round of gunshots sounded in the distance. Her eyes locked with the guard's. "Are they still here?"

"Your agents drove them out. There were less than a dozen of them, but they caught us unawares. Many in attendance were unarmed, per your request."

Alexandria fought to breathe. She looked around the room, praying she would not see Leianna in the pile of bodies. She could not find her. The realization that her captain was still fighting the assailants set her in motion.

"Give me your gun," she ordered the guard, desperation seeping through the cracks. "*Please.*"

The Premier moved first. He pulled a revolver from under his uniform jacket and handed it to Alexandria. She faltered, surprised by the gesture.

"Take it. We go together," he said in the common language. When he pulled another out of his jacket, Alexandria briefly bristled at the fact that he ignored her *no weapons* request, but she was glad he did.

They moved out of the throne room, clearing each hallway as they neared where they had last heard gunfire. Alexandria wished she had her sling for an extra layer of protection. With her arm hanging by her side, she felt imbalanced. Especially as she cocked the revolver with her thumb.

Amira reached from an alcove and pulled her inside. The Premier pointed his weapon at her in a split second, but Alexandria quickly told him she was safe, setting her own gun on the floor. He nodded and glanced around before drifting further down the hall. The women embraced tightly, Alexandria's chest heaving with the weight of her panic and the draw of her bodice.

"I thought they killed you," she whispered, tears trailing through the powder on her face. She would find a mess in the mirror later.

"I'm too valuable to Natania alive. One of her guards took a bullet for me." Amira's voice was bright despite the death around them. Her weary expression had eased with their reunion, but in a fraction of a second, her face grew serious. "They have more bombs, but only two have the radioactive cores so far. That's what makes them dangerous. I work with those because her scientists are too afraid to do it. All they need is more of the mineral and they'll be unstoppable. If they keep mining, it's over for us, even if I find a way to destroy the bombs she already has."

"Don't destroy them. It'll only put you in danger, and we don't have the means to attack just yet." Alexandria pieced together her thoughts, the distant sounds of gunfire breaking her concentration. "And if we do dismantle them, she'll just make more. We have to destroy the mines, too."

Amira bit her lip. "I might have made them easier to break, but I won't know until you try. I can't do anything too drastic, or the other scientists will notice. What else can I do to help you?"

"Whatever you do, don't put yourself at risk. You're worth more than winning this war." She hugged her friend again, memorizing the way the embrace felt. Her chest ached when she removed herself. "Just do whatever is safe."

"We have to go," the Premier interrupted. "Now."

Amira took Alexandria's hand, desperation flashing behind her eyes. "I love you."

"I love you, too. We'll make a way back to each other soon. I know it." She ruminated over that promise as she followed the Premier, gun back at the ready.

A man lay motionless down the hall, a trail of blood behind him as if he had tried to crawl. The Premier pointed his weapon at the body as they passed. No movement. Alexandria's stomach turned at the sight.

Shouts erupted as they rounded another corner. Alexandria gripped the gun tighter. Up against the wall, Leianna held a writhing woman's arms behind her back. Her black jacket looked familiar, and when her shoulder bucked backwards, Alexandria noticed a blank rectangle where an Argentum name badge would be.

"Let me go!" the woman yelled.

"Since you're asking so nicely," Leianna muttered. She motioned for the two other Argentum agents to handcuff her, and as they escorted her away, the woman glared at her.

Alexandria finally exhaled, though her nerves were still on fire. Strands of Leianna's dark hair fell haphazardly out of her updo. When she saw Alexandria, her eyes narrowed.

"I need to speak to you, Your Majesty." The title was only a formality with the foreign leader beside her. Leianna met the Premier's stare. "The last of the assailants have been neutralized."

The Premier nodded and turned to Alexandria. "We will be leaving immediately. Until this situation has been handled, I cannot foresee our nations having any further relations."

Her mind raced and her heartbeat threatened to rival it. "That woman will be questioned, and I can assure you we will have answers for today."

"Answers will not change what has happened. That boy will have to take on his father's title. We must return and tell our people of the damage that has been done." He set his shoulders in a sharp line, and his stony voice raised the hair on the back of her neck.

Before she could respond, the leader walked out of sight. She froze, her thoughts traveling a thousand places at once, until Leianna gripped her shoulder.

"I told you we couldn't trust him," Leianna said.

Alexandria swallowed hard. "The Premier did nothing wrong. I understand his decision, though it makes my job impossible." Another failed alliance. One less person to help her fight Natania.

Natania. Was she alive? Somewhat guiltily, she hoped that the queen had been caught by a bullet. But that might not solve Kevelda's problems at all. The Coalition would still exist, just led by another Genean monarch.

"Not the Premier. Carter."

"He didn't..." She couldn't say that he wasn't a part of the attack. He had known what was going to happen, and he did nothing.

Not nothing. He had saved *her*, and no one else. Now, she had one less potential ally. Perhaps two, if Argon made the same decision the Premier did.

"I don't know," she said. "I don't know how he's connected to all this. Tell me if Natania lived. That's the answer I need right now."

"She did, as far as I know. When the attack started, her guards stood in the way of the bullets."

"Where is she now?"

Leianna pushed a piece of hair out of her face, smearing blood across her pale skin. "I'm sure she will show up when she wants to."

After hours of checking on injured agents in the medical wing and sending off the surviving members of the Victorin and Duarmmian delegations, she could not breathe, let alone talk. Her words had become repetitive, meaningless apologies and platitudes.

They died because of me, she thought, as she made her way to her quarters. Five of her own agents had died, two on her personal Guard. Watson, the agent that had let her into Mendoza's cell six months ago, replaced Lawton for the night shift. She would have to pay a visit to his family in the morning, if he had any.

Leianna and Watson swept her room before she entered. When they emerged, Leianna whispered, "She's here."

Alexandria's stomach dropped. She clenched her jaw, hoping her exhaustion wasn't written on her face. Watson stationed herself beside Prior as Leianna shut the door behind her, leaving the two queens alone.

Natania beckoned Alexandria over to the window where she stood. She could do nothing but answer the woman's call.

"It was the rebels, wasn't it." Not a question. Her cold eyes narrowed as if she could perceive every minute movement that Alexandria made. She hardly looked disheveled at all. The silver crown rested evenly across her ash brown hair, curls perfectly pinned atop her head. A red scratch lined her jaw. It was the only sign that she had been under attack.

Alexandria could not meet the queen's gaze any longer. She looked through the windows and out over the city, far beyond the white buildings to the pitch-dark sea. "We don't know. My agents are questioning the surviving assailant as we speak."

"*You* will question them. I do not trust your agents, and neither should you."

"If I don't trust them, I have no one."

Natania shook her head, the corner of her mouth lifting in what could hardly be described as a smile. "No, that's not correct. You have me."

"Of course," she muttered.

"Alexandria, you're aware of the weapon my researchers are building. The one your friend is helping with. If these rebels continue to give you trouble, I have the means to dispose of them.

And if anything happens to me," she paused, slicing her with a glare, "I will dispose of *her.*"

Alexandria's heart sank at the mention of the bombs, but it shattered at the reminder that the queen held Amira in the palm of her hand. "What will that weapon do to the rest of my people? Poison them? If it doesn't burn them until there's nothing left but ashes, that is."

"We all have to make hard choices for the good of the world."

"Not the world. Just your country."

"You haven't yet realized that my country *is* my world, and yours should be, too. Until you do, you will never be able to make the best choices for your people."

"What is the best choice for my people, Natania? Sending them to die so you can create a weapon that will kill all of us?"

Natania straightened her shoulders. "You are of no use to me if your people are not also on my side. If you do not get these rebels under control, I will burn your kingdom to the ground. Then, in a century or two, once the wind has carried away the ashes, my descendants will prosper on the land that once was yours. You will be the end of Kevelda, the queen who eradicated her people. Is that clear?"

She could do nothing but nod. The queen left without another word. Alexandria heard her guards shuffling when Natania passed through the door, and then it was silent.

Her arm burned as she untied her dress, pulling out the laces with as much force as she could muster. The repetitive motion and awkward angle made her bicep twitch, but she could not face anyone else. Once the garment hit the floor, air rushed back into her lungs. She crumpled to the ground and cried.

Nausea rose in her chest with the force of her sobs, but she swallowed it down. She crawled over to the side of the bed. The frame pressed into her back as she wrapped her arm across her chest. She wanted the nightmare to be over. She wanted her people to come home, for Amira and Phillip to be alive and safe. And against all the logic she could muster, she wanted Isaac to hold her like he did those months ago in the cabin.

What has he gotten himself into?

Isaac had knowledge of the attack, and the rebels trusted him enough to let him go off on his own. That meant he must have some kind of power or ranking among them. He had promised to protect her, and now he was in an organization dedicated to killing her. And he had *left*. She had hoped that, somehow, he would have decided to stay. That he would have come with her when she went to find Leianna, or at least waited in her room to see if she returned intact. But he was gone.

She pushed herself off the ground in one movement. Sitting still would do her no good. Her legs ached as she paced back and forth across the room.

Was James with him? Did *he* join the rebels? James had expressed his anger at Queen Evangeline since they were in secondary school. He hated the way that Kevelda was run, the pain its people were put through with the Draft. Yet she never expected he would feel that way about *her*.

Her throat tightened. She held her breath until the tears went away. As she wiped the wet trails from her cheeks, she noticed a folded piece of paper on her nightstand.

Isaac. He had left her a note. Maybe he still cared. No, she knew he cared. That was why he had warned her. Heart pounding, she opened the page.

It wasn't from him.

Alexandria,

If you're reading this, Natania is alive, and we still have work to do. I'll send someone to you over the next few days. Then we'll finally meet.

See you soon,

E

The pieces clicked in Alexandria's head. Isaac would have moved up in the organization rather quickly. It had only been six months since he left, and she did not know how long the rebels had been active before that. One person trusted him above anyone else, enough to ask him to fake her death.

Evangeline was a rebel, and Isaac had chosen her.

SEVEN
ISAAC

You let Natania get away." Evangeline rarely let her emotions get the best of her. Now, they spilled into her words, lining her pointed finger.

She and Isaac were alone in her office after she ordered the other soldiers to leave. He steadied himself, focusing on the flickering lamp lighting the dim room, mind turning over ways that he could spin this. With breath in his lungs, he still had a chance to save himself. "I was busy securing Vale and McMadden. Without me, they'd be rotting under the palace."

He had knocked out the agents guarding the cells and freed the two soldiers. One had been arrested for her role in the first attack on Alexandria. The other had been assigned to the mission with him—the sole survivor, the one who could tell Evangeline what had truly happened, how he had disappeared instead of attacking with them. It had taken a few days for him to be able to sneak back in and break her out. He should've left her. Saved himself.

Now here he was, on the wrong end of Evangeline's fury. Except, he realized with a shock, it was not anger engrained in her expression. Her mouth curled into a smile that made him recoil.

"It was Alexandria, wasn't it?" She did not give him a chance to calm his racing thoughts. "Of course, it was. I knew you would get her out of there, one way or another. That's why I sent you."

His heartbeat staggered. If she questioned his loyalty, Reagan and the turned rebels were at risk, too. But if she didn't want Alexandria dead, why lead the rebels against her?

He crossed his arms. "Don't pretend to be in my head."

"I don't have to. It's written all over your face."

"I would have died with the others. Does that even matter to you?"

For a moment, he thought his attempt at deflection worked. Her face softened, the crease disappearing from between her brows. "It does. I'm glad you're here." She cupped his chin, softly at first, then with more force. "I need you on my side. Don't disappoint me again."

"I won't." He wouldn't be around for the aftermath when he did. When she let go, he released his held breath, shoving down the years of pain and regret that threatened to resurface whenever she touched him.

Those memories grappled at him with such force that he didn't realize they were no longer alone.

James's brow furrowed as the door clicked shut behind him. "You wanted to see me, General?" he asked.

"Yes, Collins. I have a job only you two can accomplish."

Isaac's gaze shot back to her, but her expression was frustratingly blank. If she put him on another mission that targeted Alexandria, Evangeline knew he would save her. What else could it be?

"An agent is bringing Alexandria in as we speak. You need to convince her to join us."

"We just attacked her a week ago. A grudge like that doesn't just go away, especially with her," James argued. His attempts to pretend disdain for Alexandria were transparent, at least to Isaac. He would have to work on it if they were to be of any help at all.

"That's what makes your job so important. I need her on our side."

"Why attack her, then?" Isaac asked. He cringed at his tone, muscles taut as he waited for her response.

"I need the rebels, too. The only way we can win is if we're united. Once I know Alexandria is willing to fight for us, I'll change their mind." She arched an eyebrow. "Are you in, or do I have to convert her the hard way?"

He flexed his fingers and steadied his breath. "No hard way. I'm in." He glanced at James, who seemed to be avoiding his eyes. "Are you?"

"I'll try my best."

"Good," Evangeline said, "because she should be here any minute." She left without another word.

The two retreated to the back of the room for fear of the soldiers listening on the other side of the wall.

"Our plan doesn't change," Isaac whispered, his voice barely audible. "Never trust a word she says."

James opened and shut his mouth, an indignant look on his face. "You think I'm at risk of that?" He neutralized his expression when the door opened.

Two soldiers carried a blindfolded, thrashing Alexandria into the room. James lunged forward the same time he did. They were both bad at acting, when it came down to it.

"Let her go," Isaac commanded. The two soldiers simply shared a smirk. He was not their general.

Alexandria kicked out her legs one final time before they dropped her on the ground. "That was unnecessary!" she shouted, ripping off the blindfold. The soldiers left, slamming the door hard enough to make Isaac's teeth rattle.

Her breath caught when she laid her eyes on James. "James? Where am I?"

The brightness on her face faded when she saw Isaac. Her mouth pressed into a flat line. She didn't say a word, ignoring his outstretched hand. He swore he could smell alcohol on her breath as she stood.

"Nice to see you, too," he said. His chest tightened, a sharp pain spearing through his heart. "You're at a rebel base."

"I knew you were one of them." She turned to James. "I didn't expect it of you. Not with Evangeline in charge."

Isaac tensed. "How did you know Evangeline was a rebel?"

"I know *you*." That was all she needed to say. "Why did you choose her, after everything she put you through?"

I didn't, he thought. He couldn't risk saying it with the soldiers so close. "You two both want Kevelda to be free."

"But she wants that at the cost of *my* life. And now, James, after hating her for years, you've joined her, too?"

James finally seemed to figure out how to speak. "I have the chance to help my family. She's the only one who's doing that."

Okay, don't try that *hard, James.* The words stung him, and he wasn't even the recipient.

Her face fell, voice quieting as she toed a sparse patch of carpet. "I had no choice. You have to believe me."

"You have a choice now. What will it be? Natania or Evangeline?"

"It's not that simple."

"It *is*." James's proclamation sparked a fire behind her eyes. Isaac had the instinct to jump between the two of them, but he simply watched.

"You don't know what kind of position she put me in," Alexandria said. "She has Amira."

James's jaw slackened, eyes wide. "Is she okay?"

"I. Don't. Know," Alexandria gritted out. "With that attack, her death could be my punishment. Why did you think I joined the Coalition?"

"He didn't think," Isaac said. "That seems to be a problem of his."

Her hand flew up. "You stay out of this."

"We have to get her out of there," James said.

"Obviously. That's what I'm trying to do. I'm holding this kingdom together by threads. If I let go, or if your rebellion decides to strike again, Natania will kill us all. Starting with Amira."

"Join us, then. We can come up with something together."

"Evangeline is no innocent in this." She shot a look at Isaac as she said it.

All he wanted to do was apologize, but the words would never be enough to cover for what he had done. For what Alexandria thought he was doing now. "The only thing keeping you alive is that Evangeline doesn't want to come out of the shadows yet," he said. "You're more valuable to her in the palace."

"Is that a threat?"

"It's the truth. I will do everything I can to keep you alive, but you have to work with us." He pressed forward, lowering his voice. "Make her think that you're on her side."

Whether she understood his intentions or not, she nodded, right as the door clicked open behind him. Evangeline walked in, her strides long and graceful. Her mouth twitched in that too-sweet smile.

"Finally, we meet in person," she said, taking Alexandria's hand in hers.

"Not a pleasure." Alexandria ripped herself away and reeled backwards. "I'm with you, on one condition. You keep your rebels at bay for the next few months while things cool off with Natania, or we won't have a country to fight for."

Evangeline pressed her lips together. "I will try my best."

"Try harder."

"Don't speak to me like that."

"One of us is the queen in this room, and it is no longer you," Alexandria snapped.

The look on her face was enough to make Isaac step forward between them. His heart lurched. He always thought her to be beautiful, but that fierce look was something else entirely. Being the recipient of it in the cabin had scared him half to death and brought him to life all at once.

Evangeline clicked her tongue. "But it could be. The Dais would be glad to have me back."

"How do you think they would feel to know you willingly abandoned them? Or that you hid the state of the war and the real purpose of the Draft?"

"They won't care when I bring Genea to its knees."

"Great work on that so far."

"I could say the same to you."

Isaac put his hands out. "Okay, *Your Majesties*. Can we take a minute?"

"*No*," they said in unison. Alexandria narrowed her eyes at the former queen. Evangeline crossed her arms in response.

Then, her anger faded, or at least, she hid it well. "You're right, Isaac." She sighed and faced Alexandria again. "You're the last of my family. I want to protect you, but I can only let Isaac save you so many times before the rebels start questioning us. You must give them something in return."

He ground his teeth at the notion that she had manipulated his decision in the palace. Yet she had built him—all but raised him—over the past decade. What if he was nothing more than another piece of her plan?

"What do you want from me?" Alexandria asked.

"We will delay any further attacks until you give us word, *or* until we feel the situation has become so dire that we must respond. You will give us all possible information on Genean activities and weak points."

"Deal." Alexandria straightened her shoulders. "As long as your soldiers don't kidnap me a second time."

Evangeline nodded and turned to go, but Alexandria spoke again.

"How am I related to you?" Her voice had none of its former steel, replaced by heavy curiosity. As if her entire life balanced on it.

Isaac held his breath. A knife could slash the silence.

"You're my half-sister. Tomas's child."

"Who's my mother?"

Evangeline just winked. "Convince me that I can trust you and I'll tell you the answer."

PART II
THE REBEL

EIGHT
ALEXANDRIA

As waves thrashed the ship, threatening to send her sprawling across her cramped quarters, Alexandria thought a heart attack might kill her before any of her enemies could.

Her brain already hammered against her skull from her month-old concussion whenever a minister spoke too loudly, but the liquor she had a habit of drinking before bed added palpitations to the mix. She clutched her chest, praying that the sharp pain there would cease before they docked in Victori. Her first words would be her most important. An apology for the attack that took the kingdom's last heir. Empathy for their grief. Acknowledgement that she would do everything in her power to bring the attackers to justice.

That was a lie. Though she did not know how to locate the rebels, she could find them if she wanted to. But if she turned them in, Natania would win. She was not ready to commit the final betrayal of her people.

The Dais had warned her of what could occur when she attended Prince Louis's memorial. *They could imprison you. Or assassinate you.* She did not let those thoughts linger in her mind for too long. This was something she had to do, a true test of her queendom.

One more name to add to the list of people she had failed.

She hadn't thought she would be invited to the ceremony simply because she could not fathom a way for the Victorin royal family to get the news to her in time. The trip between Regia and Biscay, Victori's capital, took a week in perfect conditions. As the Victorin delegation hurried away after Coalition gala, she did not know when, or if, they would speak again.

A day later, one of the Genean diplomats had informed her that the telephones in the palace could now communicate across the Coalition territories. *"A gift from our queen,"* he had said. The sentence sent a shiver down her spine. Though communication with the other kingdoms was beneficial, Alexandria had no doubt that Genea monitored every conversation—and that Genean spies would use the technology to relay messages back to Natania. They likely had been for years. Perhaps even Mendoza had possessed his own personal telephone connecting him to their enemy.

Her palm stung as the corner of the wooden chest she supported herself on dug into it. Humidity flooded her lungs with every deep breath. The closer they came to the peninsula, the more the warmth jarred her. She missed the way the cold bit her skin. It kept her alert, even as she spent her days numbed to the things she had to do. Greeting her sick people at the clinics. Visiting underperforming greenhouses. Sitting in meetings with ministers who shouted about the things they thought she could actually change. Spending her nights alone, eyes wide open, waiting for an assailant to come and kill her once and for all.

She told herself she was lying in wait, that she had a plan, that she would save her people, but she had never been a good liar. Just good at being lied to.

Someone knocked on the cabin door, the rapping sound cutting through her thoughts.

"Come in," she croaked. Her heart still felt like it was being sliced open. Maybe another sip from her flask would help.

Before she could act on that thought, Leianna peeked her head into the room. "Minister Greer would like to see you."

"Again?" She straightened her shoulders, swaying slightly. "I almost wish he hadn't gotten used to being on a boat."

"He wants to make sure you know what could happen when we dock, and if you're really ready to face the king."

"That's exactly what he said the last time. Tell him I'm busy. Please."

The captain nodded. Instead of leaving, she hesitated. "Are you alright?"

Alexandria couldn't take her eyes off a fixed point on the wall. It was the only thing keeping her balanced. "Of course. Don't worry about me."

"I take my role as the Captain of the Queen's Guard very seriously. If I stopped worrying about you, I would be the first person to tell you to replace me."

"Well, don't worry *in particular* about me right now."

Leianna crossed the room and pulled the flask out of her hand. She hadn't realized she had taken it out of her coat pocket.

"This is going to be one of the most dangerous situations you've ever been in, if not for you, then for your kingdom. Go into it sober or I'll personally make sure you don't go into it at all."

Heat rose up her neck, stomach churning in embarrassment. "You're not in a position to give me orders."

"No, but you put me in a position to keep you safe, and that's what I am doing." Leianna narrowed her eyes and tossed the flask back to her. "Fine. Keep it. Just don't drown yourself in it. We'll be in Biscay by tomorrow morning."

The disappointment on her face forced Alexandria to speak before her captain could turn away completely. "Nobody understands the position I'm in."

She looked back from the door. "You're right. They don't. *I* don't. But do not pretend I don't know what it means to feel pain."

Alexandria stared at the empty space long after she left.

Through the night, she watched the open ocean narrow into a suffocating canal, bracing herself for the ship to crash into one of the barren banks. Crumbling buildings haunted the shore. She startled at the sight of a woman weaving among the ruins, before realizing it was only her reflection in the window.

Just when the river widened, they maneuvered into a smaller channel, and she squeezed her eyes closed until Leianna informed her of their imminent arrival.

King Argon greeted them at the dock. The circles under his eyes matched his silver hair in the darkness. His cheeks were gaunt, as if he hadn't eaten since the attack three weeks ago. They hollowed even further when the corners of his mouth tightened in a pained smile.

Alexandria dipped her head. She scoured her mind for the speech she had prepared, but nothing came.

"I'm so sorry," she said, her throat raw. The humidity pressed against her, making her buttoned blouse stick to her skin, sweat thick as blood dripping down her spine.

"It was not your fault. There are always growing pains with a new sovereign. I cannot blame you for the actions of a group you do not claim." An unnatural steadiness surrounded the words, a sign that he had practiced them.

Her stomach twisted, a thousand needles pricking her abdomen at once. She may not have claimed the rebels, but she did nothing to stop them. Just like she did nothing to stop Natania. The latter's violence could not justify the former's, not when it took innocent lives.

"I know I cannot bring him back, but I will do everything I can to ensure your trust in Kevelda. The attackers will be brought to justice." It would be impossible to convince the king if she did not even believe it herself.

The two attendants flanking him moved forward as he gestured to them. "Please bring Her Majesty's delegation to their quarters. Queen Alexandria, I will show you to yours. I hope to speak with you a bit more."

A vehicle waited for them by the road, and though the city's rounded archways and limestone brickwork were jarringly unfamiliar, the rust-covered car reminded her of home. As Leianna moved to follow her, Argon sent Alexandria a glance that she took to mean he wanted to speak with her alone. She held up her hand, hoping that the apologies written on her face would let Leianna know that she wasn't brushing her off.

Salt and mildew bombarded her nose as she ducked into the car. An opaque sliding window connected the back seat to the driver, but when he closed it, Alexandria could see nothing of their surroundings. Argon took the seat on the opposite end.

"Miller, take the long way," the king said to the driver. He did not respond, and if he nodded, the black screen separating them blocked the motion from sight. Argon turned to her, the jovial expression from the Coalition gala now dead serious. "How much do you know about the history of our kingdoms' relationship?"

Her heart stuttered at the shift. Alexandria racked her brain for a response. "I know that we used to be allies before Victori joined the Genean Coalition thirty years ago."

"Yes, we did. You must know that we did not join the Coalition of our own volition. My country did not have the resources to fight back, even with Duarmme on our side."

"Duarmme didn't choose either?" A glimmer of hope sparked in her chest.

"No," he said. "When the war broke out and decimated the Old World, Duarmme lost too much. That, combined with the wealth of the people who made bunkers in Genea, gave Natania's predecessors enough of an advantage to overtake Duarmme and force them into the Coalition."

"What price do you pay?"

"A portion of our crops. We can survive it." The shadow that crossed his face hinted otherwise.

"Natania requires that I send laborers to mine radioactive material in Thaertos. She's building weapons." She paused, hoping that Argon would confirm what she thought his intentions were. If she was wrong about him, Natania would destroy her.

Argon's skin turned deathly pale, moonlight reflecting off the sharp edges of his cheekbones. "It's going to happen again."

"What?"

"The end of the world."

Her breath hitched. "Help me stop it."

His head shook like a tree branch in a summer storm. "No, no. We cannot. Not if what you are saying is true. She will destroy us."

"Not if we all fight back together. Kevelda, Victori, and Duarmme. We can have peace."

"We have peace now, even if it comes with a cost. There is too much at stake."

She clenched her fist to keep her hand from trembling. "My people are already dying. Are yours?"

He locked eyes with her for only a moment before rapping his knuckles against the window. "We're ready to return, Miller."

"Please." Alexandria reached out to touch his arm but decided against it. She twisted to try and catch his line of sight. "I know what you've lost. We can end this. Together. I cannot save my people without you."

His eyes darkened and Alexandria drew back. The shift in his demeanor made her squirm. It brought her back to that dark night in the palace, when she witnessed Mendoza turn his anger onto Isaac. "I am saving mine."

The rest of the trip passed in silence. When they finally made it to the palace, Alexandria caught only a glimpse of the beige brick building and its rows upon rows of balconied windows before she was ushered inside through the arched wooden doors. She fought to come up with the words to plead for the king's help, but when she turned to him, he had already disappeared.

Leianna and Watson had stationed themselves outside of her temporary quarters. The captain raised her eyebrow, and Alexandria only responded with the inclination of her head toward the room. Watson stood straighter as Leianna left her alone at her post and followed Alexandria inside.

With the door shut, Alexandria explained everything she had learned. "I shouldn't have told him about the mining. It made us seem weak," she said as she unlatched her traveling case.

"You couldn't have known how he would respond."

"I should've thought about it, though. I never think."

Alexandria anticipated a sarcastic remark, but Leianna only squeezed her shoulder. "Get some rest. I have agents set to guard your door through the night."

"Thank you." She sighed and flicked her eyes up to Leianna's. "I'm sorry about earlier."

"What happened earlier?"

"On the boat. I know you know what it's like to be in pain. And I care."

"Oh." The captain shifted her gaze around the room. "You don't have to apologize."

"I won't be the kind of queen that doesn't acknowledge her mistakes. Or the kind of friend." Her eyes traveled down to the nightgown in her hand. She heard Leianna clear her throat, but when she looked back up, the captain was gone.

Once again, she was alone.

NINE

ISAAC

Reagan kicked the beat-up football toward Isaac, a cloud of dirt exploding around it. He dove, missing it by a few centimeters.

"Nice work," he said, tweaking her braid. "You're getting good at this." His fingers found his side instinctually as he dropped onto the ground. While the pain of the bullet wound had ceased, the memory remained. The scar tugged at his skin when he moved too rapidly, more unpleasant than debilitating.

"Because football is definitely a necessary skill," she mumbled as she sat beside him.

"When I was young, it was the only thing I wanted to do." *When I was young, I hated being called that,* he scolded himself. Everything he said to her was wrong. He didn't know how to raise a child, especially a teenager, no matter how much he tried to guide her. She wasn't technically his to support, but she had no one left. They were both orphans.

"I want to be helpful. Earn my place here."

"You don't have to *earn* anything. I'm here because I have to be, but as soon as I'm done, we're leaving. This isn't a life you want to live." When Alexandria was safe, he would take Reagan far away from Evangeline and the Argentum. They would find a new home.

"What if I'm a really good fighter, or something? My brother always talked about finding the rebels. Maybe this *is* what I want. I can help save us."

"The war isn't your burden to bear. It isn't even mine. We didn't start it." He plucked a piece of grass and twirled it between his fingers. "Don't let it break you, too."

She put the soles of her boots together and swayed back and forth. "Is she really a good person?"

"Who?"

"The queen."

He had tried to explain to her that Alexandria wouldn't have joined Natania without a reason. Even though he attempted to convince Evangeline that he didn't care about Alexandria, he couldn't sit by and let the former queen manipulate Reagan, too. He wouldn't let her grow up with the same regrets he had. "She is. She's just stuck between a rock and a hard place, same as us."

"I don't know what that means."

"It's from a book. Doesn't matter." He flicked the blade of grass at her, and she laughed. "She was forced to make an impossible decision. Keep a friend alive—keep us *all* alive, really—or start a war."

"And you trust her?"

"With my life." *Now, don't ask if she feels the same way.* He did not deserve Alexandria's trust, not after all the secrets he had kept from her.

A lopsided smile dimpled her face. She rammed her shoulder into his. "Do you like her?"

"I'm not having this conversation with you," he chuckled.

"Fine. Have it your way." Her eyes settled onto the water in front of them, a certain weariness dragging down her grin. "How long do we have here?"

"I don't know. As long as it takes."

"I don't want to be homeless again. I can't watch the hunger take anyone else."

He wrapped an arm around her shoulder. "As long as I'm here, you'll be taken care of. And I don't plan on going anywhere."

"You better not." Her words were thick. A tear landed on his leg.

"I'm not leaving you, kid. That's a promise."

After a few minutes, they went back to the hotel. Being outside for an hour made the mustiness worse. Combined with the acrid smell from soldiers on their smoke breaks, he almost gagged. He had tried smoking once, back at his post in Lyrica when he was seventeen, but his lungs couldn't handle it.

He was about to drop Reagan off at her room down the hall from his, but the sight of James at his door made them pause. "Is something wrong?" he asked, making sure no one was around.

James lowered his voice. "Come with me."

Reagan looked at him with raised eyebrows.

"Go to your room," he whispered. "I'll catch you up later."

She opened her mouth to argue, but the tension in the air seemed to make her think twice. The three walked together until she reached her door, and then James and Isaac walked alone.

James led him to a room he didn't recognize. Taking one last look down the hallway, he slid a piece of paper from his pocket underneath the door.

In a second, the door opened. An arm pulled him inside, and Isaac followed quickly behind. He froze when he saw the room full of rebels.

"What's going on?" he whispered to James. They all spoke in low tones, shooting him sideways glances. There were at least twenty soldiers in the tight space, crowding the table and using the bed as extra seating. The woman who let them in locked the door and set a chair under the handle, which she proceeded to sit on. She swept her cropped, brown hair behind her ears.

"I found your army," James said.

Isaac's jaw clenched. This was a terrible idea. If anyone listened through the walls, they would all be done. His muscles tensed, but instead of getting him out of there, they planted him to his spot. "How do you know we can trust them?"

"I've been working with them for the past five months. They slip up in conversations, say something bad about Evangeline before they remember they're working for her. They want an alternative. The issue is," he paused to look at the woman, who smiled back, "they don't trust *you*. Not until you tell them the truth about who you are and why you're Evangeline's right-hand man."

He could've asked why, but he knew the answer already. Mendoza's name stained him, and even without it, he was still the trained killer who had risen through the ranks too quickly. His past would never let him go. "What's your name?" he asked the woman instead.

"Isla," she replied, reaching out a hand.

"We grew up in the same town," James said. "If we can trust anyone, it's her."

"Okay." Isaac blew out a breath and pushed into the center of the room. When he stood in front of the table, everyone hushed. The silence drummed into his ears. He didn't know how to address a crowd. This was the opposite of what his father had forced him to do. Most of his life had been spent avoiding others' attention, not drawing it. Certainly not convincing people to follow him.

"You know who I am," he spoke in a low voice, quiet enough that it could not be heard by anyone passing by. "I'm the son of a power-hungry manipulator. I'm the person that Evangeline trusted enough to help fake her death. I'm the agent who was sent to deliver our current queen to Mendoza so that he could take the throne for himself."

He leaned back against the tabletop, clutching it to keep his hands steady. "I'm a liar and a traitor. I know you don't trust me. I don't need you to. All I need is for you to trust *them*." He pointed at James and Isla. "The two people here who grew up with Alexandria. Who know that she is better than Evangeline ever can be, that she can make a difference for us. These past few months, Evangeline has tricked you into forgetting that she sent your loved ones to die. That she is the one who burned this organization to the ground at the start. She might want to save her people, same as us, but what will she do when we are free? This fight for power never ends."

A man to his left murmured, "Alexandria is no better than her. She's working with Natania."

"We've given her no choice. How is she supposed to defeat a kingdom that's been killing us for years if we aren't on her side?"

"What if we give her a choice and she still chooses wrong?"

If she had an ounce of self-preservation, she would. The smart thing to do would be to let Natania keep taking her people, and to live without fear of retaliation. But he knew her. She may have been hesitant to sit on the throne, but now that she was here, she would destroy herself to keep them alive. These people could only judge her and Evangeline by their actions, and unfortunately, the latter seemed to be the one fighting back.

He pushed off from the table, leaning toward the group, speaking directly to them. "She won't. I know that better than anything else. But if she still chooses Natania, then we do it ourselves. Not Evangeline's way, but ours. We plan. We get others on our side, from within this building to the cities and towns outside. And when the time comes, we bring our people home."

TEN
ALEXANDRIA

The black satin brushing against Alexandria's knees nearly suffocated her in the Victorin humidity. She took in a deep breath, pressing her ribs against the fabric, begging it to make space for her. But it was not the dress's fault that her lungs ached for air, nor was the heat to blame.

Her eyes drifted from the priest in front of her to the painted frescoes in the dome above him, displaying multi-colored sacrifices that made death seem sterile. Thinking of the blood she had spilled, and that which had been spilled because of her, made her skin crawl.

I shouldn't be here.

Prince Louis had been in the wrong place at the wrong time, and because of Evangeline—because of Isaac—she wasn't there to save him. She clenched her black-gloved hand. Even the fabric there had been touched by the prince's murderer. All her clothing had been borrowed from the former queen.

She had been to a few memorial services in her life, mostly those of mayors and officials. There had been a collective service for the lives lost in the Genean attacks. The memory of the black veil across her mother's face, the tears sliding down her cheek, could not be shaken away. Her mother hadn't been friends with the Dais ministers who had perished; her grief was for something else entirely. An ideal. Alexandria fidgeted now as she did then, her fingers grasping her dress, pleating the delicate satin.

This memorial was different. As per Victorin tradition, the body had been interred as soon as they reached their shore. There was no casket here, only a priest, an altar, and Argon's scattered cries rising from the first pew. The Premier sat to her left, far enough that she could forget he was there. Natania blocked her way to the aisle. Even if she wanted to escape, abandoning propriety, she would not make it far.

The weight of the silence fell off her chest when she finally stepped out into the morning light. She gasped, pulling her high collar away from her neck. Leianna moved forward, weapons rustling, but she held up her hand.

Someone touched her shoulder, and she startled.

A woman looked at her with kind, though reddened, eyes, silver hair done up with a simple comb. Her long-sleeved black dress absorbed all sunlight. She bowed her head slightly. "I've been longing to meet you, Your Majesty."

Alexandria glanced at Leianna and held out her left hand for the woman to shake.

"My name is Sofie," the woman said. "I am Argon's sister."

She stiffened and dipped her head. "My condolences for your loss."

The shadowed skin around Sofie's eyes crinkled. "Thank you for being here. It is a dark day for us. Losing the last heir is difficult."

She nodded, unsure what to say next. "If there's anything we can do for you personally, please let me know."

"Tell me about you."

The words made Alexandria flinch. Sofie's expression held a mixture of pain and determination, though she could not imagine what the latter was for. "I grew up as the daughter of a mayor. Seven months ago, I survived the Campaign and ascended."

"I heard of this *Campaign*." The princess seemed to consider her next words for a moment. "Your own Prime Minister challenged you."

Word travels fast. Whether Victori had spies in Regia or Argon had deduced it from his time at the Coalition gala, Alexandria frankly didn't want to know. She needed Sofie, and by extension, the king, on her side.

"Yes, he did." She battled against the tug of memories threatening to yank her back into the throne room, the little girl's screams piercing her eardrums. "I could not have made it on my own, though I was supposed to. We could do better than our past. I pray I have the chance."

Sofie's eyebrows softened at what she found in Alexandria's face. "I see. Who helped you?"

Where the princess wanted to go with this conversation, she didn't know, but she had an idea. "My family. My friends." She gestured to Leianna. "Another reminder that we cannot survive alone. We always need allies."

Sofie followed her gaze as her eyes found Natania in the crowd. "No, we cannot. We are stronger when we work together."

"We agree on that, Your Highness. Others don't." There she was, scheming in the midst of this woman's grief. She swallowed the bitterness in her throat. "I hope to see more of you in the near future."

The princess squeezed her hand once more. "We're only an ocean apart. Remember that." She left Alexandria and her guards standing at the edge of the crowd.

Prior spoke to Leianna in a voice she likely wasn't intended to hear. "Friendlier than others."

"My thoughts exactly," Alexandria replied.

He drew a step back and straightened his shoulders. His snap to attention filled her with unease.

She merely started walking to the car that would take them back to the palace. "Let's just hope she stays that way."

"You did well," Leianna said as they stopped outside her temporary quarters. Alexandria noted that the captain was staring at her shoulder bag, probably expecting her to bring out the flask right in the hall.

"I did my duty." She didn't have the energy to hide her cynicism. Attending the memorial took every ounce of pretending she could muster. The facade had crumbled beyond repair, and now, all she wished to do was lay in the dark.

Leianna followed her inside, checking the space before she retired for the night. She seemed to hesitate in places. Alexandria peered over her shoulder and found nothing concerning. Realization dawned on her, punching her in the stomach. Will never received a memorial like that.

"Prior, would you mind closing the door?" she asked, giving him a small smile.

The agent looked between them and nodded. When they were alone, Alexandria dropped onto her traveling case. "Are you alright, Leianna?"

Leianna stiffened, eyes darting to the door as if she needed to escape. Still, her face exuded the seriousness it always did: the flat line of her mouth, slightly furrowed brows as she assessed the world around her. But if she was anything like Alexandria, underneath her armor there was a shattered woman clawing, screaming, begging to be heard. That woman could not survive their world, but Alexandria hoped she felt safe enough to come out, if only in this moment.

"I will be," Leianna replied. "Are you?"

"No. We've both lost so much, and it seems we'll keep on losing." She tapped her fingers against the chest to fill the resulting silence. "Have you visited Bailey recently?"

Leianna shook her head. "He's been busy. Lots of people wanting someone to save them." Her eyes flashed and she looked down. Alexandria didn't take offense. She understood.

"Do you need more time off?"

She crossed her arms and sighed. "The last thing I want to do is worry about you from a distance."

"But if you need a day, take it."

"I will miss my husband for the rest of my life. No amount of time will make it hurt any less." After finally meeting Alexandria's stare, she continued, "Will was the first and last person to know who I really am. Mendoza didn't just kill him. He killed a version of me I will never see again."

She knew how that felt, not recognizing her reflection without having Phillip's shadow beside her. No longer being able to access a part of herself, because he was gone, and no one could unlock the exact facets of her personality that he did.

"I know it's not the same, and it won't ever be, but you don't have to hide. Not from Bailey. Not from the other agents. Not from me."

She thought Leianna might run, but instead, she leaned against the wall. "I come from a long line of Argentum agents. We specialize in hiding."

"Is that why you joined so young?"

"Yes. I had a legacy to fulfill, and I was close to doing it. Evangeline knew my name, knew my parents. Attended my grandparents' funerals. I never understood why she would choose Carter over me, until we realized whose son he was." Leianna cut herself off, avoiding Mendoza's name.

"You're here now." Alexandria attempted a reassuring smile. "I won't judge you by a legacy. You've done a great job in your own right, and I'm glad to have you here. In fact, I don't know what I would do without you."

Leianna laughed. It was a small sound, restrained, but it was stark against her captain's uniform. And it suited her. "You would be fine."

"I won't ever have to know, will I?"

"As long as you keep paying me." Her mouth twitched as she joined the agents outside, leaving Alexandria alone with her thoughts.

Briefly, their conversation had made her forget about the flask in her bag. Shame froze her fingers as she reached for it, but in the sudden silence, the guilt she buried at the memorial overtook her. Her excuses screamed the loudest.

Just one more time.

ELEVEN
ISAAC

Isaac's plate clanged against the table. He dropped down onto the bench, Reagan taking the space to his left. She didn't make much room for herself, squeezing where she could, trying not to be a burden. If he wasn't there to check on her, she might disappear entirely.

"What'd you get up to this morning?" he asked, stirring the soup in front of him. The cook, a former chef for one of the ministers, threw together whatever they could steal from the palace's food shipments without raising suspicion. There were a few farmers in their ranks that contributed supplies, but they could not give enough to sustain them all and still make a living. Today's combination included fish and a leafy green substance that melted into stringy goop if it sat for too long. If he ate it quickly, he could enjoy it. It was better than what they were fed in Argentum training.

"The General had me run messages for her."

He clenched his fist against his knee. "Anything exciting?"

"Top secret," she said with a mischievous grin. "Making sure people were in the right place. Guards at the front, helping clean up the first floor, that kind of thing."

"Just don't get into any trouble."

"I can't get into trouble if I follow her orders."

"You sure can." He spooned the soup into his mouth, ignoring the burn. "I would know."

A clattering sound turned his head. James sat across from them. The mess hall had started to fill, now that everyone was returning from their duties for lunch. He had made a deal with the second soldier assigned to watch Evangeline's office that if she covered for him leaving a few minutes early, he would put in a good word with the General. Every day, he did the same thing, so that he could find Reagan and keep her away from the other soldiers. Some were nice, like Isla, but that wasn't his main concern. Most of them thought serving Evangeline was an honor, especially the Argentum agents who had either deserted or retired when Alexandria came along. He wouldn't let them poison her mind like that.

"I heard Evangeline was looking for you," James said.

"I just left her door fifteen minutes ago." He shoveled another spoonful into his mouth before sliding the rest of the bowl to Reagan. With his spoon in his hand, he stood. "Down for more football later?"

She nodded as she poured the soup into one bowl and handed the empty one to him. He laughed. Before he left, he looked at James and inclined his head to the girl. James nodded, understanding what he meant. *Keep her close.*

The water chilled his hands as he rinsed out the bowl. When summer ended, he expected an influx of new recruits. Whether they came out of disdain for Alexandria or hunger, it didn't matter. More people for Evangeline to use either way.

He climbed the stairs, the old ache in his calf panging with each footfall. Evangeline's door opened before he could knock. Two soldiers left, with the familiar look in their eyes like they had been told something important. He set his jaw and entered.

"I heard you needed me," he said.

She didn't look up from the paper she was holding. "Why weren't you at your post?"

"I was hungry."

"Tell me the truth."

"I didn't want to leave Reagan alone."

"As long as she's here, she's safe." He didn't voice his opinion about that. She dropped the stack of papers on the table and turned to him. "Besides, you're going to have to leave her. I'm sending you to the palace."

"Why?"

"To make sure Alexandria sticks to her word. Can I trust you to do that?"

This was a test. Proving he was loyal to Evangeline by reporting on Alexandria's activities. Of course, there were rebels in the palace. The General had eyes everywhere. He would not know who they were, because they would be watching him, too.

"Yes, but only if Reagan comes with me."

"She'll hinder your mission."

"I'll find a place for her. If I'm back in the Argentum, I'll use my pay to send her to school."

"She's valuable to me here."

"*I* won't be valuable to you if I'm worrying about her."

Evangeline searched his face. She must have accepted what she found there, because she conceded. "Take her, but keep her out of the way. I need all your focus on Alexandria. That shouldn't be too hard for you."

He swallowed down his words.

"It's okay to have feelings for her. We all have our faults," she said, stepping closer. "But if your feelings get in the way, I'll have no choice but to remove you from the situation."

"I understand."

"You don't. Not yet." Her breath caressed his cheek. "The time will come when you have to decide who you love more. Her, or the family her ally stole from you."

~

Isaac's eyes strained against the light as Alexandria threw her bedroom door open, the curve of her shoulders showing the strain of her travels. Her curls swept down across her collarbone as she plucked the pins from her updo one by one and tossed them to the side. The damage from the bleach lingered in her limp hair, peeking through the dark brown dye in scattered orange blotches.

She supported herself against the door, head leaned back, eyes squeezed shut.

He had been waiting in the chair by her window for hours, having taken the tunnel passageway that led straight to her quarters. Either due to Evangeline's insiders or a lack of agents, the door was unguarded. Before he left, he promised Reagan he would return for her once he knew how Alexandria would receive him. James would take over their unofficial army for now, gathering new recruits as best he could without Isaac as a safety net. He wasn't worried about that. He spent the silent wait ruminating over how he could keep the young girl safe.

When Alexandria saw him, she stiffened.

They held each other's gaze.

Isaac couldn't move, even though he meant to explain what he was doing in her bedroom. He always had a list of things he wanted to tell her, but every time he saw her, he forgot how to say anything of substance.

His heart stopped when she began to sob.

She collapsed, her face buried in her palm. "Why can't you all just leave me alone?"

He rushed over before his mind could convince him otherwise. There was nothing he could say, not with the guards right outside the door. Her skin was cold as he wrapped his arms around her. Goosebumps trailed across her shoulders.

"I'm tired," she said, the tears thickening her voice. "I'm so tired."

"I know," he whispered. He held her tighter as she rocked back and forth. Brushing aside her hair, he pressed his mouth to her ear. "I'm with you. I promise I'm with you."

"No, you're not." Her lips pulled into a frown. Every time she echoed that disbelief, he repeated his promise, until eventually she stilled, and the room went quiet. She stumbled as she stood. He watched as she picked up her traveling case and set it on the bed. The soft click of the latch was the only sound in the silence, beyond her heavy breathing. Her fingers fumbled with the buttons of the sling that held her other arm in place. A discolored pink scar pulled a swath of skin together in a jagged line across her bicep.

They had stood side-by-side once, in the throne room where she received that injury. He would stand by her now, even if she didn't want him to. Even if he had to do it from a distance.

When she dropped onto the edge of the bed and met his eyes again, he joined her.

She fiddled with the cap of a metal flask, her pointer finger and thumb twisting it back and forth. "What are you doing here this time? Tell me there's not another attack."

"Evangeline thinks it would be helpful for there to be two sets of eyes in the palace." He lowered his voice. "She wants me to keep an eye on you. Make sure you're on her side."

"I would ask whose side you're on, but I wouldn't believe your answer anyway."

His mouth tightened into a sarcastic smile. "I've never been a good liar when it comes to you."

A muscle in her jaw twitched when she looked at him, her brows furrowed, redness rimming her irises. "Really? I seem to remember differently. Even now, I don't know what was true and what was fake."

"I wish it was all true. I wish I wasn't Mendoza's son. I wish I hadn't been manipulated by him and Evangeline for twenty-three years of my life. Do you really want to know the truth? Because I don't. I don't want to think about it any longer than I have to."

He shifted away, not able to bear her expression now. His hand trailed the sharp stubble on his chin. For so long, his father had been his only guide. If he didn't follow the man's every word, his family would never be avenged. His mother and his sister would have died for nothing. And he believed it, even as he bore the scars and bruises from Mendoza's wrath.

"You protected me. I know that. But I can't rely on you again, not when I can't trust that you're not hiding something."

"I won't ask you to trust me. I don't deserve it. Just know that I'm here if you decide to." He nudged her shoulder. The action was too lighthearted with his heart cracking open in his chest. "Deal?"

She squeezed his hand once. "Deal. I guess I'll have to convince the Dais not to execute you."

He stiffened. "Is that a possibility?"

"They wanted someone to blame for Evangeline's death, and since Natania had Mendoza killed..." She paused when he inhaled sharply. "Which you didn't know about. I'm sorry."

The weight of her words rammed into his stomach. "Why?" he breathed. Though the man was anything but a good father, the reminder of his death and finally learning who killed him knocked the air from his lungs.

"He made an arrangement with her. That's why he wanted you to bring me to Regia so badly. If he killed me and took the throne, he was going to hand it over to her. Of course, what I did is hardly any different. We just have a facade of control, and I didn't get anything out of it besides keeping Amira alive."

A hollow laugh bubbled from his throat. He bowed his face into his hands, rubbing circles around his temples. "Of course he did." Mendoza always had a plan. No matter how much he promised his son, those plans would only ever benefit himself. Isaac knew this, but still the unhealable ache grew in his diaphragm, that knot of complicated emotions about his father that he could never unravel.

To his surprise, she rested a hand on his back. The sensation lit up his senses. It was warm and comforting, but also exhilarating. It was her. "One day we'll have a conversation that isn't about someone dying."

"Is that a promise?" His muscles strained with the effort of his grin, but once he looked at her, it was easy. Easy to remember what they had felt the last time he spoke those words, while she was sitting on the countertop in Bailey's church. Easy to forget that he had ruined everything.

"Unless I figure out how to keep Natania and Evangeline happy, it's hardly a possibility."

"Well, I'll be here for a long time. I like my chances."

Cold crept along his skin when she pulled her hand away. "I'll call for Leianna and have her put you in the guard rotation. On her watches."

Because I still don't trust you, he imagined Alexandria saying.

"I have to go get one more person before I'm here for good, but please keep her away from the Argentum at all costs."

Her eyebrow arched. "Who?"

"Reagan."

She nodded and turned away before he could catch a glimpse of her reaction. "I'll find a safe place for her. If safe places even exist anymore."

He knew they did, because she was his. And he was not leaving her again.

TWELVE
ALEXANDRIA

It's a threat to Your Majesty's security," Minister Sawyer said.

Alexandria sat once again in the throne room listening to her advisers argue. This time, they debated Isaac's fate. Looking back and forth between them would make her dizzy, so she kept her eyes firmly planted on the middle of the table. Her head no longer ached, filled with a lightness that could only be attributed to the long swig she took out of her flask before entering the room. Most of her energy was focused on keeping herself steady instead of hearing what the Dais had to say.

Above her, a breeze blew in between the chipped edges of the stained glass. The walls had been replastered after the gala attack, but Minister Agate could not find a glazier to reconstruct the intricate panes. It would have to be fixed by winter, or perhaps they would let the snow pile in, burying her and her throne in a frozen tomb.

"He should be punished. We cannot confirm his innocence in the late queen's death," Wagner argued.

She brought her hand up before the discussion could continue. "You can't confirm his guilt, and I am under the impression that is necessary for a proper execution."

"We have enough evidence that he was working with his father the entire time he was in the Argentum."

"If I have to remind you, the Minister of Justice, one more time about how our laws work, you will no longer have that title." She cleared her throat. "Besides, I think his presence in the palace will do us good. He's a survivor of the Genean attacks. That could signal to the rebels that we are moving forward."

"Are we?" Minister Greer asked. "You still have not divulged your conversation with King Argon."

The Minister of Defense, Kari Daniels, lifted her head. Of course, an agreement with Victori would interest her the most. The woman had been vocal about her disapproval of the Genean Coalition, especially considering her entire position had hinged on the war for the past two decades. "What did he say, Your Majesty?"

"Nothing that can help us with the bombs hanging over our heads." She leaned forward onto her elbow. "Even more proof that Isaac should be here. He is a sign that we will not allow our history to define us."

Her logic was shoddy at best, and the warmth flooding through her skull only made it more difficult to figure out how to justify his presence without outing him as a rebel *and* without directly opposing Natania.

Minister Agate came to her rescue. "I agree. He's not a fugitive, and he did protect Her Majesty throughout the Campaign."

"Even into the throne room. Unprecedented." Minister Wagner's flat voice held anything but amusement.

Vada raised her hand. "This is not up to a vote, is it, Your Majesty?" She inclined her head as if giving Alexandria room to speak.

She shook her head. "No, it's not. Isaac will not be punished for his father's sins. He has already been incorporated into my guard rotation."

"You're letting your emotion cloud your judgment. It's obvious that you have some kind of attachment to him." As Wagner said it, Sawyer took in a sharp breath.

Minister Agate opened her mouth to respond, but Alexandria spoke first. Perhaps it was her lowered inhibitions that made her rise and walk over to Minister Wagner's seat. "Go."

Wagner's eyes narrowed. To her credit, she didn't argue. That was a first. She simply pushed back her chair, the legs screeching against the obsidian tile, gathered her papers, and strode out of the throne room.

Alexandria released a deep breath. "Anyone else?" she asked the table.

The corner of Minister Agate's mouth turned upward. Sawyer's eyes widened as they darted back and forth between her and the slamming wooden door. Her question was met with silence.

"I have another meeting to attend. Vada, please find a replacement for Minister Wagner. Minister Daniels, you'll oversee the Argentum's operations in the meantime." Under her breath, she added, "It may soon need to be a defense force, after all."

As she walked away, Minister Greer called out, "One more thing, Your Majesty." He coughed as his voice cracked. "Duarmme will host a celebration to signal the end of grieving for the Southern Councilchair in a month. How should I respond to the invitation?"

Alexandria bit the inside of her cheek. Another Coalition gathering could go terribly wrong. Yet it would give her a second chance to change Argon's mind, and maybe she could gather more information on where the Premier stood.

"Tell them we'll be there."

Wheels spun in her mind, until everything clicked, and she knew exactly how to convince Natania and Evangeline that she was on both of their sides.

Leianna pulled her aside when she entered the hallway. Her captain gave the other agents a look that made them disperse.

"Carter's too much of a risk and you know it. What's the real reason he's here?" she asked.

"He saved me from the attack, and he'll do it again. He's valuable," Alexandria replied.

"If he's a lead to the rebels, I have to investigate. Even if Minister Wagner's not working on the investigation anymore, the rest of the Dais won't let this go."

"Give me time. I'll get as much information out of him as I can, and then you can take it from there. Okay?"

Leianna's eyes narrowed. She searched Alexandria's face, then let out a small exhale from her nose. "I don't trust him, but I have no choice with you."

Alexandria prayed that was enough.

After enrolling Reagan at the capital's academy, Alexandria locked herself in her quarters, kicked off her heels, and collapsed onto the bed. With her face buried in the quilt, she did not realize she wasn't alone until she heard someone tap on the bedpost.

In an instant, she was on her feet, the blade she kept sheathed at her thigh pointed at Isaac's neck. Her quick movement made the room spin.

"You should know by now that I don't like to be surprised," she muttered, her heart in her throat.

He pointed at the sitting area. "I was waiting right there. Completely visible. Not my fault you weren't paying attention." His gaze trailed her hand as she withdrew her dagger.

"Shouldn't you be off guarding something?"

"Yes. You."

"Oh, right." Though she wasn't in any real danger, her body had yet to catch up to that knowledge, and the ravine's damp odor assaulted her nose. She fiddled with a loose thread on the quilt. "I met with the dean of the academy. Reagan is settled in her dorm, and she'll begin tutoring next week. She hasn't been in school for the past few years, so she'll have to catch up before they can start her in official classes."

His shoulders relaxed as he exhaled. "That's great. Thank you."

Something in his expression made her chest ache. Reagan was around the same age his sister would be if she had not been killed when Genea attacked years ago. She did not know how he had found her again, or what the girl had been up to for the last seven months, but it was impossible to miss how much he cared about her.

"I told her I would remember her. At least that's one promise fulfilled."

They stared at each other in silence. Alexandria waited for him to make the first move, but as soon as he opened his mouth to speak, he closed it again. Her wariness had not faded completely, but something about being in the same room as him, and him alone, made it impossible for her to think about any of her other problems. The only issue she could be concerned with was forgetting the past seven months had ever happened and returning to how things were between them in the cabin.

Her country had been against her then. Now, it seemed like the whole world wanted her dead. Or even worse, they wanted to use her in a way that got the people she cared about killed.

She shifted her eyes away and the tension broke. "How do you feel about taking a trip to Duarmme?"

"We both need a vacation, but I assume that's not what you're talking about." When she explained about the celebration, he said, "I'm sure Leianna can fit me into her security detail."

"Actually, I have a better idea, one that will make Evangeline happy. I need someone on my arm, and I don't think Leianna's much of a dancer."

"Are you asking me to be your date?" He smirked, but guilt gnawed at her stomach when she noticed the brightness in his eyes. She wished she had no ulterior motive.

If only it were that simple. "Yes. Now, take me to Evangeline so I can say it to her face."

"What if she plans another attack?"

I'm betting on it, she thought. "Then at least I'll be prepared this time."

They waited until nightfall before taking the tunnel into the city. The waning of summer afforded them more hours of darkness, but they still had to move fast. She had changed into a comfortable outfit that would allow her to blend into the crowds. Donning her old denim and mended jacket felt like putting on a costume, same as wearing Evangeline's dresses.

Convincing Prior and Watson that everything would be alright if she and Isaac went out alone proved a difficult feat. The sly look Watson had given him told Alexandria that Minister

Wagner's earlier sentiments about their relationship were not restricted to only her.

Alexandria pulled her hood closer to her face. "This feels familiar," she murmured, careful not to make eye contact with anyone as they traversed the edge of the shadows.

The distant echo of laughter left a bittersweet taste in her mouth. She yearned to dance with Amira again, to joke with her and James. All-consuming memories of flickering lights and blaring music and blurred faces filled her with a tricky sense of longing. The woman she was then no longer existed, but she could feel like her, if only through the familiar burn in her throat.

Three months of sacrificing everything for Natania, and she still had not learned anything about Phillip. His bright smile did not greet her at the docks when the laborers came home from their shifts in Thaertos. *He wouldn't still have that smile if he spent three years in those mines.*

She stumbled over a loose stone. Isaac caught her, his arm tight at her waist. "You okay?"

"I'm fine." Forcing herself to focus, she realized they were on the outskirts of downtown. Eerie silence met her ears. "How much farther?"

"Not long." He let her go. A small part of her, like a gnat buzzing at her thoughts, wished he hadn't. His eyes widened as he glanced over her shoulder.

She only saw a shadow before he pushed her against a wall. The chill of the plaster crept through the fabric at her back. Taking in a deep breath, she found Isaac's forearm blocking her face from whoever walked by. The scent of old leather washed over her: his jacket, so close that she could nearly taste the smell.

A familiar voice spoke to her right. "I can see you."

Isaac lowered his arm, Leianna appearing at the end of the alley. She crossed her arms. Her dark hair shone blue under the streetlight. Alexandria's heart jumped, blood rushing in her ears.

"Hello, Lei," Isaac said. "Beautiful night, isn't it?"

"Quit stalling. Tell me why you kidnapped the queen."

Alexandria scoffed. "I'm not that easy to overpower. Give your training some credit. I came willingly."

"Why did you avoid notifying me?"

She flicked her eyes to Isaac, who watched her with an expression that she assumed to mean she would have to explain this all on her own. "We just needed to get away from the palace."

Leianna had never done anything to make her trust waver, but Evangeline being alive would complicate their partnership. Nothing she could do would earn Leianna's full loyalty when she had practically been raised to serve the former queen, and Alexandria was not ready to lose her captain yet.

"Without protection?"

"He's my protection."

She raised her eyebrows. "Is that what they're calling it these days?"

"I promise I won't die. We'll be back soon." Her skin itched under Leianna's stare. If the woman questioned them more, she wasn't sure how long their story would hold up. "Just don't follow us. We want to be alone."

Recognition crossed Leianna's face, and Alexandria hoped she remembered their earlier agreement, despite however reluctant she might be about leaving them on their own. "I wouldn't dream of it."

When she had faded into the shadows a few blocks down, Alexandria sighed. "You didn't look behind us that whole time?"

Isaac leaned against the wall. "Never underestimate Leianna."

"She did track us all the way to Hult. I should've expected it." She brushed the windswept curls away from her face, starting back down the alley. "That was a terrible idea back there."

Footsteps sounded across the path as Isaac matched her stride. "I just confirmed what the agents have been whispering since I got here."

"I don't need any more whispers. Things are already bad enough. Now they think I'm letting my emotions get the best of me."

"Are you?"

She wished she could wipe the smirk off his face. "No. Not at all."

"That's a shame. I'd like to be able to say I distracted a queen."

"You wish." A laugh escaped her mouth before she could stop it.

He chuckled. "That we can agree on." A dimple dotted his smile as the melodic sound stretched between them. She rubbed her fingers together to avoid touching his face.

If the nighttime breeze did not hold such a chill, she liked to think that she would not feel her blush as acutely. Her cheek burned when she brushed the back of her hand against it.

As she took her next step, someone grabbed her arms. Her shouts echoed through the alley as she struggled against the force pulling her to the ground.

A figure dressed in black clamped his hands over Isaac's mouth. He drove an elbow into the person's side. Alexandria could not watch the rest as she fought off her own attacker.

She threw her arm back. The assailant loosened their grip enough for her to turn and launch the flat of her palm at his nose. It cracked loudly. He stumbled backwards, holding his hand against the steady stream of blood. His eyes watered.

Grunts echoed behind her. She turned for a split second, but that was all it took for the man to rush her again. Burning pain lanced up her arm as he clawed her skin.

She slammed her head into his broken nose. Light flashed behind her eyes. He yelled and drew back. Blood dripped hot and thick down her forehead. His blood, she hoped.

"Who are you?" she snarled. The lack of air in her lungs made the words come out in sharp staccato.

"They're rebels," Isaac said. She kicked out at the attacker's knee, and he crumpled to the ground. Then, she turned to face Isaac.

Red lines split his lip in two places. His assailant's hood had fallen away to reveal a man with silver-streaked hair. Unlike her attacker, who was currently cowering against the wall, he was unconscious.

She grabbed the conscious man by the back of his jacket, dragging him off the cobblestone. Her fingernails scratched the cracked leather as she pushed him to walk in front of her.

"Of course they are," she muttered. "Evangeline can never make things easy."

THIRTEEN
ISAAC

The rebel Isaac recognized as Fitzgerald stumbled ahead of them, nose dripping blood onto the stained carpet as they navigated the abandoned hotel. Alexandria clenched her teeth so tightly that he could see her jaw working as she kept the man in line by the collar of his jacket.

James watched them from his doorway, Isla peeking over his shoulder. Isaac wondered what they were plotting so late in the evening, before coming to an altogether different conclusion. He inclined his head ever so slightly in their direction.

When they reached Evangeline's office, Alexandria didn't bother knocking. The click of the doorknob could've been gunfire with how quiet the hall was. Multiple doors were cracked open, but no one dared to move with the deadly look on her face.

"Did you put them up to this?" Alexandria's voice cut through the room.

Evangeline tossed a file onto the table and folded her arms on the surface. "To what do I owe the pleasure of this visit?"

"I had some information you might like to know, but after you sent people to attack us, I don't feel like being generous."

"I didn't send anyone to attack you." She sighed and stood. Her long strides brought her in front of Fitzgerald in the span of a second. Ice flooded Isaac's veins as she gripped the man's jaw, fingernails digging into his skin. The blood from his shattered nose spilled down her hand. "Who was a part of this?"

He coughed, his voice raspy. "Just me."

Evangeline glanced at Isaac. "Is that true?"

Whatever she intended to do with the two men couldn't be good. Isaac's stomach churned at the thought of giving them up for punishment. She hadn't been a gentle queen, and especially now that she didn't have the eyes of the country on her, who knew how she would react?

But they could have killed Alexandria.

"Carlson," he said. "Carlson was with him."

"Where is he now?"

"In the alley. Unconscious."

Her irises glimmered. "Nice work. I've always appreciated your strength."

The praise nearly brought a smile to his face out of habit, but her assessing expression made him nauseous. He inspected the carpet to avoid meeting her gaze.

Alexandria moved closer to him, her arm brushing against his. "I don't believe you, Evangeline."

"I can prove it." She let go of Fitzgerald's face to take his hand. A saccharine smile tugged at her lips. "Come with me."

Fitzgerald's eyes widened. They pleaded with Isaac, but his feet wouldn't move other than to make way for the two as they left the room. Alexandria closed her fingers around his wrist. Her touch sparked his muscles. He followed Evangeline numbly, feeling only the gravitational pull that meant Alexandria was still by his side.

Evangeline shoved the man into the mess hall. Under the dim lights, his pale skin turned a sickly shade of yellow. Silverware clattered as people stopped eating.

"You all have been such good allies," Evangeline said, stopping in the middle of the room. All eyes turned to her, their bodies like the sea, ebbing and flowing as each snapped to attention. "Without your loyalty, we would never stand a chance against Genea, to end the suffering they are putting our families through."

Silence.

"This man has put our mission in jeopardy. He was caught planning to give critical information to our enemy. I cannot allow him to compromise us further. How do we deal with a traitor?"

Stares.

Isaac noted the lies from her lips. The man had betrayed them, but not as egregiously as she wanted them to believe.

Her voice grew deathly quiet. "I asked, 'How do we deal with a traitor?'"

"We remove the threat, General," a woman responded from the crowd.

A rumble rolled over the rebels, growing louder with every second. They chanted the words. If the man in front of them gave Genea even the possibility of an advantage, then he needed to die. Some stood silently, their eyes meeting one another's with wary glances. Isaac recognized most of them from the meeting back in James's room.

Their battle cry stole all the oxygen from his lungs. His chest tightened, and he suppressed the reflex to gasp for air. Light glinted off the gun in Evangeline's hand as she raised it steadily up to the man's head.

"You fought with honor," she said, "but we'll take it from here."

Alexandria lunged toward her. He grabbed her wrist, pulling her away as the shot erupted. Other than the ringing in his ears, nothing made a sound as Fitzgerald crumpled to the blood-slicked tile floor.

His heart pounded so hard it hurt. Violence never got easier to handle, no matter how much he was its perpetrator or its witness. One final breath left the man's body in a rattle that made him flinch.

Evangeline holstered the gun at her side and turned back to them. "Now, what information do you need to give me?"

In that moment, Isaac realized just how she had gotten under his skin for the past decade.

Love and fear.

As soon as Alexandria disappeared into Evangeline's office, he nodded to the soldiers at the door, told them he was going to grab something from his room, and slipped away. His pulse thudded painfully as he fought to keep his countenance calm. He needed to find James and Isla *now.*

Fortunately, by the time he knocked on James's door, they were already on their way out. Isla jumped when she saw him on the other side. Her muted smile failed to cover the fear in her eyes.

"We heard a gunshot. Are you hurt?" she asked in one rushed breath.

"No. Fitzgerald is dead. Where's James?"

She pushed the door open wider and James appeared behind her. His usually pale face matched the red of his hair. "We were just–" he started before Isaac cut him off.

"I'd love to hear that story another time." Footsteps pounded in the distance, and he lowered his voice. "We need to talk."

Isla stepped into the hall and glanced around, sharing a look with James. "Follow us."

He obliged, though a nagging sensation in his gut implored him to stay behind. Moments ago, he had gotten someone killed and ratted out another. Who knew what Evangeline would do next?

Alexandria can handle herself. The thought didn't placate his dread.

The old wooden staircase squeaked beneath their feet. He held his breath until James stopped two landings above and whispered, "No one uses these rooms but us."

Immediately, Isaac could tell why that was. Water stains spread from the ceiling like dark clouds, trailing in lines down the wall. The stale air burned the back of his nose. He imagined a sealed coffin would smell better.

James pushed open a cracked door at the end of the hall. Inside, three people had gathered. He recognized them from the first rebel meeting. His heart sank at the idea of their group diminishing that quickly, until Isla explained that the three were an inner circle of sorts—the most trusted individuals who would carry on their mission if anything happened to them.

A middle-aged man stood, arms crossed, in the center of the dilapidated room. "Tonight, Evangeline has made it clear that Alexandria is on her side." His harsh whisper sounded like a worn car engine. "Why protect her if the General already is?"

"Evangeline has done nothing but prove that she's willing to kill to get what she wants," Isaac said. "She wants Alexandria to trust her, and that will never happen." He looked over his shoulder into the hallway, searching for anyone who might have followed them. "We don't have much time until Evangeline persuades everyone into thinking she's doing what's right."

One of the two women stepped forward. Her angular black brows and pulled-back hair made her appear eerily similar to Leianna in the darkness, but her soft voice distinguished her immediately. "If we're lucky, this will disillusion more people with Evangeline. If we're unlucky, which I expect to be, this will make them hate Alexandria, too. Fitzgerald's execution was in her name."

The man turned to him. "Have you told her about us yet?"

Isaac had considered it multiple times, thinking it might regain a sliver of her trust, but he couldn't give her false hope. The group seemed wary of her at the start, and this conversation made it apparent that some of them still were. "I won't tell her until I know you won't turn on her."

This time, it was the second woman who spoke. "Don't tell her until you know she won't turn on *us.*"

A door slammed somewhere in the hotel. Lightning struck his nerves. It sounded too similar to a gunshot, and even though his brain tried to be rational, his reflexes were convinced Alexandria was bleeding out on Evangeline's floor. He couldn't leave her alone with the General any longer. Not when he knew firsthand what that woman could do.

He rushed to the door, looking back over the group once more. The three shared heavy glances. He could only hope they weren't questioning their decision to join him.

"Evangeline will do whatever it takes to come out on top. Don't let them forget that."

"Go. We'll handle things here," James said.

Isaac started running before he could finish the sentence.

FOURTEEN
ALEXANDRIA

Alexandria's mouth went dry as she stood in Evangeline's office, muscles primed to bolt.

"How could you?" Her voice was ragged around the edges. She wiped at a stray drop of Fitzgerald's blood on her sleeve, but the stain remained.

Evangeline silently poured an amber liquid from a decanter into two chipped glasses and slid one across the wooden table. *Maybe she* can *read my mind.* Alexandria tried to hesitate before she grabbed it. She failed.

The burning taste gave her a brief moment of clarity before her head went fuzzy. Evangeline beckoned for her to sit, and against her better judgment, she did.

"I saved you," Evangeline said. The three simple words sent Alexandria over the edge.

"You killed him," she ground out. "You killed all of them. You sent them to die."

"Yes, I did."

"Why?"

Evangeline rolled the crystal stopper under her palm. "You're sacrificing our people to the mines, just like I did. Why is it different when you pull the trigger?"

"I'm doing it for the people I love."

"Everyone has someone that loves them. This job is impossible when you care for some more than others."

Her glass clinked against the tabletop. "I suppose the alternative is caring for my crown above them all."

"You must care for the throne if you expect to serve it well."

"We have two different ideas of what it means to care." She cursed herself for ending up on the defensive again. Evangeline was just toying with her. They could not be more different, she and her half-sister. Or so she hoped.

Evangeline hummed a noncommittal noise. "I should have identified you as the heir sooner. You could have learned so much in the palace."

"There's nothing I want to learn from *you*." She swallowed down the rest of the liquor and set it aside. Her fingers trembled against the arm of her chair.

"That's because I haven't started teaching you yet."

"I'm waiting." The bitterness of the drink coated her words.

"Tell me yours and I'll tell you mine."

With a jolt, she remembered why she was there to begin with. Buried underneath Fitzgerald's corpse and the alcohol coursing through her veins, she had a plan–one Evangeline would be forced to play along with, if only due to her pride. "The Premier invited the Keveldan delegation to a celebration for the end of mourning in Arhaven. I'll be leaving in a month. Your turn."

Evangeline pushed her chair back and started walking around the table. "There's a loose floorboard under the desk in my study."

"And?"

"What you find there will help you make the right choice in the end." Evangeline plucked the glass from her hands. The woman scrutinized it and set it back on the table. "You know what they say about old habits," she murmured.

Alexandria stiffened. "You don't know what you're talking about." It was a terrible bluff.

"Sure, I do. I'm not judging. Just stay focused. I need a kingdom to come back to."

She wasn't sure if the command made her want to stop her spiral or continue out of spite. After years of being ignored by Evangeline and living under her reign, she could not imagine the former queen giving advice without an ulterior motive.

"We're done here. I've kept up my end of the deal." The chair rattled when she stood.

"For now. You'll be back here soon enough, won't you?"

She didn't bother to glance back at the smug look on Evangeline's face. Before she knew it, she had slammed the door behind her and started stumbling through the halls. The soldiers tried to follow her, but Evangeline must have ordered them not to, for some reason. That was even more concerning, that she trusted her enough to let her go easily.

Alexandria would return, after all.

Isaac found her by the time she realized she didn't know where she was going. His hair had fallen in his face, and his rapid breathing made her look over his shoulder. He took her face in his hands and asked, "What happened?"

"Nothing worse than what we've already seen tonight." Her brows furrowed. "What happened to you?"

"I thought–" He cut himself off and dropped his hands. "Never mind."

With her thoughts muddled, she didn't have the energy to question him. She looped her arm through his. "Take me home."

~

The papers hit the floor with a crinkling sound that reminded Alexandria of leaves falling.

Not of the rebel's body crashing down a week prior, blood seeping into the cracked tile around him. Definitely not that. She forced herself to think about something different, returning to the ordinances and letters scattered on the ground.

She crouched, knees cracking with the effort. When she was younger, she thought she would have a couple of decades before her bones started to protest every movement, but being attacked more times than she could count aged her beyond her years. Instead of picking up the papers, she dropped to her stomach and rested her cheek on her arm.

Her eyes caught on the uneven edge of the floorboard peeking out from beneath her solid wood desk. It had been calling to her ever since Evangeline brought it to her attention. Spite kept her from exploring what lay beneath. That, and fear. Her half-sister seemed confident that whatever she stowed away there would change Alexandria's mind about something, and she could not let her or Natania hold any more power over her.

Still, *not* knowing rattled her. It stole her appetite and consumed her thoughts. Isaac and Leianna tried to speak to her, but she responded only with short sentences and inattentive nods. Her people's restlessness permeated her own skin, an ache that urged her to run, to scream, to go anywhere but the one place she was obliged to remain.

The palace walls closed in around her a little bit more every passing day. She could go and gather her people, visit incoming workers and send off their replacements, but her words would harm more than salve. Giving them a blessing from her lips while signing their lives away with her pen... She would rather be a distant shadow than a present hypocrite.

She laughed harshly. Evangeline had done that exact thing, hadn't she?

It would take all her strength to move the desk on her own, especially with one arm. She shoved away the idea of asking for help as quickly as it entered her mind. Witnesses might be dangerous depending on what she found.

With her hip pressed against the side, she thrust her bodyweight into the desk, knocking over a cup of pencils. They rolled off the side one after another. The sturdy legs scraped against the wood.

Her personal study was connected to her quarters by a side door; undoubtedly, the guards posted in the stairwell would still be able to hear the noise. Watson and Beckett were on duty, and they would hesitate to ask her questions—unlike Isaac and Leianna, who would barge in without a thought. She wanted to be annoyed by that but couldn't bring herself to it.

Finally, she had moved the desk enough to access the panel. Her uneven fingernails were just long enough to slide underneath and pop it free. She set the floorboard to the side. The small rectangular compartment, barely as long as her forearm and less than half as wide, held a worn leather notebook and a yellow-tinged folded paper. Dust coated the cover of the notebook. It transferred a grey film to her fingers as she assessed it, holding it steady against the floor.

The brittle paper had started to tear in places. Upon further inspection of the binding, she noticed a ragged edge, as if pages had been torn from the front. She studied the smudged ink on the first page. The date in the corner was illegible, and deciphering the condensed cursive gave her no other details about the notebook's origin. One paragraph struck her attention:

BURNED QUEEN

The Varnard has been more forceful as of late. Commander Arlington is turning Keveldans away from the base, no matter how young or ill. I sit and watch, tending to their wounded while watching my people starve on the outside, all for the promise of scraps. They have enough rations to feed all of us. The long winter will be over soon. We just have to survive until the crops start growing again. Mikel wants me to join him in Regia, but I can't leave them here. Without me, they'll have no one on the inside.

Her eyes ran over the passage multiple times. She thought back on what her father had told her about the world after the Fall. Thousands of Keveldans died in the aftermath, not because of the bombs themselves, but because snow and ash had fallen in equal measure, suffocating farmlands and making it all but impossible to fish. If that was the *long winter* the author referred to, then they were writing within a few years after.

But who were the Varnard? They didn't seem to be Keveldan, not with their commander turning her people away. Her father had never mentioned them, and neither had Minister Daniels. She thought perhaps they were an earlier version of the Argentum, but if that was true, the name would have been mentioned in her documents somewhere.

After skimming for a minute, she landed on another mention of Commander Arlington—of his death in an attack. The next page made her pulse race. She fought to keep from skipping ahead, even though she suspected where it would end.

The Varnard's parliament is prideful. They claim Arlington's son is the rightful successor. Mikel and I proposed a deal: Whoever is strong enough to beat John will rule over all of Kevelda, including the base. Arlington's selfishness killed my child. It's only fair that we do the same.

Alexandria almost ripped the page with the force of flipping it. The author had set up the Campaign, at least, an early version of it. She held her breath as she read the rest.

I won. As always, there was a cost. My husband took a fatal blow for me. I killed John in turn. I'm their Commander now, but even that title is colored by their control.

It's time Kevelda returns to the age of kings and queens.

She closed the book and rocked back on her heels. Her head ached as she tried to piece the entries together. The author was the first monarch after the Fall and had proposed the Campaign to take control back from the Varnard, whoever they were. Still, that did not explain why Evangeline thought finding this would make Alexandria sympathetic to her. It simply meant that there was yet another group she had to worry about. Dealing with Natania and Evangeline was complicated enough without history coming back to bite her.

Before she could flip back to the last page she had read, muffled footsteps sounded through the wall. She slammed the notebook closed and slid it back into the compartment as someone knocked at her study door. Alexandria looked at the clock, realizing she should have been getting herself ready for training.

When she opened the door, Leianna glanced beyond her. "Should I even ask what you were up to?"

"Renovating." A couple of curls had sprung free of her updo in her effort to move the desk. She brushed them out of her eyes and exited the room, sealing the notebook and its secrets away.

Until she figured out what Evangeline would do with the information, no one else could know.

FIFTEEN
ISAAC

Seafoam sprayed tiny droplets over the ship's railing. The water swirled and simmered, waves cresting too close to Isaac for comfort. Over the past few hours, the bright sea had turned midnight blue, the sky darkening to a ghastly gray. His first time on a ship, and of course, there would be a storm.

He thought of finding Alexandria to take his mind off it, but she had been so preoccupied with preparing for their visit to Duarmme that he would only be a bother. Their brief moment of camaraderie had dissipated as soon as Evangeline put a bullet in Fitzgerald's head almost a month ago.

Despite his best efforts, she closed herself off again. He would do anything to regain her trust. Countless hours guarding her door, his nerves standing on end, all senses attuned to potential threats. Just as he had for Evangeline.

The reminder of who he had once been made his blood run cold.

As he turned toward the cabin, the door opened. Leianna strode up to the railing and rested her arms on it. The wind whipped her black hair across her face, stark lines on the paleness of her skin.

When she and Isaac went through Argentum training, they had been forced to do conditioning under the summer sun. For most of the first few months he had known her, her complexion was a bright shade of red. It turned even more so the one time he had overcome her while sparring. He never won a second time, not until he tricked her in Bailey's church during the Campaign. Almost as if she had remembered all his moves enough to know when he would make them again.

"Needed air?" he asked, returning to his previous stance.

"No. I need your help." She spoke the words as if they were a gnat she was trying to swat away.

"You need *my* help? You don't need help from anyone."

"Though I don't trust you, Alexandria does. I'm worried about her."

He had seen Alexandria become a shell of herself over the past month, that was true. Often, he tried to break through to her, but she did not reach back. It broke his heart over and over again. Not her pushing him away, but her *fading* away.

"That makes two of us."

Her head shifted slightly toward him. "Evangeline never had times like this, did she." Isaac wasn't sure if it was a statement or a question.

"I don't want to talk about Evangeline."

"I know. I miss her, too."

His shoulders straightened. He had forgotten that many people still did not know the former queen was alive. More shocking than that was Leianna admitting her own emotions.

"Evangeline didn't feel things the way Alexandria does. The war weighed on her, but even at her worst, she never had to face the pressure that Alexandria's under now."

Leianna's fingers made circles on her sheathed dagger's handle. "I don't know how to help her. Perhaps it's not my job to protect her emotional wellbeing. She only hired me to keep her alive."

"I'd argue that's an important part of it." He ran his hand over his jaw. "If I knew a way, I would tell you. I would be doing it already."

"You do help. I see it."

"She's hardly talked to me over the past few weeks."

"What happened between you two? The last I saw, you were getting too close for *my* comfort."

"That's the nearest thing to a joke I've ever heard you say." He plastered a smile on his face as he shook away the memory of Fitzgerald hitting the floor. Carlson had likely been executed the same way after they left. Alexandria had been silent the entire walk to the palace, locking herself into her room without looking back at him. "Nothing happened between us."

The silence stretched out until Isaac could not help but shift uncomfortably. "What about you?" he continued. "How have you been?"

"That doesn't matter," she said.

"It does. Will was the best of us."

She snapped her head toward him so quickly that he thought she might punch him. Instead, her face softened. An unguardedness flickered across her eyes before they steeled again. "He was."

Will had enlisted at an older age than they had, when Isaac was nineteen and he was twenty-one. He always assumed that the man had family to provide for, or maybe he had lost them all. It wasn't until the Campaign that he realized Bailey was Will's father.

For the most part, Isaac had stuck to watching the other agents interact to avoid saying anything that would connect him to Mendoza. He joined groups in the mess hall and on training fields, but he rarely spoke a word. That is, until Will came along and actually started asking him questions about himself. The man was more outgoing than anyone else he had met in the Argentum, easily forming friendships in an environment that usually destroyed them before they began. Never cutthroat, never cunning, just Will.

"Things remind me of him all the time," she said, "even these uniforms." A dry laugh joined her words. She turned and opened the door without another sound.

Before she could cross the barrier, he asked, "Were we ever friends?"

Her eyes focused on a point beyond him, and she nodded.

The metal railing chilled him to the bone as his fingers tightened around it. "Do you think we could be friends again?"

"Yes," she said. "I do."

~

He found Alexandria on the upper deck the next morning, the staggered green trees of Arhaven blending into a port of brick-roofed buildings in the distance. Her mouth was drawn in a harsh line, and she squinted against the glare of the sun on the water below. She tensed as he came up beside her.

"Almost there," she said. A slight tremor underlined her words. Shadows trailed under her eyes, dark against the bronze of her skin.

"Did you sleep?" he asked. As they neared the city, his heart began to beat faster. Evangeline knew about the gathering ahead, and she was not one to waste an opportunity, no matter what she promised Alexandria.

"Did you?"

"No. The storm kept me up." And he spent the night worrying about her, but she didn't need to know that.

The corner of her mouth twitched upwards. "I guess one thing never changes."

There was the way for him to get through to her. "What about you? Do you still talk in your sleep?"

A swath of deep red blossomed across her nose. He never mentioned it, but he noticed it every single time. If his flirting distracted her from the looming threat of their destruction at either Natania or Evangeline's hands, he would do it without hesitation. He would do it without that motivation, too.

"I wouldn't know." She turned her face away from him. He followed her gaze back to the line of buildings, which were propped haphazardly along the water in various shades of brown.

A soft breeze whispered along his skin. He had expected this place to feel different from Kevelda, given that it was his first time out of the country, but the dry, cool air had not changed over the course of their journey. As they drew nearer, a cobblestone promenade appeared. Few people milled about it in the early hour. This was a glaring contrast to the line of soldiers in green military uniforms standing at attention on the dock.

The two silently surveyed the soldiers as the ship drifted into port. When the attendants secured the mooring lines, the ship swayed, and he caught Alexandria's arm to keep her from stumbling. He kept his eyes on the group, noticing a woman about their age with light brown hair and a crown atop her head. Her icy stare was joined by a smile that Isaac did not find very convincing.

To her left stood a man in a dark grey uniform of similar style to the others. Another man with honey-blonde hair stood on her other side. He smiled brightly, though Isaac recognized the pain in his creased brow. His grin faltered when he locked eyes with Alexandria.

Alexandria looked like she had seen a ghost.

SIXTEEN
ALEXANDRIA

The pain in her stomach sent her sprawling from the railing.

Her vision blurred. The sky and sea warped in her sight. What was once up was now down. The world had irreparably altered, and the fraying thread that tethered Alexandria to it had snapped when she set her eyes on Phillip.

Phillip.

A dam broke in her chest. Every painful memory rushed back through her, all the nights she had forgotten spent half-drowned in a bottle. He was *here*. She had long lost hope of ever seeing him again, but when she discovered what Natania was doing with the drafted soldiers, a spark had lit in her heart. Yet she had not truly expected him to come home.

It took her a moment too long to realize there was something wrong with the scene.

Why is he standing next to Natania?

Her heels clicked on the deck as she stepped forward. Though the boat no longer moved, she could not find her balance. Ringing in her ears muffled the sounds of the crew setting the gangway. She did not realize her nails were digging into Isaac's arm until her fingers grew sore.

Sorry, she meant to say, but her words were lost among the thoughts racing through her head. A garbled noise escaped her mouth. Tightness in her throat blocked air from reaching her lungs. All the while, Isaac clutched her to his side as if his own life depended on it.

"Is that the man from the pictures in the cabin?" he asked.

Nodding her head took too much energy. She simply lifted her face and blinked.

"Phillip," he said. He tightened his grip around her shoulders before she could respond.

After a minute, the chaos in her mind had subsided enough for her to form a sentence. "She knows it's him. She knows what he means."

"I'll distract them."

Her voice cracked as she spoke. "No. I can't let her see my guard down. Nor the Premier. I need him. I need to be strong."

"You *are* strong. This would hurt anyone."

She choked on a laugh. Her feet balanced on the edge of sanity, and one slip would send her to a depth from which she could not emerge. "Can I tell you something, Isaac?"

His eyes widened as he searched her face. She could not know what she looked like, but with the way her eyes burned and her cheek muscles strained, she could only imagine.

"Anything."

"If Natania didn't have Amira locked up, I would throw myself overboard rather than deal with this. Because if Phillip's on her side, then we're in the wrong. That's the only explanation. We're the bad guys. And if we are, I've already lost."

A wave of nausea crashed into her. She clutched the fabric at the back of his jacket. To those gathered on the pier, she prayed this looked like nothing more than a queen holding her potential consort.

That's how she would have to play it. Like she didn't care at all that Phillip was *right there.*

"Get me through this," she whispered, taking his arm.

He clasped his other hand over hers. "Of course."

Leianna approached them as they moved toward the gangway. "All clear," she said, before pausing to look at her. "What happened?"

Alexandria's legs had not stopped shaking. She hoped her face did not betray the storm in her mind. "I'll explain later. Nothing that concerns my safety right now." Her heart was an entirely different matter.

As she stepped onto the dock, knuckles pale against the black of Isaac's jacket, Natania's stare sliced through her skin like a blade. She bowed her head to the Premier, who did the same with an unreadable expression. Phillip stood on her periphery. He drew closer, but she averted her eyes, instead focusing on Natania. The sole person responsible for whether her people lived or died.

"Nice to see you, Natania." No emotion rimmed her words, her tone completely flat.

"Always a pleasure, Alexandria," the queen responded. "I believe you haven't met my fiancé, or maybe you have. Phillip grew up in Kureya as well."

A small, strangled sound started in her throat, but she swallowed it down. "We've met."

Minister Greer spoke, his monotonous voice shattering the line of their stares. "How wonderful." For once, she was grateful for his comment.

Natania's sharp eyebrow twitched as she turned to Isaac. Her eyes narrowed in a way that only heightened the dread building in Alexandria's chest. "I don't believe *we've* met."

She reached out a hand and he shook it. "Isaac," he said.

"Of the Mendoza family?"

His fingers tensed at the small of her back. "That's the one."

"Such a shame what happened to your father."

Alexandria bit her tongue so hard she feared it drew blood. She turned to the Premier and recited her condolences; Greer did the same, much more eloquently, though it did not appear to affect Duarmme's leader one way or another.

The Premier clasped his hands in front of him and lowered his head slightly. "We appreciate your joining us for the end of mourning. The Vice-Premier will escort you to your lodgings and brief you on the schedule." When he finished speaking, he turned and walked up the dock, flanked by two guards.

A man of few words.

A woman Alexandria hadn't noticed emerged from the line of the remaining soldiers. She wore the same grey uniform as the Premier, yet a bright blue lacquered pin on her jacket differentiated her. The woman quickly introduced herself as the Vice-Premier, Therese Gram, and then she explained what their day would look like. They would all gather for breakfast in the Great Hall and would be free to do as they pleased until that night's gala in the Grand Ballroom. There would be a tour of the palace grounds and capital, of course, if they so desired to join.

The Vice-Premier led them to the guest wing, which had so many doors lining the walls that she could not count them all. Fortunately, they were numbered. Once Leianna swept Alexandria's room and declared it all clear, a Duarmmian soldier took her and Natania's guards to the barracks. She had argued that she should wait until Prior or Watson was available to stand guard, but Alexandria vowed to lock herself into the guest bedroom until breakfast in two hours.

Isaac stood at the threshold, watching her frantically pace around the room. He inched forward, then paused. She shook her head. His mouth pressed into an unconvincing smile, and he murmured something about being next door before backing out of view.

Much to her dismay, Phillip tapped on her door as soon as the hallway was clear. Her heart hammered against her chest. She needed more time to prepare. A part of her ached for him, for who they had been, but she was no longer that girl, and if he was on Natania's side, the boy she knew no longer existed.

She shattered when he closed the door behind him. His face had hardened over the past three years, sharper angles cutting his cheekbones and jaw. But his smile was the same. Broad and bright, with nothing held back.

He broke the silence first. "I don't know what to say."

Everything would change when he explained himself, where he had been the past few years and how he became Natania's fiancé. For a moment, just a moment, she wanted to be unconditionally happy that he stood there before her. *Alive.*

"Don't say anything."

The tension snapped. His arms circled her waist as her hand found his face. She crashed her lips against his, fiercely enough to hold back the tide of memories–all the pain that had brought them to where they stood. He held her so tightly that her feet were light against the ground. If she had to support herself, she would have collapsed. Tears rolled down her face and onto his cheeks.

They pulled apart in waves, a short break followed by a longer one, until they separated completely. His fingers still brushed the fabric of her jacket. Her chest heaved.

Something between them, something beyond their circumstances, had changed. He was different. *They* were different. As much as she had longed to hold him again, she now wished for nothing more than to know how he had found himself betrothed to her enemy.

"Why are you here?" Her voice cracked before she could ask about Natania.

He tightened his fingers around her waist, as if he knew his answer could make her run away. The urge to do so was only tempered by the pull of their past. "Queen Natania found me in the mines a year ago. I didn't know what her interest in me was until I heard you were the heir and that you had survived the Campaign. How are you the heir? I know you were adopted, but no one ever told your parents that you were related to the queen?"

"I'm King Tomas's daughter," she said, before she could think it through. Of course Natania was using him, but she did not know to what extent she could still trust him. It had been three years. If her entire life had changed in a month during the Campaign, who could tell how different they both were now?

"You're Queen Evangeline's sister?"

She nodded. It was easier for her not to explain that she still didn't know who her mother was. There was no way to find out, not unless she groveled her way into Evangeline's favor.

"What does Natania have over you?" she asked.

He let go of her jacket as if it burned him. The distance between them grew, and though he took but a few steps backward, it seemed uncrossable. "Nothing."

Her heart stuttered. "There has to be something." The words were thick in her mouth.

"There isn't."

"Why?"

"It's for the better. Believe me." He was never good at shielding his emotions. His face displayed them all, eyes exposing the fact that he needed to convince himself, too.

Her tears fell hot against her hand as she wiped them away. Anger tightened her stomach, though her brain could not determine who the target should be. Natania, maybe. Never Phillip.

Never the Phillip she had known before.

"How can you say it's for the better when I'll spend the rest of my life regretting that I fell in love with you? You were everything I wanted. It was always you. Do you know what I gave up for you? For who I thought you were?"

She faced his back now. He reached a hand up to brush his hair in place. "Don't give up anything for me. Or anyone."

He was gone before she could respond.

SEVENTEEN
ALEXANDRIA

Isaac found Alexandria in her room before the gala, as she was struggling with her corset and trying to fix the puffiness around her eyes. She might have asked him to help her with the garment if she had actually cared about it at all, but with her lungs already incapable of filling any time she thought of Phillip, the lacing would only send her lifeless body to the floor when she saw him on Natania's arm.

The dress was another thing entirely. While the palace tailor had adapted most of her clothing so that she could fasten it with one hand, he had not yet figured out Evangeline's evening gowns. She stood motionless as Isaac deftly secured the row of buttons lining her spine over her slip. Silence hung in the air like humidity before a storm.

"Have you ever done anything like this?" she asked.

"Button a woman's dress?" His sly grin could be heard on his voice.

"Not that." Though now that he mentioned it, she was curious, but that would be a discussion for another day. "Escort Evangeline to a gala."

"On the Queen's Guard, I had to attend them. Never *with* the queen, though."

"Do you know how to dance?" She did not remember seeing him dance at all when he was a boy. The memory of him and his mother standing by Mendoza's side—silent pillars the former Prime Minister shoved the weight of his anger onto—pushed to the forefront of her mind.

"I've seen enough people do it to know the basics. The agents would throw their own parties after we ended our shifts, but it was a different kind of dancing."

"Well, don't worry about it too much. If you make a mistake, it'll be a good distraction."

"Glad I can help." He rested his hand on her waist to indicate that the buttons were fastened.

She twisted around to face him. "How does it look?"

Her dress came from before Evangeline's time, likely decades earlier. Large flowers patterned the silky fabric, creating a faded rainbow that draped to her ankles. Once again, she decided to keep her motionless arm unrestrained, if only because the billowing sleeves would be difficult to fit into the sling. She regretted not choosing a dress that displayed her thick scars, one on her upper arm and one at her shoulder.

Any sign of strength would help her face the night that would almost certainly end in disaster. She had hoped to find out something, *anything*, about Evangeline's plans for the evening, but none of her agents had acted suspicious during their journey. If the rebels were to attack again, she would have to think on her feet.

Isaac's eyes trailed the dress from collar to hem. Finally, they landed on hers, after a lingering glance at her mouth that sent her heart racing. "You look beautiful."

Don't give up anything for me. That's what Phillip had said. Why couldn't she listen to him?

Because she could not trust anyone. If the man that had been her best friend her entire life could betray her, she would be a fool to believe that Mendoza's son and Evangeline's confidante would not do the same. Even James, the closest person she had to a brother, was under Evangeline's spell now.

Still, seeing Isaac in his dress uniform lit a flame under her ribs, and no argument she dredged up would extinguish it. Four brass buttons secured the front of his tailored black suit, leading up to the matching tie at his neck. Leianna and the rest of her on-duty agents would be wearing similar uniforms. His hand grazed the knot at his collar as if he felt her gaze on it.

She cleared her throat but didn't pull away. "I better. If I have nothing else going for me tonight, at least I have that."

"You have more things going for you."

"Name them."

"I'm stuck on the 'beautiful' one, but I'll let you know."

A laugh bubbled from her lips. It melted away the memory of her earlier tears. Her brief remembrance must have flickered across her face, because his grin grew serious.

"Do you know why he's here?" he asked.

Her whole body sighed. "No. He said she doesn't have anything on him. He's with her because he wants to be."

"After everything she has done, both to him and to his country, he's choosing her of his own free will? He's a fool." Anger laced his voice. It pushed her to the edge of a smile, to know he cared that much.

"It doesn't matter. Three years is a long time to miss someone. We're not the same people we were. I know for a fact I want different things now. It makes sense that he does, too." His eyes brightened so briefly she could have missed it if she wasn't staring at him. "Unfortunately, the thing he wants is a conniving queen who happens to be holding my best friend captive and creating a weapon that could kill us all."

"What can I do?"

There were many things he could help with, she imagined, the most important being assassinating Natania, which they could not feasibly accomplish even while working together.

"Nothing." She forced her mouth into a neutral line and extended her arm. "Let's not be late."

When he opened the door, she noticed a thick square of paper on the ground. Isaac met her gaze, looked around the hall, and picked it up. Amira's signature was scrawled in the corner. Upon unfolding it, she discovered a rudimentary map scribbled in graphite. It seemed to be the layout of a building, though the top floor was labeled *ground.* The bottom of the drawing had an arrow pointing downward, beyond the twentieth floor, indicating more of the structure below. Amira had circled the thirteenth floor and written *lab.*

"It's underground," she said. Isaac read over her shoulder, but she could not get herself to close it. The fear that it would disappear spurred her to memorize every detail.

"Do you know what building this is?" he asked.

"No." She folded the map and stuffed it between the clothes in her trunk. "We still need more information, and we don't even know if we can trust this. What if Natania forced her to write it and planted it?"

He squeezed her shoulder. "It's a start. I can ask the other agents if they saw anyone come by here earlier, though I'm sure they would have picked up the paper."

"Keep this quiet. I'll talk it over with the Dais when we get back." She couldn't help smiling at the thought of the tide turning in her favor. "If this is real, we have a friend in Genea, and they're here right now."

The contents of the letter swirled around her mind as they navigated to the Grand Ballroom. Her breath caught as they entered. It had once been a theatre, one of the guards had said. A spacious half-circle of pale wood led to a wide platform that she assumed had formerly held an orchestra. Balconies lined the walls above them, carvings in the stone cascading into an ornate chandelier surrounded by clay swans. Some of the pieces had chipped off over time, cracks forming between their wings. She returned her gaze in front of her after she nearly tripped over a step leading down to the floor.

As they descended, a man in a dark grey uniform announced their arrival. "Queen Alexandria of Kevelda, with her escort, Isaac Mendoza."

Her adoration of the room faded. She touched the man's arm, whispering, "It's better not to use that last name."

The man's face went white as snow. She smiled apologetically, wondering if any of the other royals had given him reason to be fearful.

Isaac brushed her hand and murmured his appreciation. She could not tell what made her heart tumble: him, or the seating chart placing them across from Natania and Phillip.

A violent urge to vomit seared through her chest. She drank the water in front of her without a second thought as to whether it was poisoned. *It would get me out of here faster,* she justified.

The man to Natania's left watched Alexandria with an assessing gaze, but when she caught his eye, he turned away. She drew a blank when she tried to remember the chart. From where she sat, she could not read his place card. She averted her attention to Greer, who sat on her right, already conversing with the Eastern Councilchair.

Leianna pointed out where she, Prior, and Watson would be positioned throughout the room. Alexandria nodded, unable to speak. Despite conversations carrying on around her, the silence between the four of them was deafening. Typically, Natania would talk first–usually an unsettling comment, but at least it gave Alexandria material to work with–yet this time, she just stared knowingly at her. Phillip examined his empty plate.

The girl next to him tapped her fingers against the table. Her light brown hair matched Natania's, and the longer Alexandria watched her, she looked more and more like a copy of the woman. Rough calluses lined the skin between her thumb and index finger, and her chipped nails seemed so unlike the queen that Alexandria briefly second-guessed her original assumption.

"Hello," she said, and the girl raised her head, "My name is Alexandria. I don't believe we've met."

The girl's eyes darted to Natania before a sharp smile crossed her face. Alexandria hoped that was a good sign. "We haven't. I'm Cassandra, Princess of Genea."

"You're Natania's sister?"

The queen shot daggers at her with a look. "Yes, she is."

Alexandria gripped Isaac's hand under the table, the sole display of her excitement. Cassandra was the crack in Natania's armor.

This was her way in.

"How old are you, Cassandra?" she asked.

The princess glanced at Natania again before she straightened her shoulders. "Sixteen. I suppose I'm not allowed to ask the same of you."

She laughed. "You can ask me anything you want. I'm twenty-one."

"You're young."

"It happens."

"I'm sure Natania can't say anything. She was my age when she–"

Natania cut her off. "That's enough, Cassandra."

"Why?" Cassandra crossed her arms. "It's just a history lesson."

Alexandria continued pushing. Even if she did not gain any important material, at least she could set Natania on edge. If Phillip was not sitting between the sisters, she could have forgotten him in her elation. "My father's a history professor. Trust me, I'd love to know."

For the first time, Natania looked shaken. Her face turned pink as her sister spoke. "She challenged our father for the throne six years ago. Killed our parents and took his place. Of course, it's not murder when it's tradition."

"That's enough," Natania repeated. Her tone was deadly. She did not slam anything or shout, yet her whisper sent a rush of cold through Alexandria's body.

She cleared her throat and decided to change the topic. That information would be helpful enough, though she was not sure how she could use it yet. Perhaps she would get Cassandra alone to learn more.

They discussed the princess's education and hobbies until dinner ended and the dancing began. Phillip remained silent aside from a split-second interaction in which Natania whispered something into his ear. Alexandria squeezed Isaac's hand so tightly that her fingers ached when she let go.

The music started and he asked her to dance, a request she happily obliged. He led her to the clear section of scuffed wood in the middle of the room, where couples already strode and spun. When his hand grazed the small of her back, all thoughts of the princess left her head. Her heart panged when she realized she could not put her other hand on his shoulder. Instead of holding the proper formation on that side, he took her hand in his. With their fingers laced, she wished even more that her nerves would restart. Imagining his touch could never replace the real thing.

"I saw the wheels turning in your head," he murmured. "What's your plan?"

It took her a moment to realize he was talking about dinner. "I don't have one yet, but I will. There seems to be contention between them. I can exploit that somehow. I'll need more time alone with her."

"I'll ask Natania to dance. That should give you time."

"Thank you." The thought of him dancing with the queen set her on edge. Exposing him to her poison was something she wanted to avoid at all costs, though she reckoned that happened when the woman killed his father.

The song ended and he escorted her back to the table. She slumped into her chair, her feet already blistering from her shoes. Kicking them off surreptitiously, she watched Isaac approach Natania. Right before he could, however, Sofie greeted him. The two moved to the center of the room and began to dance. They still had a few hours to set their plan in motion, so Alexandria did not worry.

Her pulse accelerated when Phillip sat next to her. With her blood rushing in her ears, she almost couldn't hear him.

"Would you like to dance?" he asked. He did not appear to be thinking of the last time he asked her that. Images of the beach in Kureya flashed in her mind.

The man in front of her was a ghost of the boy he had been then. Her traitorous heart tried to drag her back into that moment, despite knowing who he allied himself with. If he could not be *her* Phillip, he would have to be her villain. That was the only way she could live with the pain burrowing into her veins.

Still, she could not help herself. "Sure."

Nearly hitting her head on the table, she bent over to put her shoes back on. One of them was missing. She stretched her arm, reaching farther. A flashing red light caught her eye.

Attached to the center of the table, right next to Natania's seat, was a black metal box with red numbers counting down.

Evangeline's rebels had planted a bomb.

She had ten minutes to get the enemy queen out of there if she ever wanted a chance to get Amira back.

EIGHTEEN
ISAAC

After a conversation with Princess Sofie that made him lightheaded, Isaac scanned the room for Natania. He would have to tell Alexandria eventually, but he couldn't, not in the middle of the crowded ballroom. The princess's revelation lingered in his mind even as he tried to focus on the task at hand.

He found Natania talking to Argon, worry lines on his face making him look even older than he was. Isaac still had not had the chance to speak to him. Another time, perhaps. If he could avoid it, he would. He wanted to forget everything he had just learned.

When he came close enough, Argon said his goodbyes and went to find his sister. Isaac bowed his head to Natania and held out a hand. "Care to dance, Your Majesty?"

A brief flicker of confusion darkened her features before the ice-cold smile returned. "Of course."

Her hand froze his skin. Calluses lined her fingers, a sign that she had trained with various weapons.

Despite knowing how terrible his father was, he had loved the man for a very long time. Being this close to the woman that ordered Mendoza's murder made his blood run cold. He forced a grin onto his face. "I must confess, I haven't danced much. Forgive me if I step on your toes."

"The Prime Minister didn't send you to lessons?" she asked, though her face bore no curiosity.

His teeth grated against each other. "I'm afraid not."

"I apologize. It slipped my mind that he didn't like for you to be seen in public. Are you still in the Argentum? Or has Alexandria promoted you to a more *personal* position?"

He ignored the first half of her statement, as well as the smirk that accompanied the second. "I can't speak for her. I do my duty to serve my queen in whatever capacity I can."

"Judging by the way she looks at my fiancé, I would argue that she appreciates you serving just the way you are."

He didn't want to give any credit to her verbal spars, but he searched for Alexandria instinctively. She and Phillip were dancing at the edge of the floor. Her mouth was drawn into a smile, yet her eyes looked pained. They scanned the room until they landed on him and Natania. She squinted and turned her attention back to Phillip.

Isaac wasn't worried.

"And what about your fiancé? When did you decide to promote him from prisoner to lover?"

Her grip tightened on his shoulder. "When it suited me most. Is that not what all us royals do? Even your Alexandria isn't opposed to a power play. Keep that in mind."

"I trust her."

"No," she laughed, "you don't. You might think so, but I know enough about you. I have had you watched for years. You do not know what it means to love. You only know desperation. Desperation for someone to sacrifice for you, for her to protect you the way she does her friends. Because maybe then all of the things you have done to avenge your mother and sister will be worth it. You'll gain a new family to make up for the loss you can never undo."

His throat constricted. He could not reply.

Seeing his torment, she continued, "You thought your father loved you, but he only wanted power. You thought Evangeline loved you, but she only wanted power. Third time's a charm?"

"You don't know me," he whispered.

"I do. I know everything you've ever done, every way you've earned your family name. The people you killed out of vengeance for what you thought was *our* attack. Here I am, not judging you for any of it. I admire you for doing what you must to get justice for your family. Would she say the same?"

He stood silently. They had stopped dancing, but he could not discern when that had happened. Her words meant nothing, but his stomach tensed all the same.

"Right," she said. "You can't speak for her."

Knowing they were finished, she sauntered off the dance floor, leaving him alone in the center.

She walked over to where Alexandria and Cassandra now stood and took her sister's hand. Before she could drag the princess away, Alexandria said something that made her pause. Natania's brows furrowed and her mouth drew into a tight line. When the two moved again, she spoke sternly to her sister, but Cassandra's earlier heated sarcasm had morphed into an expression of thinly veiled fear.

He didn't need to wonder for long. Alexandria strode up to him, holding his arm and standing so close that he nearly lost his footing. After the pain of his conversation with Natania, her cheek brushing against his gave him whiplash.

"We need to get out of here," she whispered, her voice shaking, "but we can't set off any alarms. If the guards have any reason to question why we're leaving, then this is all for nothing."

"What's going on?"

"I can't tell you right now. Do you trust me?"

Without Natania's words ringing in his head, he never would have hesitated. He hated that it took him a moment to nod.

"Do you have any ideas?" she asked.

If they needed to leave quickly, they couldn't say proper goodbyes to the other officials. The celebration was almost over, but their unannounced departure would be surprising either way. Unfortunately, he could only think of one thing. *Might as well shock a few people while we're at it.*

"Can I kiss you?"

A deep red blush rose to her face. If she didn't look so scared, he might have joked about it. "Good idea. It'll look like I have no regard for etiquette, but that will help, in this case."

Awkward tension filled the gap between them. Back when they were in the cabin, he had thought this would eventually happen, but with time separating them from how close they had been then, his hope had faded. Something like disappointment clung to his ribs. He didn't want it to be like this, a ruse to stop some mysterious disaster from occurring.

Another thing he refused to think about: the fact that he didn't know what he was doing.

In the Argentum, he never had time for romance. He was there to serve Mendoza, and anything else would have been a distraction. Several times, he had been tempted to make moves when his team went into town on their nights off, but he always fought it. He had a higher purpose, answering to a man that used him for power and called it justice. Now, he answered to no one, or so he tried to tell himself.

He wove his fingers into the hair at the nape of her neck. She leaned into him, snaking her arm up his back. His heart pounded so fiercely he thought she might hear it. He glanced over to where Natania and Cassandra were, but they had already left. Phillip stared at them from his seat, and then he, too, moved to exit the ballroom.

Nobody else watched besides their agents. He hadn't known Watson for long, but Prior had been on the Queen's

Guard with him before the Campaign. Whatever was going to happen, he hoped they were aware.

He stalled for too long. She pulled his mouth to hers and the rest of the room faded away.

His first impression, when he got his mind working again, was that her lips were soft. She tasted of mint with something sharp underneath, which struck him as odd because they had eaten steak and potatoes for dinner, but then again, he didn't recall seeing her touch her plate.

His second impression was that he never, ever wanted to stop kissing her.

For the first time in his life, he felt like he could breathe, even though he couldn't catch his breath. It was as if his head was above water at last, and when they broke apart, he would be caught underneath the waves again.

She ran her palm against the stubble along his jaw, entwining her hand in his hair. He wasn't sure how long they had been standing there when she pulled away. Before he could inhale, she kissed him again, quicker this time. Like she needed it as badly as he did.

"Let's go," she spoke between breaths.

She played her role well, clutching the fabric of his suit jacket with a drunken swagger. He snuck his arm around her waist. They departed the room without a word to anyone else. He didn't even think about them until they crossed the corridor leading to the guest wing.

When they entered the hallway, his muscles tensed, unsure what to do next. The kiss had wrecked his senses. They had been escaping something, but the irrational part of him didn't care.

Alexandria glanced behind them, concern painted across her face. "She didn't follow us."

"Who?"

"Leianna. She always does. I have to go back." Her tone grew more nervous, every word coming faster than the one before.

Isaac grabbed her arm before she could take off running. "What's really going on?"

Her eyes searched his as if weighing what would be worse—trusting him or leaving Leianna behind.

"There's a bomb. The rebels planted a bomb. I'm assuming they didn't tell you."

"No, they didn't." A surge of panic rushed through his core at the thought that Evangeline didn't trust him anymore. He had brought it upon himself. Still, he needed to know what the former queen's plans were in order to keep Alexandria safe. "How did you know?"

"I found it underneath the table. It would have killed us, too."

He remembered her conversation with Natania moments before their kiss. "You warned her. Why?"

"We can't talk about this now." She pulled herself free from his grip. "I have to go back for Leianna."

They raced back to the Grand Ballroom. He pulled in front, knowing he wouldn't let her go inside. There wasn't enough time. If Leianna knew he allowed Alexandria to run toward death for her, she would haunt him, dead or alive.

A loud booming sound echoed through the corridor. His heart sank. Alexandria cried out, falling to her knees. The doors rattled, pushing outwards. Everything was drenched in an eerie silence.

Then the screams started.

He pulled her up by her shoulders, his hands shaking. It would be too dangerous to let her go in without knowing what kind of device it was. "We have to leave."

"I left her behind." It sounded like something was caught in her throat. "After everything she has done for me, I left her in there."

Smoke curled from the crack under the door, scorching his lungs. His eyes burned for a different reason. He and Leianna were never that close, but she had been a constant in the Argentum. And because of Alexandria's decision, one his mind couldn't grasp, she might be dead.

A woman spoke behind them. "Left who?"

They whipped around to find Leianna standing there, Prior and Watson flanking her. Alexandria ran and hugged her. The woman stood with her arms by her sides, startled, before patting her on the back and releasing her.

"We were investigating a suspicious device left outside. I should have known the real threat was in the ballroom." She stared right through them. "Why did you two leave?"

"It doesn't matter."

"It does. Did you know what was going to happen?"

Alexandria swallowed hard. "No. Of course we didn't."

Isaac watched as she fidgeted with the sleeve of her dress. A sign of her guilt. She would have let them all die, and she had not yet given him an explanation.

For the first time, he thought that Natania might have been right.

NINETEEN
ALEXANDRIA

An acrid smell singed the back of Alexandria's throat when the doors opened. The man who announced their names earlier stumbled out, soot staining his cheek and smudging across his uniform.

She rushed into the room. Smoke cast a heavy cloud that blinded her. Her chest ached as shouts and whimpers alike rose from the chaos. She could have warned them. No one had to die today. If only she had been more prepared, had discovered the rebel plan beforehand, like she had thought she would be able to when she told Evangeline about the gala in the first place.

Evangeline would use any excuse to cut her off, which is how she had justified only getting Natania and Cassandra out of the room. Despite the danger, she couldn't bring herself to leave Isaac behind. If Evangeline had reason to believe that Alexandria had known about the bomb and chosen to save the queen, the target would be on her back next.

To keep both queens satisfied, she had killed innocent people.

Greer. Argon. Jude. All the Duarmmian people who had come to end their mourning.

They could all be dead.

An arm appeared at the edge of the black fog. Her legs buckled as she raced toward it. She could get someone out of here. She could make things right.

The arm was no longer attached to a body.

Bile crept into her mouth, staining her tongue with its bitterness. She swallowed it down. Screams meant someone was still alive. She could not stop until she found them.

Broken glass sliced her hand and knees as she pushed off the ground. Her vision cleared with the door open, the smoke having somewhere else to be. Heat clung to her skin like a burial shroud. It dried her mouth, leaving her unable to call for survivors.

Her lungs could not fill with air. No matter how much she coughed or clawed at her chest, it would not clear. She sank to her knees, chipped wood biting into her skin, glass embedding further. Pain seared through her palm as she crawled further into the room.

A croaking sound rose from her throat when she spotted a shadow ahead of her. The shape had four arms and four legs. She blinked hard and realized it was a man and a woman.

Argon and Sofie.

They stumbled forward, Sofie supporting the king with his arm around her shoulders. Alexandria fought against the heaviness of her limbs and took his other arm. He grunted as they limped to the doors.

When they reached the threshold, her head instantly cleared. Phlegm caught in her throat as she choked on the clean air. Prior held her steady as she fought for breath.

A swarm of soldiers and surviving attendees crowded into the corridor, spilling outside into the night. Her eyes burned as they swept the room. The insides of her eyelids scratched like needles. She straightened, still leaning on her guard.

Isaac and Leianna were nowhere to be found.

"Where are they?" she asked, a weight in the pit of her stomach.

Prior flicked a glance at the ballroom. "They went to find you."

Her heart cracked. Without a word, she took a deep breath and staggered back into the smoke. She called their names until her voice was nothing but a whisper. The thick air sliced the lining of her throat. They could have gotten lost in the darkness or succumbed to a lack of oxygen. She shook the thought out of her head, pushing forward with no destination.

A hand caught her arm. Watson. The woman's blonde hair looked gray through the foggy veil. Suddenly, a roar exploded deeper in the room, accompanied by a rush of crackling. Her skin lit up in orange and red. Alexandria could not breathe, and it was not the smoke that suffocated her this time.

Fire grew, tearing along the curtained balconies, scattering ash on the ground. Water poured from the ceiling. The flame faltered but persisted. Her dress clung to her as she moved toward the fire.

"We need to leave," Watson shouted over the cacophony, but Alexandria chose not to hear. She would not leave until she found them, even if her lungs burst and the flame rendered her to dust.

She found Isaac carrying a woman in a Genean uniform. Someone Natania left behind. Her chest constricted. She would be a hypocrite to cast any judgment on the queen.

Leianna limped next to him, ash stark against her pale skin, her dark eyes reflecting the fire as they scoured the room.

Their eyes met and she tapped Isaac's shoulder, pointing to Alexandria and Watson. "This way!"

Alexandria let out a sob. A deafening crack above them motivated her to move. She took Leianna's hand and raced to where she thought the doors were. They reached only a curved, soot-stained wall. She cursed, her mind paralyzed under the weight of the frenzy. She followed the wall, praying it would lead them to safety. Leianna was the only anchor keeping her steady.

A rectangle of light appeared ahead. The sound of voices grew louder as she forced her legs to move faster. Another crack came from above, followed by a slithering metallic sound. She turned to find the chandelier careening down.

The seconds drew out into minutes as she flung Leianna in front of her. Isaac tossed the Genean soldier to Watson, who had made it past the threshold. Alexandria shoved him through right as the chandelier crashed behind her.

Pinpricks tore through her back and shoulders, culminating in a burst of blinding pain. Stars dotted the edges of her vision. Blood rippled down her knees, lingering at the points where shards of glass stuck out of her skin. It could not compare to the other side of her legs. Warmth pooled at her back, her head light and fuzzy, until everything went dark.

Pointed light shone in her eyes. The woman on the other end of it wore a green Duarmmian uniform with a white band around her arm. Her brows furrowed as she looked at Alexandria, who, in shattered waves, came to the realization that she was laying on her side. She did not remember falling. The tile floor chilled her fire-warmed skin, soothing the singed top layer. She pressed her hand against the ground, sucking air through her teeth at the sensation of a thousand sharp needles driving into her palm.

"Lie still," the medic ordered. Alexandria braced herself as the woman dug glass out of her hand with a pair of tweezers. Little by little, the burning sensation traveled downwards, from her arms to her knees, following the path of removal. The sleeves of her dress had been cut away. Alexandria passed out when the medic started pulling glass from her neck.

She awoke to find her head on someone's knee. Her sweating skin stuck to the fabric as she lifted her face to find it was

Isaac smoothing down her hair. A sickly pallor washed over his face, and when she followed his gaze, she watched the medic twist a large piece of splintered wood out of her unfeeling arm. The phantom pain echoed long after she put the tweezers away.

The medic wrapped clean white bandages around her arms, legs, and neck, taping a swath of it against her back where her dress lay unbuttoned. She would have been embarrassed to be so bare in front of the crowd, but no one paid attention to her—besides Watson and Prior, who watched the procedure in equal parts disgust and concern. Watson had a bandage at her neck, but otherwise, her uniform had kept the chandelier shards from penetrating her skin.

Leianna spoke sternly with the Duarmmian soldiers who had been guarding the door. Greer stood nearby, ash darkening his grey hair, but he looked fine otherwise. One of the soldiers, whose face shone a bright red, argued that they had swept the room before everyone arrived and checked all of the guests. There would have been no way for the bomb to get in.

Alexandria wanted nothing more than to sleep for an eternity, but she rallied her queenly graces and sat up. The pressure of the motion set the backs of her thighs ablaze. She twisted onto her knees, deciding that the pain there would be more bearable than putting her weight onto her palm, and after a few moments to catch her breath, she stood.

Isaac reached out an arm and hesitated. "How do I help without hurting you?"

Wordlessly, she gestured for him to put his arm under her shoulder. Every few steps, he would brush against her back, and she would clench her teeth against the stinging. Her legs were stiff. Anywhere her skin stretched, it burned.

"Are you alright?" she croaked when they reached Sofie. Soot shadowed the woman's pale face, but she appeared unharmed, if a bit frightened.

Sofie nodded. "Argon and I were on the other side of the room when it happened. Others were not so lucky."

A chill raced up Alexandria's spine. "Where is Argon?"

"He went with a medic. His heart did not escape unscathed." She sighed, her eyes watering. "But he'll be alright. He always is."

Alexandria bid her farewell, leaning against Isaac as much as she could. She beckoned Leianna to let matters rest for the night. There was nothing for her to find out that Alexandria did not already know, and everything Leianna learned would bring Alexandria's decision to let people die further into the light.

Leianna dismissed Prior and Watson to the barracks, and the three staggered over to the residential wing. A pang of guilt twinged in Alexandria's chest at the thought that she would have to walk back to the barracks alone, but when she offered to let her captain stay, Leianna declined.

"I need the air," she said, breathing out a sigh. Being surrounded by death could not be easy for a woman who had lost her husband under a year ago.

Isaac guided Alexandria to lay on her bed. She would have to move eventually, as she was lying the wrong way and her legs dangled off the side, but she had no energy left to spare. The softness of the bed made her wounds hurt less, like the bite of a midge rather than the slice of a blade. Sleep would be impossible even so.

He laid his jacket across an armchair and leaned against the bedpost. His face wasn't visible from where she lay, but she did not want to see his expression, to know what he thought about her. She could not stand to watch the puzzle pieces fall into place.

I could have saved them.

In the morning, someone would tell her the death toll, the number of injuries, and she would have to act the part of a queen. Sad for the loss but relieved none of her people had died. She could not break down. They would all know the truth if she did.

"You warned Natania," he said.

She inhaled. "I did."

"You didn't tell anyone else. We could have evacuated everyone."

"I know."

"Why?"

Her skin seared as she forced herself upright. "I need Evangeline to trust me. I need Natania to trust me. Two birds, one stone." She left out the *killing* part of the phrase on purpose. The word held too much power.

"Why did you get me out?"

"You know the answer to that."

His shoulders rose and fell. He turned, bracing himself on the frame. "My father and Evangeline used me as a weapon against each other. I will never forgive myself for the things I *chose* to do at their command. I refuse to be a pawn any longer. Don't you dare make me one of yours."

The sheet wrinkled under her grip. "Do you really think I'm playing games? This is war, and we have to win. Our people will continue to die at Natania's hand if I don't stop this." Her voice cracked. She swallowed, her throat tight. "I don't want you to follow me unconditionally. Argue with me. Challenge me. Tell me I'm wrong, I don't care. As long as you're by my side, I'll listen. I just need you there."

They stared at each other for too long. Silence stretched until the thought of saying anything at all was pointless. Her heart fluttered at the thought of their earlier kiss. One that had simply been a strategy to keep him safe. One that she had been longing for since they parted those months ago.

Everything had changed in little over an hour. Fear pricked in the back of her mind that he would never again look at her the way he had when she pulled him in. She did not deserve it.

"I'll see you in the morning," he said, leaving her alone.

Her nightmares lasted until sunrise, but she never fell asleep.

TWENTY
ALEXANDRIA

The bandages stuck to Alexandria's wounds. Where the medic pulled them away, crusted brown blood formed a second skin. She steeled herself as the woman swept a warm, wet cloth over her injuries, following up with an antiseptic that sent stars to the corners of her vision.

After being rewrapped with clean bandages, she buttoned up her shirt and sling, pulled on a loose skirt, and limped to the Premier's war room. Of course, Duarmme had not seen war since the Fall, but old habits die hard. The name had been passed down along generations of leaders, and Duarmmians were not the kind of people to shirk tradition.

The Premier had called a meeting to address the prior day's attack. Around the ornate wooden table, she found Minister Greer, Natania and a Genean soldier, Argon and one of his guards, the Premier, and the three Councilchairs. Jude, the

Southern Councilchair now, sat with a grim expression painted on his young features. He had aged quickly after the attack that took his father's life, but it was impossible to ignore that he was just a boy.

Alexandria took a seat at the end of the table, as far from Natania as she could be, with Leianna and Greer on either side of her. All eyes landed on them. Her pulse quickened. She feared they had already started discussing the attack without her, and that did not put her in a good position. She needed to control the narrative. Natania would spin it to suit herself, somehow.

"Alexandria," Natania started, "how are your wounds?"

"Healing," she replied flatly. She shifted her eyes to the Premier, who stared at her with a hardened, unreadable gaze. "How many casualties?"

"Fifteen dead, thirty-three injured."

Her heart sank. "In what condition? Are they here in the medical wing?" She thought for a moment that she might make a visit, then remembered that she was nothing but a foreign queen to them. She should not care this much. Not if she wasn't to blame.

"They are in the capital hospital. Some are critical, but many received minor injuries. What I care to know is how the instigator evaded our security." His eyes swept across each of their faces.

Natania spoke. "Fortunately, my team has already begun investigating."

"And?" Argon asked.

"The device was created using wiring from an intercontinental cellular system." She did not look at Alexandria, but her throat went dry at the queen's subtle smirk. "Specifically, the phones that Genea installed in the palace in Regia."

Alexandria gripped the arm of her chair. The motion sent pain up her wrist and through her fingers. "I know nothing of this."

"That does not mean your guards are innocent."

"I can attest to their innocence. My team would never do such a thing," Leianna said. Alexandria wished she could hold that much conviction, but she had always suspected one of them to be a rebel. Now, she was not so sure that the rebels were behind the attack at all.

"How can you be sure they came from Regia?" she asked. "That seems like an awfully fast assessment. I'm sure your soldiers were happy to be the first and only ones at the scene."

Natania raised her thin eyebrows. "Are you accusing Genea of tampering with evidence?"

Images of Amira in shackles sprung to her mind. She pressed her lips together. Nothing she could say would save them all. Either one of her agents must take the blame, or she would be putting her friend and her people in Thaertos at risk.

"No," she said at last, "I am simply shocked at the idea that any of my agents would do something like this."

"Not just any of your agents. I believe her name is Harper Watson."

She inhaled sharply. The woman had run after her into the blaze. Even if she was Evangeline's insider, she was a good person. It was impossible to imagine the woman carrying out the attack.

"How do you know this?" the Premier asked.

"The surviving soldiers saw her lead Captain Olivier and Agent Prior out of the room before the explosion."

Leianna clasped her hands together until her knuckles turned white. "One of your guards told her that there was a suspicious device left outside the room."

"I personally interviewed every one of the guards and heard nothing of the sort," the Genean soldier said.

Leianna started to speak again, but Alexandria put out her hand. "If this report is correct, what is our next move?"

"You will execute the criminal. Phillip and I will be married in a month. These rebels must be eradicated before then." Natania said it as though it was the most natural conclusion.

Alexandria understood then that this was a test. One she wished she could fail, but with her people in Natania's hands, her options were few. "I look forward to the results of a secondary investigation."

Natania leaned forward onto her elbows. "It is better if we put this behind us. Let Duarmme heal. Do we really need another investigation? My soldiers have the most experience and resources, no offense intended."

Leianna scoffed. "Your Majesty, a secondary investigation is basic protocol. The leaders here would all agree."

The Premier's expressionless facade cracked with a subtle flare of his nostrils. "Your investigation is unnecessary, given the evidence at hand, and with your history, we are sure it would be an inept one."

Alexandria took in a deliberate breath. After all that Genea had done to Duarmme, his agreement with Natania shook her. She opened her mouth to speak but was almost grateful Natania cut her off with the wave of her hand, as she could form no coherent lie. He was right; they had not supplied any real information about the rebels, because she had covered up Evangeline's crimes.

"Let us vote, then. The four leaders of the Genean Coalition can surely come to a consensus." Her eyes glinted in a way that made Alexandria's skin crawl. "All in favor of convicting Keveldan Agent Harper Watson of mass murder, raise your hand."

Alexandria stared at Argon, hoping she could sway his decision with her mind. His pale skin flushed. He held a hand to his chest as if saying a pledge. Sofie had said that the attack affected his heart, but Alexandria thought, even worse, that it had dampened his spirit. He raised his hand.

The Premier made eye contact with her as he raised his hand. He did not hesitate long enough for her to hope.

Natania watched her, waiting, looking right through her. She knew what choice Alexandria would make, even if the numbers already counted against Watson.

Alexandria raised her hand. Greer watched her from the corner of her vision, his hands clenched on the table. She would not meet his glare.

"That settles it, then. Harper Watson will be executed for her crimes within the day. If not, Kevelda will be held in contempt of the Coalition, and all privileges and protection afforded by it will be forfeit."

"Give me more time, please. Let her execution take place in her homeland." She grew nauseous at the sound of her own begging.

"I no longer place confidence in your ability to carry out orders. If you were competent, this attack never would have happened."

"That's not fair."

"It is not fair that fifteen people were murdered at the hand of one of your citizens."

Argon cleared his throat. "If I may, I have to agree with Alexandria. The agent should be punished in her own territory. All our nations afford criminals the right to say their goodbyes."

Natania shot him a look that quieted him. "Very well. You have until the end of the week, but I will be there to see the execution with my own eyes."

The Premier adjourned the meeting, and Alexandria went to her room to pack. She had hardly taken anything out of her case, considering they had only been there for a day, so she finished within the hour. Her excitement at receiving Amira's map dampened under the weight of Natania's ultimatum. Her body ached as she sat upon the bed.

She had not drank from her flask since the previous afternoon, and the tremors that overcame her chafed her wounds. All the agony of the ballroom—the echoing screams and quiet whimpers—had holed up in her stomach, and now it tried to claw its way out. For months, the world had been filtered, the rough edges burned away until nothing could hurt her, but with those fifteen lives ended, her choices became painfully clear.

What have I done?

Leianna opened the door without knocking. "It's time," she said, not meeting her eyes.

Alexandria followed her to the barracks, where Duarmmian soldiers circled the building like buzzards. She could not blame them for doing their jobs. Everyone was playing a part in Natania's game.

Leianna knocked at the entrance of the guest corridor. A Victorin guard answered, his dark eyes narrowing in confusion. When she announced that she was there to carry out an arrest, he backed away and let her enter. Two Duarmmian soldiers trailed after her.

Alexandria's heart tapped out a staccato rhythm as she waited. The unfinished beats left her dizzy and lightheaded. She did not breathe.

So many deaths at her hand. What was one more?

The man in the ravine.

The mayor's son.

The agent who served her well.

Another notch in her crown.

Leianna had not told Isaac, she presumed. He would have been there if he knew, or maybe he wouldn't have. Maybe he had decided Alexandria was not worth comforting. Why would she need to be? She had raised her hand to vote for Watson's execution without a second thought.

The better explanation, the one she hoped for, was that he was unaware that his colleague, his friend, was being arrested for a crime she likely did not commit. A good call on Leianna's behalf. He would have fought it.

Alexandria stood still, a cool breeze the sole motion around her. Phillip brushed his hand against hers. Only a split second of contact. Probably an accident, with Natania on his other side. He did not care about her anymore. It was for the best.

Through the glassy fog of her thoughts, Leianna emerged from the barracks, holding Watson by her wrists. The accused agent's tears reflected the brightness of the sun. She pleaded with the soldiers around her, shouting that she was innocent, that none of this was her fault, that she had been framed. They did not listen. Nothing would make a difference, not when Natania had her Coalition on her side.

Watson lunged at Alexandria, but her face held no threat. Her mouth opened in a plea silenced by her sobs. Alexandria's nails bit into her cut palm. The pain was a good distraction. It allowed her to hold her tongue until the woman had been shoved into a rusted military vehicle.

Without much fanfare, the crowd disbanded. The soldiers went back to their usual posts, the visiting guards to their rooms.

Natania touched her shoulder. "Careful, Alexandria. One more step and you'll become a real queen."

Her ribs strained with the effort of keeping her breaths steady. Natania walked away, leaving Phillip behind. Of course, she wouldn't care if he spoke to Alexandria. The ultimate goal, it seemed, was to make her break. He could do that just by looking at her.

When a few minutes passed without him moving, she looked up. His skin was pale green, with a sheen of sweat despite the breeze.

"Are you alright?" she asked. She wanted to be angry with him, but her voice portrayed none of that conviction.

Their dance last night had been cordial, though distant. He had brought up the time that they, James, and Amira had snuck out in the middle of the night when they were in secondary school. They had met at the park, and though they hadn't done anything illegal or scandalous, she would forever remember how red Mrs. Collins's face had gotten when she and James crept back into the living room early that morning.

Her chest panged at the memory. It was harder, she thought, to grieve someone who was still alive, standing right in front of her.

He plastered a smile on his face. "I'm fine. Are you?"

She nodded, as if talking to a stranger. "I will be."

They started walking toward the docks. Everyone would be waiting for her. Her stomach twisted at the thought of seeing Isaac after all this. Leianna, too.

She imagined the captain watching silently as Watson was hanged the same way her husband had been. The image sparked an idea, one she did not have the time to unravel in Phillip's company.

"How is Amira?" Bitterness laced her words, but perhaps even in their distance, Phillip could give her a clue as to who had delivered her friend's letter.

"Well," he responded. "As well as she can be."

"What does that mean?"

"She's helping develop weapons of mass destruction. It weighs on her, even if it's not—"

"Not what? Her choice? I know that. What bothers me is that you know the same, and yet, you're still by Natania's side."

"I can't explain, so don't ask me to."

"You told me she wasn't holding anything over you, but I don't understand. If you can't tell me the truth about that, just tell me this. Are you in love with her?" Tears welled in her eyes. She blinked them back.

He stared at the ships ahead of them. "Love is never a part of these things. Who knows what it really means, anyway?"

She gripped his arm, her voice a shattered mess. "I know what it means. Or I thought I did."

His eyes fell to the cobblestone beneath them, lashes fluttering as he blinked. "Remember me like that, then."

"No. I will remember everything."

It was the last promise she gave him before she boarded the ship back to Kevelda, where she would execute her friend.

TWENTY–ONE
ISAAC

Isaac waited the entire six-day journey for Alexandria to talk to him, to even look at him. She never did.

Watson was set to be executed on the day they returned. Leianna and Prior led her to the cells below the palace. She was placed in the same one Mendoza had been in.

The memory hit him like the shrapnel that had lodged in his leg eight years ago. This grief was different than the one he experienced for his mother and sister. More complicated. They had never asked anything of him. He had freely given his protection, bearing the brunt of his father's anger. The man had been kinder then, but only because he kept his bruises in places that could be hidden. Never before did he cut as deeply as he had when he tried one last time to manipulate his son in this cell.

Alexandria went down to speak to Watson first. Her jaw was tight when she emerged, a faint shimmer in her eyes. Their gazes met in the space between seconds. She did not say a word before leaving.

He tipped his head toward the agents at the top of the stairwell. One of them had been with him at his second post, as a guard in the medical wing. The other, a woman with silver hair, had been in the Argentum for most of her life, and she had declined a Queen's Guard position multiple times before Evangeline stopped asking. Too much responsibility, for the same pay and benefits she received where she was. Honor did nothing when standing on the wrong side of the queen at an inopportune time could earn an agent a bullet hole.

The dim fluorescents underground made him squint to make out Watson's shape in her cell.

"It's nice of you to visit." She was not typically outspoken, but her words were barely audible now, all thick and nasally.

He smiled as best he could. His usual course of action when it came to making Alexandria feel better was to offer some lighthearted comment, but it felt wrong when the best outcome for the woman in front of him would be a quick and painless death. He couldn't save Watson from her fate, only assure her of what most agents wanted: that her family would be provided for, and that he would do everything in his power to save her name from disgrace.

"We all need company from time to time." He pulled up a chair in front of her.

"No offense, but I wish my mother had come."

"Did they keep her away?" His defenses raised at the idea. He would fight anyone who stood in the way of Watson saying her final goodbyes.

"No. She's ill. Has been for a while." She wrapped the end of her blonde braid around her finger. Her eyes grew distant as they fixated on the wall. "It's a good thing. She'll soon forget she even has a daughter, if she hasn't already."

"I'll make sure she gets your badge." It was tradition among the Argentum, that when an agent died, their family would get the thick piece of fabric that displayed their name on their uniform. Often, it was all they had to give.

She refocused on him. "You would do that for a traitor?"

"I would do that for an agent who served her queen well. Even if it costed her in the end."

"I thought Evangeline would save me."

His brows furrowed. "Evangeline?"

"You didn't know? I thought she would have told you. You're the one she trusts the most. The whole reason I'm in this mess is because of her."

He leaned forward, restless, aching to stand. His mind raced. Evangeline hadn't told him anything. "So you did plant the bomb?" Accusation stained the question.

She shook her head emphatically. "No, I didn't. I left it on the boat. I couldn't do it. And still, I ended up here."

"Someone else took it." The pieces clicked together. He was willing to bet Natania was behind it. She had been too eager to point a finger at Watson, from what Leianna had told him of the fateful meeting.

The one where Alexandria raised her hand.

He was starting to understand why. Fighting Natania was futile. She always had a plan, a set of contingencies to ensure she got her way—just like Evangeline, for whom he had been that contingency plan for far too long. They would destroy each other and take everyone down with them.

Watson sighed. "It doesn't matter. I'm dead either way."

The agents returned shortly after to escort her to the throne room. He followed along, clutching her badge between his fingers. When it was all over, he would search for her mother. There had to be some kind of record of her family. Perhaps Leianna would know.

His pulse raced as they trailed down the center of the room. Light burst through the broken stained glass, washing them in red light. Was this what his own funeral procession was like, the one he should've shared with his mother and sister?

No one sat in the pews aside from the Prime Minister, the four remaining Dais ministers, Natania, and two Genean soldiers. Alexandria stood in the center of the platform before her throne. A crimson dress draped across her shoulders, cascading to the floor in waves like blood. One of Evangeline's dresses.

Prior watched from the far-left side, Beckett on the right. It surprised him that no other agents had come to watch, but the more he thought about it, he knew he wouldn't have attended if he didn't know Watson. Her execution portrayed her as dishonorable, but he was the only one to know that she was innocent–at least, of the crime Natania accused her of.

The air tingled with anticipation, like a held breath, a cocked gun ready to fire. A man in the corner angled a bulky camera on its stand. He set up a microphone next to it. They were broadcasting this to the whole kingdom.

Another execution. At least this time, they wouldn't have a celebration after. His jaw clenched at the thought of Will. He scanned the room for Leianna, but she wasn't present.

The agents led Watson to stand in front of Alexandria. Before he could sit in the front row, Watson broke free and wrapped her arms around his shoulders. "I just needed to hold someone one last time," she whispered.

When they pulled her away, she broke into sobs, pleading her innocence. Her cries made his muscles tense for a fight he could not win. He dropped onto the pew. The world faded around him, a vignette pointing his gaze to the throne. Watson fell to her knees a few meters in front of Alexandria.

"Face it standing," Alexandria said. Her voice had a practiced ring to it.

She lifted her gun with a trembling hand. He watched himself watch her, outside of his own body. Another part of her would die. He could do nothing but be there to pick up the pieces, as he had many times before, but it was different this time. Everyone has a point of no return, and he feared she was close to hers.

Watson rose to her feet. She swayed from side to side, then steadied herself. Her eyes squeezed shut. He was tempted to do the same, but he couldn't. He would bear witness to her final moments.

He had watched the life fade from a person's eyes so many times he had lost count. The first still haunted him, even as the rest blurred together.

At eighteen, he had become a killer. His hands had clasped around the handle of a gun, finger against the trigger. The man his father told him was a Genean agent spent his last moments begging. He had been a doctor, working in the palace medical wing, and Isaac had been tasked with protecting him not long before. There had been rumors that the man had his eyes on an advisory position, that he was trying his hand at politics, but Isaac didn't think anything of Mendoza's motivations.

He just lifted the gun.

Aimed at the man's head.

Ignored his pleading, his screams that he had a family to care for.

And pulled the trigger.

Alexandria did the same in the present, following step-by-step, as if she could read the memory he tried to shake out of his head.

She stepped close—too close to ignore the way Watson shook.

She fixed her grip on the handle.

Put her finger on the trigger.

And took the shot.

Watson fell in slow motion. He did not register the sound of the gunshot until moments later. Her hip clacked against the floor, then her shoulders, then her braid. A red pool trickled in front of her. Blood speckled Alexandria's face, dotting her lips and cheeks as if painted on. Her throat bobbed as she swallowed.

Lowering the gun, she stepped off the platform, not looking at the body. She walked up to Natania. His lungs burned with bated breath. The blood started to drip as she took her dress in her hand and dropped into a low bow. Her eyes could pierce through Natania's skin.

"I hope you enjoyed the show," she said.

A look resembling admiration flashed across Natania's face before it hardened. "Good work."

"Get out."

His blood ran cold at her tone.

Alexandria didn't check to see if the enemy queen moved. She walked straight to the throne room doors.

"Take her body to be burned," she called back, before letting the doors slam shut behind her.

Prior and Beckett lifted Watson's body and carried her into the stairwell that led to Alexandria's quarters.

Natania cleared her throat and rose. She carried her shoulders unnaturally straight, head high, as she moved to leave. She leaned to him as she passed. "And you didn't believe me."

He froze in his seat until he was sure she had gone. She was a monster. Alexandria did exactly what she had to do to keep them alive. Still, an uneasiness settled in his bones at the ease with which she pulled the trigger. The blood suited her.

His stomach turned at the thought that he had missed her breaking point a long time ago.

PART III
THE TRAITOR

TWENTY-TWO
ALEXANDRIA

The dead are so judgmental, Alexandria thought as she weighed her flask in her hand. It wasn't as heavy as she would have liked it to be.

She leaned back against the side of her bed, letting the platform dig into the cuts on her back. The pain was nothing compared to the agony those fifteen people suffered, whether they died in the initial explosion or the fire after. Behind her closed eyes, she forced herself to imagine their faces, though she knew nothing of them. Not even their names. Natania's order had never given her the chance to ask.

When the flask had lightened by half, all the people she had killed started appearing around her. The man in the ravine stood in the corner where he usually did. Her nightmares had a habit of bleeding into her waking hours. It had become difficult to decide which was worse, as of late—sleeping or being awake. At least she knew her dreams were fake.

"What do you want from me now?" she asked. If her guards could hear, they would likely think her unwell. But as her limbs grew heavy, she stopped pretending to care.

The vision of the man's father never joined him. His blood was on Carter's hands. Isaac's. They were two different men in her mind, but she thanked both of them for saving her from one more haunting.

Eighteen would be too much to bear.

I've already hit eighteen, counting the rebel I hand-delivered to Evangeline. Fitzgerald.

Fine, then. It was too much to bear.

Flicking her fingers against the flask in her lap, she found it hollow. She staggered upward. For a second, she forgot she was no longer on the ship. The room shifted from side-to-side. Her legs moved gingerly as if testing out the security of the floor.

The door had two knobs. She gathered that they must have installed a second one, for some unknown reason. Or maybe someone was playing tricks on her. Maybe it was Fitzgerald's ghost. Maybe it was the little girl who screamed when Alexandria stabbed her father.

She laughed, followed by a sharp cough. Ghosts offered no torment that the living couldn't provide.

By the third time she failed to open the door, unable to find the real handle, she couldn't breathe. The air around her pushed inward like a vise.

She found herself on the floor, crawling to the bathroom. Blood seeped through the bandage on her palm. Her elbow smacked the wood, and she dragged herself as far as she could before she collapsed. The dead men watched her.

Make it stop, she prayed, hoping God was much more forgiving than she was.

"Make what stop?" a man asked. She hadn't realized she'd said it out loud. The thought that she should be afraid of someone coming into her room crossed her mind for a second before she forgot about it.

"Get Leianna," the same voice said. It came closer this time, though she feared that if she opened her eyes, she would see the man in the ravine.

"She hasn't been back since the execution," another man said. "That's why I found you."

Someone picked her up, and then she was on her bed. She cracked open her eyelids and found Isaac standing next to her.

"Don't tell anyone about this," he ordered the other guard. "Either of you."

She didn't know who the second person was, but she didn't care. Sleep tugged at her, pulling her into the place where she would be safe. The dead couldn't hurt her there.

And maybe she would see Watson, the one person she had saved.

Light streamed through the windows, forcing her eyelids open. She squinted and rolled herself to her feet. All her muscles ached.

A new bandage had been wrapped around her elbow, but she could not remember getting it. She couldn't remember anything after she came into her room last night. Instinctively, she reached for her flask where she usually put it on her bedside table and found it gone.

She swallowed down the dryness in her throat, clenching her fingers against the ache to search for it. It was for the best. No more hiding, no more mistakes. She had work to do.

Having come back early from Duarmme due to Watson's execution, she did not have any appointments scheduled for the morning, though she knew she would have to call her ministers together to discuss what she had done. With uneasy steps, she made her way to her study, pausing to lean against various pieces of furniture before finally dropping to the floor beside her desk. A stack of memoranda rested on the corner, delivered in her absence.

The papers would remain unread for now. Alexandria had just killed a rebel, as far as Evangeline was concerned, and she wanted to brace herself for what her half-sister might do next. And there was one more thing she hadn't figured out about the former queen's motives.

A gap had appeared between the wooden floorboards, the cooling weather shrinking them. She easily lifted the loose plank. The sound of it clanking against the floor echoed in her head.

Her hand moved once again to the first monarch's notebook. In the week after she had opened it for the first time, she had been so busy preparing to face Natania again, keeping herself afloat, that she hadn't had the chance to read further. Maybe she had been avoiding it. There were no more excuses now.

She flipped to the last page she had read, propping the book open with her knee.

I received a radio signal from Genea today. I can't let the former Varnard know their people survived. Not now. They'll force us to unite with them and pull Kevelda back under their control. They'll discover what lies on the island to the north. Their new beginning will be our end.

I destroyed all forms of communication so that no one will know. In a decade or two, when the ocean is navigable, I imagine they'll come for us. By then, most of the Varnard will be dead. The next generation will not know their name. We will have always been one people.

The room spun around her. The Varnard came from Genea, or as Argon explained months ago, from the nation that had sheltered and reemerged there.

History could be covered up, but the first monarch could not stop parents from passing stories to their children. Someone in Regia, beyond Evangeline, had to know about Genea's former military presence, how the Campaign was created to protect Kevelda from their power.

And they must think I'm bringing us right back to where we started.

"There have been riots all over the kingdom. When are you finally going to take a stand, Your Majesty?" Minister Daniels pinched her red-stained lips together.

Alexandria paced in front of the throne. Natania's threats against her people were getting harder to ignore. She could not stand by and wait for the perfect moment to launch an offensive. Accepting the lesser of two evils only made the next two evils worse.

Her rebellion began when she faked Watson's death last night. Letting the agent go started her on a path that she could not abandon. The decision changed everything. She would be Natania's pawn no longer. All she needed was to figure out how to get into Dane, disarm the bombs, and bring Amira home.

"Give me a little more time. Amira's map only gives us enough information to find the bombs, but we have no way to protect against Natania's inevitable counterattack. Even then, she could just continue mining in Thaertos, and we'll be back here in a matter of months. Let me come up with a plan."

Minister Agate spoke slow and steady, but there was no apology in her words. "We have no more time. It's been four months since you joined the Genean Coalition. Our people have been suffering for much longer. Nothing you do can erase the execution of an Argentum agent at Queen Natania's orders, but you can channel their anger to the real culprit. Genea."

"Their anger will put us more at risk. We do not have any allies. War has cost us our people before, and I will not let that happen again." The pain of the Drafts was still too fresh. Fear clawed at her chest when she thought of sending her people to die, ill-equipped for a battle she knew they could not win.

"We'll give you the month to find allies, before Natania marries a Keveldan and makes this much worse," Minister Daniels said.

Alexandria whipped around. Daniels, Agate, and Greer stared back at her. Sawyer fiddled with the pencil in his hand. She had decided not to find a replacement for Wagner, despite Vada's warning that there had always been five on the Dais and that she should not break from tradition. Keeping Evangeline a secret had been easier without a minister heading the rebel investigation. Justice had no part in the position she was forced into.

"Are you giving me an ultimatum?"

Minister Agate nodded. A pitying smile crossed her face, as if saying the decision was nothing personal. "You must act, Your Majesty."

"You discussed this beforehand."

"Erna brought legitimate concerns to our attention," Minister Daniels said. "Your sobriety, for one."

"I can assure you the *former* Minister Wagner's concerns are unfounded." A low tremor undercut her stiff response, whether from fear or embarrassment or anger, she couldn't tell. She closed her eyes, forcing herself to settle before she proved her own unfitness. But if Wagner had figured out the secret she had tried so hard to hide, the rest of the Dais likely came to the same conclusion on their own. "Who will you replace me with?"

Vada sat unusually still. Of course, her Prime Minister would take over. Did she know about their country's history, about Genea's former military presence? Would that make her do something rash?

Alexandria cleared her throat, burying her rising nausea. "I see." She forced a smile onto her face. "Vada, arrange a voyage to Biscay. Minister Greer and I will leave tomorrow morning. Minister Daniels and Minister Agate, start taking inventory of our weaponry. We might need it if this goes wrong."

Minister Greer looked like he might object to the short notice, but Minister Agate touched his arm. Minister Daniels immediately began to write on the paper in front of her.

Their game had begun.

She adjourned the meeting and headed up to her quarters to pack. Her skin was slick with sweat, and it took her a few attempts to turn the handle with how much her hands shook. She itched for a drink, but she could not have another lapse like she did last night. Not now.

Isaac and Leianna, who both had not spoken to her since the execution unless absolutely necessary, stood outside her room on their guard shift.

Alexandria shifted awkwardly, hoping they didn't see her struggle. "Can you come inside for a minute?"

They followed her as she sat on the bed, Isaac leaning against the bedpost and Leianna positioning herself near the door. The latter would not look at her, and the former stared at her so intently that a tremor washed over her. She attributed it to withdrawals.

Before she could give it a second thought, she told them everything.

TWENTY-THREE
ALEXANDRIA

Fearing that Natania would question her if Leianna and Isaac assisted with the execution, Alexandria had enlisted Prior's help in securing a bulletproof vest for Watson to wear.

He had brought Beckett in on the plan. Alexandria had been wary at first; while Beckett was on the Queen's Guard, she had kept him and the others at arm's length. After threatening them thoroughly, an action that made her sick to her stomach, she was content that they would never tell, at least not for a long time.

As soon as they docked, she had hurried to the kitchen to mix up a solution of dye and syrup. She and James had figured out how to create fake blood for a prank in secondary school—his idea to get back at her cheating ex-boyfriend, since ratting him out to a teacher for the other kind of cheating wasn't enough.

When she went down into the cells, she ordered the agents to leave so that she could speak to Watson alone.

"I didn't expect to see you," Watson had said. Her eyes were bloodshot. She had been crying, thinking that there was no way out, that her queen had abandoned her. If all went according to plan, she would walk out of the palace alive, but her old identity would have to die in the throne room.

Alexandria pulled the bag of colored syrup out of her shirt, along with a roll of medical tape. "Do you have the vest on?"

Watson tapped her chest, a soft thudding sound emanating from the motion.

"Tape this over your heart and pray I don't aim too high."

Watson lifted up her uniform shirt and arranged the bag. "Thank you for doing this."

"Don't thank me for anything," Alexandria said. "You can't return to your old life or the people you knew. It'll be as if you truly died, and I'm the reason for all of it."

"I have no one outside of this palace," Watson had replied.

Isaac fidgeted with a black scrap of cloth as she told him and Leianna the last part. She vowed to ask him about it later, if he would speak to her again. Try as she might, she could not tear her eyes from the way his fingers moved over it.

She ran her hand across the quilt she sat upon. "When I left the throne room, Prior and Beckett brought her here. I cut and dyed her hair, gave her new clothes, and told her to never come back again."

"She was a rebel," Isaac said. "I doubt she went back to Evangeline after all this."

Leianna's eyes widened. "Evangeline?"

Isaac and Alexandria shared a glance. There was no point in hiding it anymore. While she certainly did not trust Evangeline, she had disavowed Natania by sparing Watson. That decision aligned her more with the rebels than anyone else.

"Evangeline is alive," she said. "She's leading the group of rebels that have tried to kill me multiple times."

Leianna pressed her hand against the wall, keeping herself steady. A flicker of hope flashed in her eyes, then they narrowed. "Were the rebels behind this attack?"

Isaac shook his head. "No. Yes. It's complicated."

"Explain."

"Evangeline put her up to it, but she left the bomb on the ship. She didn't want to hurt anyone."

Alexandria picked up his train of thought. "Natania had someone take the bomb and plant it to test me. This gives us an advantage. In her eyes, I passed." She stood and drew closer to Leianna. "Which is why no one can know what happened, not even Evangeline. I know how loyal you are to her. I can't compete against a woman you've looked up to for years. All I ask is that you don't tell her about this."

Leianna pressed her lips together before responding. "Why didn't you tell me? He's one of them. Do you trust him?"

"She doesn't." Isaac crossed his arms. "It's part of our arrangement."

Her chest burned with the desire to tell him that wasn't true, but now was not the right time. "I thought you might choose her, and I couldn't let you do that. I need you too much. Both of you."

It was their turn to exchange a loaded glance. Alexandria crumpled the fabric of her skirt as she waited for one of them to respond.

"If it helps," Isaac said, "Evangeline doesn't trust me anymore, because she knows who I chose, and it wasn't her. She's the same queen she was, the one we didn't see because we were so caught up in her attention. If you wouldn't die for her, you're her enemy. All or nothing, Lei. What's it going to be?"

"If she wanted me, she would have come." The sole crack in her armored expression was the slight quiver of her lip. "I serve the queen, and she no longer holds that title."

Her words did not give Alexandria much confidence, but if she lost Leianna, her circle of trust would become a line connecting her only to Isaac. She could not lose any more allies.

"We leave for Biscay in the morning. If you don't show up, I'll assume you've gone to find her. Your decision. I can't keep any more secrets, and I can't hold you here." Alexandria's fingers circled Leianna's wrist. "If I don't see you again, just know I'm sorry. I've been trouble for you since the moment you became my Protector."

Leianna nodded. Her dark eyes shifted between her and Isaac. Alexandria dropped her arm and watched her captain leave.

"She'll come," Isaac said, squeezing her shoulder. She had not noticed him move.

"Maybe you can read her better, but I'm not so sure."

"It's hard to tell with Evangeline. Leianna never had a chance to know her as anyone other than the leader that cared about us. She doesn't know how Evangeline used you and me, only that she grieved for a woman who's still alive. But if I've learned one thing about Leianna, it's that she's loyal, even more so to the crown. She won't just leave you."

"I wouldn't blame her." She sighed and leaned against the wall. The bandages covering her back rubbed against her wounds, making her grit her teeth in response. *Something to numb the pain would be excellent.* She pressed her palm to her forehead as if pushing the thought away.

"I would."

"Why?"

He propped his shoulder next to her. The sleeve of his shirt brushed hers. "Because no matter what you've done to keep Natania and Evangeline happy, you're not *them*. You don't look at people and wonder how they can serve you. You do everything you can to protect them."

"Not well."

"It's okay. You're good at other things."

She twisted her body in his direction and arched an eyebrow. "You need to stop saying things like that if you're not going to list them."

"One, you're great at keeping track of everything they throw at you. I don't know how you've managed to placate them for this long without help. Asking for help, now that's something you're terrible at."

She punched his arm without much force. "Totally helping."

"Two," he started with a grin. That dimple would kill her. "You're strong. Not in the physical way, though that's true, too. But after everything you've been through, you're still here. You bend, but you don't break."

"I feel broken."

"A broken woman wouldn't have set her kingdom on the line to save one guard." His fingers brushed her cheek, thumb running along her jaw. "You're not broken."

Tears leaked from the corners of her eyes. She blinked rapidly, shifting her face away from him. Her skin ached for his touch when he dropped his hand. "Is there a third?"

"Three, you're a fantastic kisser."

A laugh bubbled from her throat. "Really? That's what you're going for?" Her body felt light, a prickling sensation climbing up her arm and into her core. The illogical piece of her brain wanted to test his assessment.

"It's the truth, as far as I'm concerned."

"Tell me, where do I rank on your list?" She said it as a joke, but she scolded herself for actually caring. It was the least of her worries, but for the moment, she longed to feel normal.

His smile faltered for a heartbeat. "You're the only one."

"That was your first kiss?"

"Technically not. Minister Sawyer's daughter got that honor when I was thirteen. That one didn't make the chart."

She stared forward at the floral pattern of the quilt. The kiss had not meant *nothing* to her, but she wouldn't have done it if not for the ruse. Not then, in front of all those people. Not when they had so much history.

Both he and Phillip had betrayed her, but only Isaac was working to make it right. Unless he was just there to do it again. That didn't ring true, but she couldn't chance another crack in her heart.

"Don't feel bad," he said into the silence.

"I have a deal for you." She pushed away from the wall. "We both survive what happens next. I bring our people home. Then, I'll kiss you. For real this time."

Surprise crossed his face, and for a moment, she wished she could take the words back. They hung in the air, impossibly heavy between them, until he schooled his expression into a smirk.

"I wasn't planning on dying," he said, and she could breathe again.

"Good. Just stay alive."

His hand found hers and they shook on it.

TWENTY-FOUR
ALEXANDRIA

An icy hand clamped over Alexandria's mouth, ripping her from one nightmare and dragging her into another.

She thrashed against her sheets, the thick fabric tangling her limbs. Her foot struck something hard as she kicked out. A scream reverberated in her mouth, caught by the cloth that covered it. It tasted like a spoonful of sugar. She gagged as the cloying odor burned her throat.

A mass of shadows surrounded her, outlined by the moonlight seeping through her windows. One pressed the cloth harder. Another held her down. The third grabbed at her legs, pushing them to the bed.

Everything was too sweet. Her heart pounded, head fuzzy and eyes watering.

"Let me go," she tried to say. Her cries made no sound.

Please, she thought, when her throat would not work. *Let me go.*

The dampness of the ravine crept over her before the world faded into nothingness.

A bright light blinded her when she next opened her eyes. They strained against it, focusing for seconds at a time.

Rope rubbed against her wrist. Her fingers brushed another hand, which she came to realize was her own.

The chair her assailants had tied her to creaked as she urged her limbs to move.

She saw worn curtains frayed at the edges, joined by wallpaper torn and patched anew. Yellow baseboards lined the walls, connecting them to stained carpet.

Evangeline's office.

Her ankles stung as she tried to loosen the ropes that bound them. She gained a centimeter of space, then two. Then, the doorknob slammed against the wall and Evangeline burst into the room.

"You killed one of my agents," she said, her voice tight and low.

Alexandria whipped her head back. She shifted her hand, squeezing her right thumb until she heard a crack. Her chest heaved at the thought of what she had done, even if she could not feel it. "You sent her to kill me."

"You were collateral damage."

"I thought after fifteen years of your reign, you wouldn't underestimate anyone, especially not Natania. She took over your plan when Watson couldn't carry it out. Now, she's safe, our kingdom looks weak, and sixteen people are dead." She started to push her broken hand up through the ropes with her other fingers.

"You still underestimate *me*. I am the only reason you're still on the throne. We could have reigned as sisters." Evangeline clenched her jaw and turned her face away.

"You want to be a family so badly? Don't leave me to die and then punish me when I'm forced to deal with the consequences of *your* choices!"

"If you're not on my side, you're a liability."

"Did our father teach you that?"

"My mother did. Our father thought he could win with diplomacy. He tried to show Genea that we would benefit them more as equals, not enemies." She scoffed, crouching until their eyes were level. "Look what they did with that."

"I might have allies in Dane." That proclamation was her last plea, her final hope that her half-sister could make a better choice.

"You inherited the worst of him."

"I didn't inherit anything from any of you."

The rope fell to the floor. Alexandria lunged. Her hand found Evangeline's throat as she shoved her onto her back and straddled her. She could not block with her other hand, however, and her rival punched her in the diaphragm. Eyes watering, she gasped for air that never came.

Evangeline threw her off. Pain jolted through her hip as she collided with the wall. She rolled toward the window to avoid the next blow. As Evangeline stood over her, she ripped the curtain down.

For a fraction of a second, she feared her plan had not worked. Then, the metal curtain rod collapsed, ramming into the back of Evangeline's head. The woman cursed and stumbled backwards.

Alexandria pushed onto her feet and bolted toward the door.

The rising sun swept through the windows as she staggered down the hallway. Pins and needles crept up her legs. Her vision swam, the aftereffect of whatever chemical the rebels had used on her. Footsteps grew louder behind her. She turned into the stairwell, taking the steps two at a time. Her leg gave out on the first landing, and she scraped her knees on the floor.

She crawled, started upright, and fell again. Fingers gripped her arm hard enough to leave a bruise. Her throat burned with her shouts. Nails dug into her skin, dragging her back up the stairs.

Evangeline would kill her. She had survived the Campaign just to be killed by the queen who put her through it in the first place.

Screams echoed around her until she forgot that she was their source. The world appeared to her through water. She dug her bare heels against the stairs. It accomplished nothing but bloodying them.

When they reached the top of the stairs, she dropped deadweight. A second man took her by the waist and pulled her upright. Her voice failed. With no weapons, no leverage, and unable to call for help, she twisted her head frantically, looking for a way out. There were none.

A gun clicked behind her. "Put her down." *Isaac.*

The second man dropped her. She used the distraction to wring herself out of the first man's grip and dig her nails into his hand until he let go of her other arm. Red marks circled her wrists, peeking out beneath the bandages from her prior injuries, and she had to do a double take to make sure she hadn't started bleeding again.

"Mendoza," the first man said, "I never suspected you would be one to switch sides."

Isaac flinched at his surname. "I didn't switch sides. I was always on hers."

"You make a good traitor."

"Makes sense why I was Evangeline's favorite, then." His eyes flicked to her. He had both the men's attentions. "Do you really think she has your best interest in mind? She'll turn on you the second she has a chance at power."

She rose little-by-little, inching upwards each time they took a step toward him.

The man grunted. "She'll bring our people home."

"How? By hiding in this hotel?"

Alexandria spotted a knife at the second man's side. She inclined her head toward him, hoping Isaac noticed. He aimed the gun at the first man.

"She's going to take the throne again soon. Then, this nightmare will be over," the second man said. Right before she slipped the knife from its sheath and held it up to his neck.

"Move and you die." Sweat slicked her palm. *Please don't move.*

"That's enough," Evangeline shouted down the hallway. Her hand clutched the back of her head. "Let them go."

"Who are you talking to?" Isaac asked. "Because as far as I'm concerned, we have the advantage, and I don't take orders from you anymore."

Metal glinted in the dim light as she drew a pistol from her side and held it to the back of Isaac's head. "Alexandria, release him."

She took in a sharp breath. "Okay." Her hand shook as she dropped the knife. The second man held her arms within a second.

Isaac took his finger off the trigger, then slowly crouched and set it on the floor.

"Good." Evangeline holstered her gun. "Bring Alexandria to my office. Take Mendoza downstairs."

The man pushed her back down the hallway to the room she just escaped from. All she had gained from her excursion was a lost voice and a broken thumb she could not feel. Palpitations wracked her chest. She did not stand a chance, being drugged and going through withdrawals simultaneously.

He threw her onto the chair. An arc of pain tore up her spine. She noticed him tie her broken hand tighter, but even if he hadn't, she would not be able to pull it through anyway. The rope was too high up for her other fingers to reach it. For good measure, he laced a cable around her ankles, one on each side of the chair. It cut into her skin so deeply that for a moment she could only see white.

Evangeline cupped her jaw and yanked her face upwards. "No one else is coming to save you."

"I wouldn't be so sure about that," she ground out.

"You have a strong will, I'll give you that. It's a shame you weren't a better ally."

"Why put me on the throne just to kill me?"

Evangeline walked in a circle around the chair, surveying her. "I had high hopes for you, Alexandria. I waited more than twenty years for you to come into your potential. But I've been fighting this battle my whole life, and I'll find another way to destroy Genea."

"You'll kill them all."

"They killed us first."

She thought of Cassandra, of the pain that marked her eyes when she talked about her parents, how Natania had killed them to take the throne. And then there was the mysterious figure who delivered Amira's map. "What if someone there wants to help us?"

"You're naïve."

"You're a fool if you think our people will stand by you until the end, after everything you've done. All the people you've killed to stay in power. Do they know about the rebel you slaughtered during your Campaign?"

"We're not so different, you and me. I'm sure you have a few secrets you'd kill to keep. A few secrets they'd kill you for."

She spit in the woman's face. Even though they shared a father, Alexandria could not think of anyone more different from her. Different than she wanted to be.

Evangeline kicked the chair backwards. Her head cracked against the floor and then everything went black.

TWENTY-FIVE
ALEXANDRIA

W ake up."

Alexandria bolted upright, remembering too late that she was tied down. A muscle twinged in her neck. Her brain pushed against her skull. She sucked air in through her teeth.

"That looks bad," James said.

Her body tensed at his presence. Did Evangeline send him? The former queen knew how much it would hurt to see him after what he said the last time she was here. *She wants to break me before she kills me.* The cables sliced deeper into her ankles as she tried to free herself.

"Can she hear us?" a familiar female voice asked.

Of course, I can hear you. Her words came out in a jumbled mess. She would do anything to make the pain stop. Pressure built in her temples until it felt like they would crack open.

James held his hand under her head. "Help me untie her."

The two pulled the chair to its feet. When he moved his hand, blood coated it. *Is that mine?*

A brunette woman stood in front of her. She crouched, her hands working at the cables. "Do you remember me?"

There was something about the woman that reminded her of home. Of Amira. Of poppies.

Isla. She ran the flower stall at Kureya's market. Why was she here?

Alexandria had the sudden thought that she was dreaming. No words came out of her mouth, at least not ones that made sense. That was a recurring theme in her nightmares.

James did not really come to help her. He hated her for the Genean Coalition, so much that he joined Evangeline, the other queen he despised. Right?

"Isla," she said at last. The one word she could get out. Her tongue regained control with every breath. "You're a rebel."

"Have been since I was born," Isla said with a smile.

Alexandria's skin stung when the cables fell. She flexed her ankles until they recovered a semblance of feeling. "For Evangeline?"

Isla shook her head. "There were pockets of people across Kevelda, but we hadn't been organized since my brother died. Rather, since Evangeline killed him. After you ascended, she swooped in and brought us together. She told us that she was the only one who could end the war, and we believed her. At least, some of us did."

"She killed your brother, and you followed her?"

"I never truly did. I was just here until someone better took over. We had to do something after you joined the Coalition, so when she sent out the call, I came here. Besides, he was the one who decided to challenge her." Despite the neutrality of her tone, her eyes watered.

The rebel in Evangeline's Campaign.

"That day at the market, you warned me about the man watching me. Did you know he was sent by Mendoza?"

James finished with the ropes around her hands. She stumbled when she stood, and Isla caught her.

"No, I didn't know. That wasn't a rebel thing, not in the organized way. 'The most powerful act of rebellion is caring about one another.' My father used to tell us that."

Alexandria gripped James's arm to keep from falling over. "Why are you two here? Does she know?"

"Isaac didn't tell you?" he asked.

She remained silent until he guessed her answer.

"We've been working to turn people to your side. To convince them that you're the queen they should fight for."

"I thought you hated me. You said I wasn't doing anything to save our people."

His face blanched. "I thought you knew I was acting. I had to make Evangeline and the others believe it."

"No!" She would have punched his arm if she wasn't leaning on him.

"You seriously thought I would turn on you?"

"I don't know, we've had our arguments over the years."

"About who was cleaning the dishes. Not about whether or not I wanted someone to kill you!"

Isla chimed in. "I love that you two are reconciling, but can you do it at a lower volume? Also, having this conversation after you get out of here would be great, too."

"Right," Alexandria said. "I'm sorry, James. I don't know who to trust anymore."

"I'm the one who should be apologizing. I didn't know I was such a great actor." He wrapped his arm under her shoulders to support her. "Let's get out of here."

"We have to find Isaac."

"You're not in any position to fight."

"Does it look like I care?"

His eyes searched hers. "No. God help whoever stands in your way."

They passed a few others on their path to the basement. Most just nodded in acknowledgement, but one asked where they were taking her. James and Isla acted as though they were moving her for Evangeline. The woman did not question them any further.

Her head throbbed in tandem with her descent down the stairs, each step like a shard of glass. She grimaced and felt for a wound. The blood had mostly dried, but a few streaks transferred to her hand. A bitter smell emanating from the basement made what little food was in her stomach rise into her throat.

The fluorescent lights flickered, disorienting her. Everything had blurred edges in her vision. Isla went through the door first and disappeared. Seconds passed, long enough for Alexandria's pulse to double. Then, Isla beckoned them inside.

Dark blotches stained the concrete floor. Pipes ran along the walls in a labyrinthine pattern. Her stomach churned when she spotted Isaac.

The men had tied him to a splintered wooden chair, and his head slumped forward at an uncomfortable angle. They had removed his jacket and shirt and tossed them on the ground. Red patches marred his skin around the ropes. A line of blood trickled from his nose onto his chest.

She gasped at what she saw there. Black and purple bruises blossomed from his shoulders to his ribs. The marks circled the jagged white scar Jason's bullet had given him. As she drew closer, the world turned on its side.

They had branded him. Harsh lines cut across his skin over his heart, drawn by the tip of a blade.

"Traitor."

A mangled sound tore from her throat. She fought to breathe. Her bandaged knees landed in the puddles of blood next to him. His skin was clammy and cold. The basement held a damp chill that permeated her bones.

"Isaac," she whispered, unable to speak at a normal volume. The room was too quiet; *he* was too quiet. His breaths were weak. Imperceptible. Only when she held her hand to his chest could she tell he was alive. He shifted at her touch, but he did not awaken.

"Please, Isaac. Wake up." It sounded like someone else's begging, coming from across a chasm. "Say something."

She lifted his chin, exposing cuts and bruises across his face. One of his eyes was swollen shut. Movement crossed behind his other eyelid. Still, it did not open.

Isla knelt beside her, a hand on her shoulder.

"What did they do to him?" Alexandria asked, though she knew the answer. They had tortured him because of her.

The blood rushing in her ears muted Isla's voice. "If people don't make an effort to do better, they will only ever be as good as those they follow. Keep talking. I think he can hear you."

"I need you to wake up now." Her fingers trembled as she held his cheek. James and Isla moved to cut the ropes binding him.

"I don't know what to say," she continued. "You always say the right thing to keep me calm. I'm not calm right now. I need you to fix it. Come back and fix everything. Fix me, please." Sobs punctuated her words. Towards the end, they all slurred together.

When James and Isla freed his arms, she took one of his hands. His knuckles tasted like salt when she held them to her lips. "I promise I'll never call you 'insufferable' again."

"I like it when you call me 'insufferable.'" He inhaled sharply, followed by a set of coughs. His mouth twisted as he brought a hand to his ribs.

"Good. I'll say it as much as you like if we make it out of here. Okay?" She picked up his shirt and clutched it to her chest. James helped him stand. If he let go, Isaac would keel over. He could not raise his arms; it would be impossible to get his shirt back on, so they maneuvered his jacket over his shoulders. She and James each took one of his sides and half-carried, half-led him to the door.

Isla stopped them. "I have to stay here. Someone has to tell our people what happened."

"Evangeline will know you helped us," James said.

"All she'll know is that I brought her down here with you, not that I helped you leave."

"She won't believe you."

She straightened her shoulders. "I need one of you to hit me. Just give me a black eye or something."

James raised his eyebrows. "I'm not punching you, Isla."

"Come on, I saw that fight you got into in secondary school. I know you can do it."

"In his defense, it was my former boyfriend," Alexandria interjected, "not our friend."

"Semantics." Her smile widened, though her body tensed. "I won't hold it against you."

James sighed and let Alexandria take the brunt of Isaac's bodyweight. She leaned her shoulder against the door for support. Isla moved a few steps back, James positioning himself in front of her. He apologized profusely, and Isla told him to get on with it. Alexandria looked away. She heard the punch and Isla's pained breath.

The skin around her eye turned bright red. A small cut split her cheekbone. James pressed a kiss to her temple and asked how badly it hurt. Alexandria's jaw dropped, sending a shock through her skull, but she did not have time to comment before Isla pushed the three of them out the door, saying she would handle things there.

They moved as fast as they could up the stairs, which did not say much. Isaac winced with every step. By the time they reached the top, her vision had narrowed to a pinhole. Darkness invaded her periphery. James had to guide them through the lobby and out the back door before anyone saw them.

Once they had traversed a couple of blocks, her legs buckled. She cried out at the feeling of a knife stabbing the nape of her neck. James helped her lower Isaac to the ground. She squeezed her eyes closed to shut out the rising light.

With her head between her knees, she muttered, "I can't make it back to the palace. You have to go get Leianna."

"And leave you out here? They'll know you're gone by now. Evangeline will send people for you." He put a hand on her shoulder. "You can do this."

Agony split her in two. Every thought came in half-finished, words in her mind blurring together. Stars flickered behind her eyes. She focused on her breaths.

"James." Nothing else would come out of her mouth.

She felt him rise next to her. "Okay, I know what to do. Bailey's church is three blocks away. Do you think you can make it?"

Her tongue was heavy. "I think so." The sounds slurred together, but he understood.

"Can you, Isaac?"

"I have to," he responded, his breaths heavy.

Her limbs moved as though they were encased in warm honey. She staggered upwards, swaying with every step. James took most of Isaac's weight. Her arm wrapped around Isaac more for her own support than his.

They ducked between the rapidly dissolving shadows, crossing empty intersections and stumbling through alleyways. If any rebel sympathizers spotted them, they could not fight back in their conditions.

Her heartbeat picked up speed when the church's entrance came into view. She set her teeth against the pain rattling her skull, which made it worse, but she did not care. With her legs on the verge of shattering, the three pushed themselves forward.

James knocked. The seconds stretched into minutes with no answer. She tapped her fingers against Isaac's waist to distract herself.

The door creaked open. She tried to smile, the stretch of her facial muscles adding to the cacophony of pain.

Bailey's eyes widened when he saw them. "Come in," he said, searching the alley behind them.

Only a few steps inside the church, she collapsed.

TWENTY–SIX
ALEXANDRIA

Light seared Alexandria's eyes. She squinted, feeling the floor around her. A cold rag fell from her forehead when she used her elbow as leverage to sit. Her muscles ached. It would be a while before she felt normal again, she imagined.

Isaac sat slumped against the wall next to her. Dried blood flaked from his nose onto his jacket. His head tilted at an awkward angle, leaning against his shoulder. She hovered her finger across the letters that had been carved into his chest. Some parts had already scabbed, but blood still welled up in spots.

"I'm so sorry," she said. "This is all my fault."

Through his unswollen eye, he watched the path of her hand. "Every scar I get for you is worth it."

"Pain is not the price you must pay to be cared for." When she lifted her eyes from the mark, she found him staring at her. She dropped her arm. "Don't martyr yourself for me. It's my

234

job to protect you now, not the other way around. I'm your queen. I shouldn't have let any of this happen."

"Let's just call it even."

The wall was cool against her back. Despite the sting of her wound, the chill relieved some of the pressure in her skull. She leaned her head on Isaac's shoulder. He shifted closer to her with a soft groan at the movement of his torso.

"Do you need ice?" Being this close to him weakened her resolve to do anything, but she would rather get up than leave him hurting.

"I couldn't hold it even if I wanted to."

"I can."

His hand brushed hers. "Are you sure?"

She nodded, putting on as much of a smile as she could muster without sending a bolt of lightning through her face. She imagined it looked rather like a grimace.

Her legs shook underneath her like a newly hatched gull's. The familiar circle of chairs told her she was on the second floor of the church. James must have carried her up. She forced a slow breath and braced herself for the trip down the stairs.

A light shone in the chapel. She stumbled toward it, stopping short when she heard voices rising from within. Her people could not see her like this. It would only cause more panic. Or worse, they would attack her here.

She did not get the chance to escape before Bailey called her name.

Her stomach tensed, making the nausea worse. With her hand against the wall for support, she set her shoulders and walked before the gathered crowd.

There are no services today, she thought. A list of possibilities crossed her mind, attempting to account for the number of people in the building—at least a couple dozen.

Bailey met her halfway. A few in the crowd stared at her, some wide-eyed, others shooting daggers with their glares. One woman bowed, the rest in her vicinity following shortly after. Alexandria waved it off with her half-formed smile.

A man asked her if she was alright. She said as little as she could, but there was no denying her appearance. It would be futile to claim she hadn't been attacked. Dried blood splotched her nightdress, and the hem had ripped in multiple places.

The priest took her arm. "Do you need anything?"

"I was going to get ice for Isaac, but what's going on in here?"

"These people have all come home ill after working in Thaertos. It appeared later for some, but they fear it is contagious. I opened the church for quarantine."

"But it's not..." She stopped herself. They did not know what they were mining for, nor that the mineral caused their sickness.

"I know. Most of the others do not bother. Yet I cannot deny these few shelter when they need it most."

She couldn't meet his earnest stare. They would spend the rest of their lives here, without their loved ones, all because she had lied to them. Over and over and over again.

The couple in the corner, leaning on each other. The woman who had bowed, coughing into a napkin. The group playing a card game on the floor. They were all her people. She would do anything it took to protect them. Unfortunately, that had not worked out so well for them in the end. Sacrifices would have to be made, even as she vowed to save as many as she could.

Grasping for the right words to say, she limped over to the cardplayers. Her knees hit the tile with a thud like a gunshot in the sudden silence. They watched her warily. The freckled woman holding the cards continued to deal them while pinning Alexandria with her stare.

The woman spoke first. "You in?"

Another woman in the circle chewed her pale bottom lip and laced her fingers as if bracing for an attack.

She didn't know what they were playing, and she wouldn't be any good at it, even if she did. The edges of the cards blurred with the dull throb at her temples. Amira had always been the one who was good at games. Alexandria and Phillip had to team up to win against her. James never stood a chance.

But she wasn't here to win. The sanctuary was not the throne room, and this was not the Campaign. She repeated that in her head, even as the eyes studying her morphed into those of the ministers and mayors.

"Yes," she said, "I'll play."

The woman dealt her six cards, three placed upside-down and three facing her. She took three more in her hand. Her hazy memory couldn't place the game, but she could gather the rules as they went along.

"Why are you here?" asked the fourth person in their group, a man with thick blonde brows and a scar on his cheek. His stern features made it difficult to gauge his attitude toward her.

She should have said she wanted to check on them. That she wanted to tell them they would never have to return to Thaertos. Instead, she replied, "I got caught up in a fight."

"I wasn't aware you fought," he remarked.

"I do now."

He grunted his acceptance, followed by a dry cough. The anxious-looking woman handed him a cup of water. Alexandria locked eyes with the dealer, who assessed her with an upturned chin.

"I don't care what brought you through those doors after all this time," the freckled woman said. "You want something from us."

"No, I don't." Perhaps she could use information about the mines, but she hadn't earned the right to their stories. They didn't trust her, and she didn't blame them. The crowd watched and whispered amongst themselves.

It was easier for her to confess to this woman than to herself. "I failed you. You should hate me. Maybe we didn't have a chance to win the war, but my predecessors never told you the truth, either. And here I am, having done the same. Worse, even."

"Don't waste your time on pity. Spend it on action." The woman slid Alexandria's cards away, shuffling them back into the deck. Their game was over. "I want to die knowing the person I love won't suffocate in that cave."

"I can't promise we'll win. I can only promise that I won't let our kingdom go quietly." She remained on her knees, but she turned her vow upon the crowd. Her words washed over their skeptical stares. "Genea has the advantage. They did not lose their progress a century ago. They have not faced famine. But we have something they don't. The power to rebuild. Whatever comes next, win or lose, we will come back."

"Will you declare war?" a soft voice asked.

She nodded. Speaking her assent aloud could kill them all, if this conversation didn't doom them already. But she could not be so afraid of losing her people that she let them—and herself—fade away. "I have one more thing to do first."

When she rose, supporting herself on Bailey's arm, their whispers morphed into loud chatter. A woman tapped her shoulder and began to tell her about the mines. And then another woman joined her, and then a man. Soon, she had heard countless stories of their experiences in Thaertos, of their lives before and their shattered hopes for what would come after. She learned the names of relatives long gone and recently born. Her head pulsed with information and her heart twisted with bitter sadness.

The seed planted long ago, by Reagan and Phillip and her family and all the people she loved and ever would love, sprouted in her chest, blossoming into a sprawling mass of anger—and when all that rage burned away, hope remained.

Her limbs grew heavy as she departed, and she caught Bailey at the door. His grey eyes sparkled, his wrinkled mouth quivering between a frown and a smile. He took her hand in both of his.

"You cannot stay here," she said to him. "Things are about to get really dangerous, and I have no doubt that Regia will be the first target. You have to go somewhere safe. Do you or Leianna have any other family you can stay with outside of the city?"

"Who am I to turn these people out?" His gaze settled on the crowd. "Besides, *they* are my family. I watched a good number of them grow up. My son is gone, but they are not. I am not afraid of what may come."

She understood, though it broke her heart to know he would be in the line of fire. "Stay safe, then." Her voice cracked. She coughed to cover it up, a stake driving through her temples. Before she would let a tear fall, she turned away and went to the kitchen.

Water dripped from the towel she carried up to Isaac. The chunk of ice began to melt, numbing her hand. He stirred, as if her footsteps had awoken him, and moved his jacket, exposing his bruised skin. The contusions had turned darker. Deep purple covered both his sides.

"What hurts the most?" she asked as she knelt beside him. They would discuss what she learned about the mines later. Once she saw his wounded state, she couldn't focus on anything else.

He grimaced. "Everything."

She decided to ice his right side and hope that James would return with Leianna soon. Ice would not be enough to heal either of their wounds. She pressed the towel against his ribs, surveying the scar from Jason's bullet. Jagged pink lines jutted from it as if it never healed quite right. His skin burned against her cold hand.

"Thank you for coming to find me." The question of what Evangeline had planned to do with her pushed into her thoughts. She blinked it away. "How did you know I was gone?"

He stared at the floor in front of him. "I check on your guards from time to time, make sure they're doing their jobs. I found them unconscious with your door open."

As much as she tried to keep a wall between them, he kept tearing it down. Proving himself over and over again. A part of her wished he didn't. It would be easier to figure everything out on her own—less people to get hurt—but that hadn't worked for her very well. "Do you think they'll do it again?" She sighed. "Who am I kidding? Of course, they will."

"I'll stay with you."

"That won't do anything besides put you in danger."

"I'm already in danger. Let it be for a good cause."

"I won't have you sleeping on my couch."

"There's a better option." He blinked, though Alexandria assumed it would have been a wink if his other eye wasn't swollen.

"Couch it is, then."

"I knew you'd come around." His hand covered hers where it held the ice. "I can talk to Leianna about setting up an internal guard rotation as well as external. Two in your room, two outside. No sleeping involved."

She liked the idea of the guards returning to their previous posts inside her door even less than the idea of Isaac staying on her couch, but it would be the safest choice. Still, she doubted she would rest at all. "I assume you'll continue checking in on them?"

"Always."

No one could promise forever, not when the world was falling apart underneath them, but the idea of his *always* comforted her. Even when she failed her people, he would be there. She hoped so, anyway. He might not have been accounting for her tendency to get people killed.

She held the ice rag against his ribs until footsteps thundered on the stairs. Her legs groaned as she stood and smoothed the hem of her bloody nightdress.

Leianna burst into the room, her lips drawn taut and brows pinched. She promised to interrogate the guards and figure out how they had been incapacitated, but Alexandria waved her off. They would worry about that another day. If the rebels wanted to kidnap her again, they could, no matter what precautions her guards took. The thought would have scared her if she had enough energy left to feel anything but numb.

As soon as their vehicle pulled up to the palace, she and Isaac were escorted to the medical wing. Leianna or James must have told the medics to place them in the same room. *Good.* She could not handle being away from him, not in his condition. Cuts and bruises covered the majority of his skin, with blood coating the rest. His eye had swollen even further. Once they set him on the cot, he passed out.

She watched the medics stitch up the deeper cuts of the carving on his chest, faintly aware that they were doing the same to her head. An IV drip ran into the crook of her elbow. One of the medics wrapped her broken hand in white gauze. If they were giving her painkillers, she would not know the difference. The world around her blurred into darkness.

Her eyes adjusted to the fluorescent light above her. At some point, she had fallen asleep. She rolled onto her elbow to find Isaac. He was still in the other bed next to her. A deep sigh drew the breath from her lungs.

She screamed when she found a figure standing next to her. Or it would have been a scream had her throat not been parched. It came out as a crackling gasp instead. Her heart thundered, calming only when she realized it was Minister Agate.

"I came as soon as I heard," the woman said. "I apologize for scaring you."

"It's okay. Everyone does." She cringed as the words fell from her mouth. Whatever medicine they gave her lowered her inhibitions. She would lock herself in here until it left her system. "Who else knows?"

"The whole Dais. They had to know. Leianna told Vada, and she told the rest of us." She draped a hand over Alexandria's arm.

"What did she tell you?"

"She said that the rebels came and stole you from your quarters in the middle of the night. We all have extra security assigned to us for the next few weeks."

Alexandria knew no one else would be a target, but that would be too much to explain, not without exposing Evangeline's fake death. That would only put her own position in jeopardy. Evangeline was right—the ministers would choose her over Alexandria in a heartbeat. She couldn't risk that, not yet.

Priyanka continued speaking into the silence. "How do you intend to fix this?"

"They will never stop, not until I act against Genea." Her mind moved sluggishly, and her tongue even more so, but she compiled her never-ending list of next steps. "We have to dismantle the bombs, but there's no way in, even with the map Amira gave me. Even if we do that, Natania can destroy us with her military. We don't have enough soldiers or weapons to protect our seas. They'll be here in days. And we'll still have our people in Thaertos."

"Ask the Dais for their guidance. It may seem like they're against you, but we're all here to help you. Use us. You can't do this all on your own, Alexandria."

"Why not? I was expected to survive on my own during the Ascension. Why would it be any different during my reign?" Her tone rang sharper than intended.

Priyanka's eyes fell to the scars covering her skin, new and old. "Strength is not determined by one's capacity for violence, nor their ability to stand alone. The Campaign is an antiquated practice. It never should have existed. Now, we're right back to where we started."

She wondered if the minister knew the true story of the Campaign, how it had been designed to protect her people from Genea's control and, over time, became twisted to keep power out of their own hands. Combat training and Protectors and bloodlines—none of it gave people like James and Reagan a real opportunity to lead. That was certainly not the conclusion Evangeline desired her to come to when she read the first monarch's journal. She was still unsure on that front.

"No matter what we do, we were destined to come back here. I just didn't want to be the harbinger. I should've known, though. From the moment Mendoza announced my name, I became a part of the game."

"If anyone can save us, it is you. You haven't played as long as we have. We're jaded. We cannot change."

"No, don't tell me you can't change. You're still breathing. You do not get to put the weight on my shoulders and back away. Even if the others can't do better, I know *you* can."

The woman's silky hair fell like a curtain in front of her face as she folded her hands. "You're right. I only mean that I watched you grow into the woman you've become. You would do anything for your family, and you care little for your own gain. A lot of us can't say the same. Tell me what we have to do, and I'll get the other ministers on your side."

She picked at the blanket draped across her lap. The stitches in her scalp started to burn. Her eyes caught Priyanka's when she finally looked up.

"Prepare for war."

TWENTY-SEVEN
ISAAC

Isaac stood at the railing of the ship, watching the receding land.

Alexandria held her hand to her forehead beside him. Dark glasses covered her eyes, making it impossible to see what she was looking at. Her migraines worried him. She had only left her quarters twice in the week since they were released from the medical wing—once to meet with the Dais, another to send James off to Hult.

The engine's thrumming pounded against his own skull. His fingers grazed the cut on his cheekbone. It hadn't healed yet, the scab still red and sensitive to the touch. He couldn't force himself to look at the word carved over his heart. When they returned, the medic would remove the last of the stitches. Maybe then the pain in his chest would cease.

"Once more to Biscay," the ship's captain shouted to his attendant.

"Once more to Biscay," Alexandria repeated under her breath.

Leianna surveyed the water from her other side. The three stood in silence. They didn't have much to say these days. No questions about plans. Especially no conversations about how they were feeling. A fog of anxiety had settled over them, prickling at his skin.

As they recovered in the medical wing, Alexandria had told him about the Dais's ultimatum. If she did not gain Victori's support, they would replace her, and they would lose their chance to act on what she had learned about the mines. Isaac got the feeling that Evangeline would be far too happy to come out of the shadows if she heard that news.

He hoped that Minister Agate would keep the Dais on Alexandria's side in their absence. With all the years that he spent serving Evangeline, he knew exactly what she was capable of. None of them would survive her return.

His conversation with Sofie in Duarmme—which seemed like an eternity ago—gave him a choice, and as the threat of Evangeline taking over grew more tangible, he knew he would have to act on it. Even if it meant complicating his relationship with Alexandria further.

She inhaled sharply, breaking him from his thoughts. Her knuckles went pale against the rail. The boat's rocking sent her stumbling into his side. Pain shot through his ribs as he caught her.

"What's wrong?" he asked. He and Leianna shared a worried glance. She motioned for Prior and Beckett to stand on watch.

"I can't..." Alexandria's words slurred together.

"Take her belowdecks," Leianna said. "The medic told me this might happen with her head injuries. We'll have to be on guard when we land. I'll brief the rest of the agents."

"I'm fine." Her breaths came short and fast. "I'll be fine. Everything is fine."

He wrapped an arm around her waist. "It becomes less convincing each time you say it."

"Rest. I just need rest." She rubbed her temple. "What is happening to me?"

He supported her down the stairs to her room. Tossing her coat and glasses to the side, she dropped onto the bed and curled her knees to her chest. He leaned against the doorway, unsure if he should come inside or leave her be. When she started shaking, he decided on the former.

She wasn't crying, though she squeezed her eyes shut. Lines drew between her brows. Goosebumps covered her arms, puckering the skin around her scars. The chill bumps and the still-healing glass cuts that littered the back of her limbs were nearly indistinguishable. If he moved her hair aside, he knew he would find similar spots along her neck and shoulder.

He rolled down the edge of the quilt, and she moved underneath it, never opening her eyes. She fumbled for his hand. "Stay," she whispered, and he did.

The softness of the mattress soothed the ache in his legs. Her hair brushed his shoulder, and when he put his arm around her, she burrowed into his side. He could tell she was trying to be gentle. They were both so fragile. His heart beat an erratic rhythm against his chest at the thought of Evangeline holding her hostage.

Traitor. The pain of the carving seared into his skin as though the wound was fresh. But he didn't mind the brand, after all. He was a traitor, and he was proud of it. It meant that for once in his life, he had truly fought. He came out of it battered and bruised, yet it was for the people he cared about. One person in particular. He would bleed for her over and over again.

Evangeline would never have another chance to hurt her. He had killed the former queen once. The guilt had shredded him, but he made it through with Alexandria by his side. He wouldn't let himself feel that same shame the second time around.

His mouth pressed against the top of her head, and he breathed in the scent of her curls. It was sharp and sterile—the antiseptic the medic used to clean her sutures. Her chest rose and fell evenly. He would give anything to freeze that moment, to live in it. As she pressed into his side, a weight lifted off him, joined by the feeling of his heart cracking open.

There was so much he needed to tell her, about who he was, about his past, about how he hoped his future would be. He just couldn't. She balanced her life so precariously; adding one more card would topple the tower.

When he had found her on her bedroom floor, arm covered in blood, he thought the worst. That someone had attacked, or that she had hurt herself. He had seen her in bad places, brought to tears by the weight of the world, but he had never seen her talk to shadows. She was already dealing with enough. The flask he kept locked in his room signaled that. Telling her the truth would only bring her more pain.

Would she care for him if she knew who he truly was?

That doesn't matter. No matter how hard he tried, the words were not convincing.

When he was confident she was asleep, he maneuvered off the bed, setting her head onto the pillow. It took a few minutes to force himself to move. He wished he could have stayed, but there was too much to do. Sometimes he forgot that he was still an Argentum agent. Protecting her wasn't just an assignment to him. The lines between his professional and personal lives had blurred long ago, back in that cabin in Hult.

He shrugged on his jacket, put his gun back in its holster, and ascended the stairs. Leianna intercepted him. "How is she doing?"

"Sleeping, thankfully. What do you need me to do?"

"I'm rounding everyone up. If she's still this bad by the end of the journey, we have to be extra vigilant."

He clenched his jaw. "Do you think Natania will do anything?"

Leianna cast her eyes toward the sea. "I don't know. If she thinks Alexandria's trying to start something, then yes, she likely will. Or perhaps she will just let it happen because she knows she can succeed against an alliance. Either scenario is frightening."

"It's hard to believe that we'll be gearing up to start a war by the end of this week."

"Not starting a war. Ending it."

She called over the rest of the Queen's Guard. The crew mostly comprised faces he recognized from his time in the Argentum, though some he hadn't worked with. A solid majority were older than him, like Prior and Beckett. There was a woman who looked to be Alexandria's age, but otherwise, they had all been established agents by the time he finished training. He was used to seeing Watson whenever they gathered. His mind turned to her whereabouts, wondering if she had survived her escape from Regia.

Leianna gave her orders to the team. They all knew the severity of Alexandria's injury, though Leianna hadn't told them the specifics of the attack. She remembered every nook and cranny of Biscay, every potential hiding place and entry point. There would be no weaknesses in their shield. During his early days of service, he had been a little afraid of her, not just for her physical abilities, but because of her tactical mind. The feeling had morphed into admiration as of late, though he worried about what would happen if she chose Evangeline in the end.

His post would be by Alexandria's side the entire time they were in the capital, from the port to the palace. Leianna did not need to warn him what would happen if he took his eyes off the queen. He would blame himself for anything that happened to her far before the Captain of the Guard ever could.

They snapped to attention and disbanded. He made his way back to her room, creeping in without a sound. Her mouth moved almost imperceptibly, though her eyes were still closed. He couldn't fight his smile.

"Still a talker," he murmured.

As much as he desired to join her, he wouldn't risk waking her up. He crouched on the ground beside the bed, stretched out his legs, and closed his eyes.

~

King Argon leaned an elbow on the arm of his wooden throne. His white shirt wrinkled slightly around the collar, and the button of the left sleeve was undone. Dark shadows encircled his eyes. Sofie stood next to him, likely there to calm him if things got out of hand. Isaac remembered the impact the attack had on the king's heart.

They had docked an hour after twilight, and Alexandria didn't want to wait to call a meeting with him, especially when Victorin soldiers harassed them about why they were there. She had donned a calf-length floral dress, though Isaac knew she wore her nightdress instead of a slip underneath, as he and Leianna had helped her get ready in the rush.

Her eyes squinted against the light of the chandelier as she leveled her gaze at the king. Isaac bowed beside her.

Despite the fatigued expression on Argon's face, the frantic tapping of his fingers betrayed his hypervigilance. "Has something happened?"

"Natania was behind the attack in Arhaven. She set up one of my guards and forced me to execute her. My people are dying under her command, either mining themselves to death in Thaertos or waiting for their organs to fail if they're lucky to make it home. Though I myself would rather face the former, because at least by suffocating underground, my loved ones wouldn't have to watch me deteriorate." Her hand clung to Isaac's. He had expected her to clear the room, but maybe allowing the soldiers to hear would force Argon into action.

She continued, ignoring the king's attempts to speak. "Yes, Your Majesty, something has happened. With each day that passes, my people dwindle into nothing. I will not pretend to play her game any longer. I was afraid that she would bomb us, send my kingdom into oblivion, but I am convinced that is a far better fate than the hell we have had to endure."

Her chest heaved after the explosion of words. Argon's mouth hung open. After a moment of silence, she asked a final question. "Will you join us, or will you stand by as we die?"

Tension hung in the air, pressing against him. His skin tingled under the weight of the soldiers' stares. He was supposed to be on the watch for threats, but he could only look at her. Her expression was as hard as stone, as sharp as a blade. But he caught the slight twitch of her left eye.

"I cannot," Argon said.

"Why?" The word was a weapon.

"She will destroy us. Without any stake in Kevelda, we cannot take the risk."

"Your material interests matter more than the lives of my people?" A dagger.

Redness rose up his neck. "*My people* matter more. That is the responsibility I must bear as king."

Isaac set his jaw and made a decision. "What stake would you need?" he asked. Sofie shot him a wide-eyed glance. He ignored it, even as his muscles tensed.

Argon's brows furrowed as he kept his fiery gaze on Alexandria. "A Victorin citizen would have to be at risk. That, or there would have to be a royal connection, and due to the attack in your kingdom, I have no more sons for you to marry."

Sofie interjected. "Argon, think about this."

"No!" The king stood, faster than expected for his age. "She does not know what she is asking of us. My answer is final. Escort the queen and her guards back to their boat. I want them gone by sunrise."

Alexandria squared her shoulders. "You are a fool."

"I am a *king*," Argon replied.

As a Victorin soldier grabbed him, Isaac shouted, "I'm your grandson."

Alexandria let out a soft gasp that made her press her fingers to her temple. The soldier hesitated, looking between him and the king with raised brows. The world seemed to freeze, thawing only when Sofie touched Argon's arm.

"I don't have any grandchildren." Argon's face paled as he said it. He turned to Sofie, mouth ajar.

Sofie held his gaze. "It's the truth."

"Both of my sons are dead."

She laced her trembling hands and took a step back. "Edgar didn't want to be a spare. I helped him start a new life. In Kevelda."

That wasn't the whole story, though he knew why she told the king that. His father had learned his violence somewhere. It didn't give Isaac any sympathy for either of them, but it did make him understand that none of the pain was his own fault.

Sofie continued, "I recognized him as soon as he was announced in the ballroom. He has his father's eyes."

Alexandria took his hand, his only support as the world threatened to buckle beneath him. He knew it would be difficult to once again be identified with Mendoza, but nothing could prepare him for the way Argon looked at him now. Equal parts anger and agony.

"You kept this from me for thirty-two years?" A strained calm coated the words. Isaac fought the urge to recoil.

"I had no choice. We could not have allied with them, not under the Genean Coalition."

Alexandria cut into the tension. "It doesn't matter now. What matters is that your only heir is fighting a war. If you won't help me, help him."

The king stared at her with an expression he remembered too well. He would have stood in front of her if not for the way she narrowed her eyes. His first impression of the king as a kind man had been wrong. No wonder no one questioned Mendoza all those years.

"Fine," the king said at last, "you have the support of my military, with one condition."

"Tell me," she commanded.

"It's not you who needs to agree." He stood, sighing with the movement, and walked directly to Isaac. "Once the war is over, you will denounce your Keveldan citizenship, return to Victori, and take on your duties as a prince."

Isaac shared a look with Alexandria, who blinked rapidly, drew her mouth into a tight line, and nodded to him. He couldn't leave her. He had promised.

But this is war.

"Okay," he replied. They shook hands, solidifying his fate.

The king's expression softened. "Welcome home, Isaac."

This was exactly what he had been afraid of.

TWENTY–EIGHT
ALEXANDRIA

After a night of restlessness, all Alexandria wanted was five minutes of sleep. But even without the light breaking through the ship's window, her churning thoughts would keep her awake.

Isaac would have to leave her. She understood why he had kept his heritage a secret from her for those few weeks, but that didn't resolve the nagging feeling that he didn't trust her as much as she hoped. Then again, she had made it evident that she didn't trust *him*, at least in the beginning. None of it mattered, because once the war was over, they would be nothing more than allies. They would brush shoulders at peace meetings and gatherings of the former Coalition kingdoms. Their history would be taught in classes, not in stories to their children.

She bolted upright, shaking that thought away. It was an entirely new imagined future, one that came too late. They were never meant for a domestic life like that, even if he wasn't the heir to another kingdom.

She swung her legs over the side of the bed, hitting her knee against the wall in the tight space. The stiff wool of her coat snagged the satin nightdress beneath when she tugged it on. Evangeline's wardrobe was too extravagant for her, but she couldn't bring herself to go back to Kureya and gather her old things. With Victori on her side, at least she wouldn't have to deal with being deposed. She couldn't stand the idea of facing her home city after joining Genea, but it would be worse to do so having failed in the end.

Wind thrashed her curls into her face when she stepped onto the deck. She picked her nails, ruminating over what would meet them on the rapidly approaching shore. Evangeline still waited for her. Fulfilling the Dais's ultimatum would not protect her from that.

Isaac tapped his knuckles against the wall behind her, alerting her to his presence. She was grateful for the warning. It gave her time to blink away the tears that had gathered in her eyes.

"We need to talk," he said.

She had avoided this the entire trip back to Regia. Any conversation they had could do nothing to change their futures. "About?"

He came up beside her, resting his elbows on the railing. "I'm sorry I didn't tell you sooner. I should have explained everything when Sofie first approached me in Arhaven."

"You were running from it, same as I did. The crown is a terrifying thing."

"It's not the crown I'm afraid of. I told you I wouldn't leave you, and I hate to break my promises."

A traitorous tear slid down her cheek. "Promises mean nothing in war. Believe me, I'm used to this. I'll be fine."

"That's the thing, Lex. You shouldn't be used to it. I wanted to be the one who stayed."

She plastered on a smile, her cheeks twitching with the effort. "You stayed as long as you could. That's all I can ask for."

"You can ask for more." He lifted his hand to cup her cheek, but she pulled away before he could. He was always so intent on making these things difficult.

"We'll make great allies. We already do." She went inside without meeting his eyes. They had a full day of planning ahead of them now that his grandfather had vowed his support.

Isaac followed her, pausing at the door to her room. She heard him shuffle as she grabbed clothes from her case.

"I'll find a way." He started to say something else, but then the door clicked shut, and she realized she was alone.

Once they had docked, she made her way across the gangway, Isaac and Leianna flanking her. With her head held high, she greeted the group of agents at the port. She reminded herself that she should feel victorious.

"Please tell the ministers that I'll meet them in the throne room," she ordered the head agent.

"They're already waiting," the woman replied.

Alexandria's stomach dropped. Something must have happened if they were all meeting without her. Or *waiting* for her. *That must be it. They're just waiting to hear what happened.*

Still, the agents watched her with grim expressions, glancing at each other as they surrounded her. They followed her closely on their walk to the car, and then again up the palace steps. Isaac lifted his hand to the small of her back. A crowd had formed to watch her return. At least, she prayed that was the reason.

The stairs blurred beneath her, a distortion not caused by tears but by the pounding of her head, ever present after the events at the rebel's base. Voices surrounded her in a dizzying chorus. Her knee buckled on the top step, but she righted herself before she could fall. The pressure of the agents' stares kept her from faltering.

Standing before the throne room doors, she awaited her fate. Seconds stretched out into eternities as the agents opened them. The feeling was all too familiar. She forced her face into a neutral expression despite the pain wracking her body.

And there, at the other end of the room, was Evangeline, sitting on the throne as if it was her own.

Time stood still as Alexandria forced herself to breathe.

"What are you doing here?" she spit out, even though she already knew the answer. Evangeline had taken the opportunity they gave her by leaving. Judging by the look on half the ministers' faces—including Minister Wagner with her red-lipped smirk—they were more than happy that the former queen had returned.

"Saving us all," Evangeline replied.

"Did you bother to tell them the real reason you left? That you abandoned us?"

"I told them the truth. Mendoza planned to kill me, and Isaac helped me fake my death in return. I came back when it was safe to do so." Her smile was as sweet as poison. "Let's not worry about that right now. What did Argon say?"

It didn't matter that Victori had allied with them. Evangeline could still have them killed. Even if Alexandria could not save herself in the end, she could keep Isaac alive. "We have Victori's support, so long as his grandson returns to his kingdom after the war is over."

Evangeline's eyes flicked to Isaac. "Who is his grandson?"

It was then that Alexandria recognized the queen's plan went even deeper than she could ever have imagined. "You know who it is. You've known all along."

"I had my suspicions about Isaac and his father. Mendoza became a prominent figure among my father's advisers rather quickly. I had a feeling he knew something I didn't, but beyond that, I'd call it simple fate."

Minister Agate's brows pinched. "If you thought he could help, why didn't you reveal this sooner, Your Majesty?"

Alexandria realized that she was talking to Evangeline, not her. She was no longer their queen.

"I could not risk a journey to Victori based on a theory." Evangeline stood, descending the steps before the throne. "How long did you know, Isaac, before you told anyone?"

Of course, she would try to shift the blame onto us.

He shifted backwards, just a half-step. "We discovered the connection on this trip. I didn't know."

Evangeline narrowed her eyes and circled the ministers' table. The seed of distrust had already been sown, and now they were on an even playing field. No, not even. They all thought Evangeline could save them, a hope they never had for Alexandria. "Well, we can be glad it came to light at last. Now, we must act. You two will be of great help as we plan to invade Dane."

"What about Thaertos?" Alexandria asked. "If we destroy the bombs, she'll make more. We have to shut down the mines. It'll buy us time."

"We need the mines." Evangeline turned to the ministers, eyeing each of them. "Genea built weapons that can destroy us. It is only fair that we do the same. We'll take them once we take the capital."

She knew then what choice Evangeline had thought the first monarch's journal would help her make. Her half-sister would decimate Genea, burn it down and scatter its ashes. The bombs would shatter the remaining shadows of their intertwined history. They would be the ones in control at last.

While Alexandria wanted her people safe, she could not follow in Evangeline's footsteps, not if it meant becoming the same enemy they feared all this time. "You can't be serious."

"What about that sounds like a joke?"

"These weapons will destroy us, even if they are in our own hands. Look at what happened last time. A hundred years is not that long ago. How will we be any different from the Old World?"

"We will be the only ones with this power. We can bring peace to all of the kingdoms. *I* will bring order and justice to those who remain."

Her stomach churned. Evangeline was the last person who should have that authority. Alexandria tried to reach each of the ministers, but their eyes were on the queen. "There will be no peace with you on the throne."

"Your delusions about me do not matter right now. I expect you to comply in aiding our attack on Dane." She approached their group, resting a hand on Leianna's shoulder. "Captain Olivier, will you take Alexandria and Isaac to the barracks? Once you return, we have work to do."

Leianna's eyes flashed with an emotion that made Alexandria's heart stop. Something like pride. Her back straightened, and she flicked a glance at the two of them before returning to her stone-cold exterior. "Yes, Your Majesty."

The captain had made her choice. A part of Alexandria was relieved. The knife hanging over her head had fallen, and though it pierced her, the wound was not as painful as the waiting. Evangeline knew exactly how to win Leianna over, a game she had never bothered to learn how to play.

They traveled into the depths of the palace, taking stairs in the opposite wing from the cells. The staircase opened into a cramped hallway lit by fluorescent lights. Doors lined the sides, paint chipping off the frames.

An agent Alexandria recognized from the rebels' hotel stood by the entrance, and she told them that Evangeline had prepared a room for her. When she took Alexandria down to it, she noticed that her meager belongings had been moved there. A picture of her and her parents rested on the nightstand, and the clothes she wore during the Campaign hung in the open closet.

She had forgotten that most of what she had grown accustomed to in the past eight months had truly been Evangeline's.

"You're not a prisoner," the agent said. "You're free to move around this hall. Her Majesty has requested that you stay here until plans are made."

"What will happen if I try to leave?" she asked.

"Don't."

Alexandria let out a dark laugh. "Not a prisoner at all."

Leianna did not give her any time to plead their friendship before she and the other agent left.

Isaac remained at the door as she sank onto the bed. "Evangeline's going to kill us all," she murmured into her hand, "and we can't do a thing about it."

"We still have time." The metal frame creaked as he dropped next to her. "Once we take down Natania, we can work on her."

"When does it end? We take these weapons out of one vicious queen's hands and give them to another. Maybe Evangeline is right, and we do need someone to keep the peace."

"Living under the threat of violence is not peace. I've spent too many years hiding to think otherwise." His conviction would have worn off on her if she wasn't so exhausted.

Eight months of playing the two queens' game and she had made no advances of her own. They were *so close*. She had Amira's map. She had a rudimentary understanding of Thaertos's layout. But she could not be in two places at once, and now she had no armies to back her up.

"What if there are no good choices? Either we let Natania keep the bombs or we help Evangeline. With them in Evangeline's hands, at least our people will be free, but the cycle will continue."

He rubbed the shadow along his jaw. "There's a third choice. The rebels James and Isla brought together, they'll follow us."

"I appreciate the idea, but they won't be enough to capture Dane." She thought about it a moment longer and her heart began to race. "That's not what we need to do, though. I can find Amira and dismantle the bombs with her."

"They'll be enough to seriously damage the mines." He started to smile. She couldn't look away from the mischievous glint in his eyes.

"Not only that, but we have people on Thaertos waiting for someone to start the fight." A weight fell from her chest as she threw her arm around his neck, basking in the breakthrough. Finally, she had a next step, one that wasn't determined by either queen.

"Fortunately, I'm great at that." He drew her in tighter.

Her joyous laughter quieted as it dawned on her what he meant.

He would lead the rebels to Thaertos, the island that had stolen everything from her.

TWENTY-NINE

ISAAC

Isaac came to the startling realization that, in all twenty-three years of his life, he had never had a woman in his bedroom.

He wasn't sure what to do as Alexandria surveyed the space. Four white walls, one flickering light fixture dangling from the middle of the ceiling, wooden nightstand chipped at the edges. It had been a couple of hours since they were brought down to the barracks, and their planning had stalled.

After a few moments, he decided to sit on the bed that had been his for the past three years, wrinkling the smoothed quilt and jostling the neatly folded blanket draped across it. The queen's top agents were lucky to get private rooms. He had disliked being surrounded by the other trainees at all hours of the day, never having a moment to himself. This had been his personal space, the one place he could be himself. Not Carter.

Her eyes landed on the picture propped on his desk. She reached to pick it up, then drew her fingers back, her gaze meeting his. "Is this your mother?"

His leg twinged rose to join her. Torture wasn't good for his old wound, nor were the memories of the attack that caused it. As he looked at his mother's face, he could only think of their burning house and the shrapnel in his calf.

"It is," he said. "She used to take me to the library when my father was working. When he wasn't, too. The librarian would let us in after hours on the nights we needed time away. That's where this picture was taken."

"What's her name?" Her voice had taken on a reverent tone. It sent a shiver down his spine.

Even after all these years, he didn't like to think of his mother as someone talked about in whispers. She brought life to their home, joy where there would otherwise be none. The ministers and mayors thought of her as a quiet woman, but he knew how loud her voice could get when she sang. It filled the room, piercing into his heart even as it hardened with age. No one could perform like her.

"Marie." He leaned against the desk, peeling his eyes from the photograph. "My sister's name was Lydia. I never got a picture with her."

He was the last person alive who remembered her face. The strain of being in the public eye was too much for a child that young, and his mother had sought to protect her from it. His throat grew tight, and he gave up trying to speak.

She set the picture back down. "I understand why you followed their orders. Everything you've done. I don't blame you for it."

They sat in silence until he was able to clear the lump from his throat. "Natania said something to me when we were dancing."

"I wouldn't believe a word she says, especially if it's about you. She knows exactly where to punch."

"She implied that Genea didn't really attack us eight years ago. Something about me getting vengeance for what I thought was their attack. Emphasis on '*thought*.'"

"You think someone else did it, then?" She touched his arm as if trying to say she believed him, but he knew she questioned the other queen's motives. He would be a fool not to do the same.

"I don't know. It's not important now. We're still at war."

She sighed and pushed herself up onto the desk next to him. "Once this is over, I'll find justice for them. Whatever it takes."

He hated the implication that she would do it alone, not because of her, but because it reminded him of his deal with Argon. The throne was waiting for him. Twenty-three years not knowing who he truly was, and suddenly, he would have to learn how to rule. If only he would have time to ask Alexandria how she did it, but there would be an ocean between them for the rest of their lives.

Metal glinted in his periphery. His breath caught. He had forgotten about the flask he took from her. She rolled it around before handing it to him.

"How far gone was I?" Her fingers fidgeted with the top button of her blouse peeking above her sling.

He cleared his throat. "You were talking to someone I couldn't see."

"Most likely the man in the ravine. That's what I call him in my head since I never knew his name. I drank to escape the nightmares he created, but then I just saw him everywhere." She pulled at the button's loose thread. "I haven't seen him since you took it from me. When I'm awake, at least. But the withdrawals are a nightmare of their own."

They basked in her confession. He dreamed about those he had killed, too, but his mind didn't conjure images of them in the daylight. He didn't know how to comfort her, how to take the pain away.

"The whole time, I knew something was wrong, and I didn't ask. I should've asked."

"Tell me you don't blame yourself." Her eyes searched his, first piercing, then softening. "Did you think I would be angry at you?"

Truthfully, he didn't know how to answer her question. Maybe he *had* thought she wouldn't react well if he pushed. His instincts resurfaced when he least expected them to—the reflexes to hide, to blend in, to not disturb the delicate balance between Evangeline and Mendoza.

She lowered her voice, meeting him in his silence. "Did you think I would hurt you?"

"No, not you. Never you. I—" He ran his hand down his face. His entire life, he'd been standing on a razor's edge, and he didn't know how to get off without cutting himself open. "I can't explain it."

"You don't owe me an explanation, now or ever. But I'll be here if you want to." Her face immediately shuttered once the words slipped out. She would be here, but *he* wouldn't be. He would be across the sea.

She started again. "It's not your responsibility to save me."

"It is, actually."

"Not like this. You keep me safe from people outside. I need to save me from myself. Don't think it's your fault if I fall back into it. Promise?"

He'd been protecting those he cared about since he was born, starting with his mother and his sister. It wasn't easy for him to accept that he could do nothing to heal her wounds. But he said, "I promise," anyway.

"Good. Now, what I was going to ask," she said, "can you hide it from me? Lock it up or throw it out a window, for all I care. I never want to see it again."

His fingers laced through hers. The flask thudded against the desk, and he lifted her chin so he could look in her eyes. "Of course. I'll be creative."

Her mouth pulled into a smile. "Do your worst."

Time stalled, freezing them in their places. Then, the moment thawed, and Alexandria drew back, as she was inclined to do.

"We need a way out of here," she continued. "If Prior is down here, he might help us."

"Let's hope helping you fake Watson's death is enough to keep him loyal." He reached out to help her down, and even though he doubted she needed it, she took his hand.

He led her to the end of the hall, second door on the right. The agent at the far entrance had her back turned. His heart pounded as he knocked, hoping she wouldn't notice.

On the third knock, Prior opened the door. The lines of his face deepened when he noticed them. With wide eyes, he started to speak, but Isaac held a finger to his mouth. The man silently ushered them inside.

"I can't help you," he said, after closing the door. "You have to leave."

"Prior, we've been through worse," Alexandria said.

"You could protect me then. Now you can't. Working with Evangeline is the only thing keeping my family from starving."

Isaac knew that was the truth, but they couldn't get around it. They needed his help. "She doesn't have to know it was you. You would just have to deliver a message."

The two looked at him expectantly. He found a piece of paper on Prior's desk and began to write. Three words in,

Alexandria narrowed her eyes and tilted her head. "I still can't read your handwriting."

He chuckled and handed the pencil to her, dictating what the note would say.

Bailey,

We're stuck in the palace. All we need is a car outside of Rosalia Station. Can you help us?

Isaac

He explained the directions to the church and told the agent to find the priest. "Don't open it if you want plausible deniability," he said, handing the folded note to Prior.

The man groaned. "You read it out loud seconds ago."

"Evangeline can't read your mind, even if she acts like it."

Prior gave Alexandria a panicked look, which she met with a strained smile. He crept up to the door, peered out into the hallway, and disappeared.

"Do you think he'll do it?" he asked.

Alexandria shrugged. "If he doesn't, what can she do to us? We're already locked up here."

She startled when the door creaked open. Prior stood in the entrance, his face pale. "Captain Olivier was in the hallway." He stepped to the side, and Isaac braced himself to see Leianna's cold expression.

But she wasn't the one behind the agent.

"Reagan?" he asked, his heart pounding against his chest. The girl's face lit up as she ran to him. He hugged her so tightly her feet came off the floor. "Why are you here?"

"We have to go. Now." And there Leianna was, her once-polished ponytail askew—the sole evidence that she had been in a fight. Usually, there was no evidence at all. He would've teased her about falling out of her prime if the thought didn't shock him into action.

"You're helping us?" Alexandria asked.

"I will never hear the end of it from Bailey if I don't. Now, come on."

Alexandria held up a hand. "I need to hear it from you. Will you fight for the queen, or will you fight for me?"

Leianna angled her head and stared in what Isaac imagined to be her version of rolling her eyes. "*You* are my queen."

A weight lifted off his chest at the realization that Leianna hadn't abandoned them after all. He laughed as adrenaline flooded his nerves. Even Alexandria smiled as the four ran down the hallway, past the now-unconscious guard, and into the main corridor.

There were no agents in sight. His joy quickly faded, joined by the prickling of the hair on his neck. His heartbeat quickened, preparing for someone to jump out at them. He held Reagan's hand. She had learned enough with the rebels to defend herself, but he didn't want her to *have* to. It was difficult for him to remember that, while she was a teenager, she had been through more than most at her age.

Leianna twisted to look around the corner. "I'll distract the two down here. You go to the tunnel." She did not wait for them to respond before disappearing.

They held their position for a few seconds. After a brief glance down the hall, Alexandria led them to the medical wing doors and nudged one open with her elbow.

Two agents stood at the end of the white-walled hallway. Isaac took in a sharp breath and pulled Reagan behind him. One of the agents spotted them, whipping a gun from his holster.

"Call for backup," he ordered the other. She spoke into a device at her shoulder. The air between the five of them froze.

Isaac stepped forward, holding up his hands. "We'll come with you. No need to point that at us."

The agent flexed his fingers and fixed his grip instead. "You think I don't remember you, Carter?"

"I don't remember you." That was a lie. He watched everyone. This agent in particular, Roman, had been a nightmare in training. A few years older, but he spent his time harassing the other trainees. Leianna broke his nose once, and Isaac nearly smiled seeing that the jagged bridge had never healed.

"Let me remind you." Roman holstered his gun, a sight that caught Isaac off guard before the agent lunged at him. The other agent yelled as Isaac slid and kicked Roman's leg out. In his periphery, Alexandria dove for the female agent.

He jumped on Roman, pinning his arms to the floor. Roman kneed him in the stomach. A spear of pain tore through his bruised ribs.

Isaac rolled onto his feet, clutching his side. He dodged Roman's fist and retaliated with his own. A cut opened beneath Roman's eye. Roman swayed but stood his ground. He drove his knee at Isaac's ribs again. His arm caught the blow.

He grabbed Roman's leg and yanked him forward. As the agent recovered, Isaac swung around to his back and locked his forearm across his neck. Roman threw them into the wall. A cracking sound erupted, either from him or the wall, but adrenaline forced him to keep going.

The muscles in his arms groaned as they constricted. Roman clawed at his skin, then he reached for his gun again. Instead of pointing at Isaac, he aimed at Reagan. Before she could scream, Isaac twisted his arm and snapped Roman's neck.

Fire spread through his chest and throat as the man's body fell. He looked up to find Alexandria struggling with the female agent, who held her paralyzed arm at a gruesome angle, sling askew. Reagan picked up Roman's gun and leveled it at the agent.

When the gunshot went off, Isaac's stomach dropped. The girl was too young to know how it felt to kill someone. He reached for her, only to find her brows pinched in confusion. They both turned to discover Leianna behind them. With extended arms, she held her pistol.

Blood bubbled out of the agent's shoulder. She looked at Leianna with wide eyes, mouth hanging open. "You?" Her voice drowned in betrayal.

"Good thing you're already in the medical wing. You'll be fine," Leianna said. "Feel free to tell them what happened. No need to lose your job."

Alexandria stumbled forward. She and Leianna nodded to each other, a silent understanding passing between them.

They had no time to celebrate their salvation, however. Footsteps grew louder outside of the medical wing. Isaac grabbed Reagan's hand, and they bolted down the steps to the tunnel just as the doors slammed open.

Once underground, Leianna jammed a knife into the crack of the door. They didn't stop running until they had escaped the train station and followed her into an alley.

His lungs burned and his calves twitched. He took Reagan under his arm when he spotted Minister Agate at the end of the street, standing next to a dented red car.

Alexandria hugged her and whispered her thanks.

"It's the least I could do," the minister said. Her pantsuit was disheveled, and she had tied her usually sleek hair back haphazardly.

"Will it track us?" Leianna asked.

"No, it's my family car. You'll be safe."

Alexandria touched her shoulder. "Will you?"

"I don't know." The minister shook her head and gave a solemn smile. "Tell Anastasia her daughter did well."

They embraced once more while Isaac helped Reagan into the car. He thought to thank the woman, but she was already gone when he turned around.

BURNED QUEEN

Battered and bruised, they drove toward their freedom. But as he caught his breath, he couldn't forget where their plan would take him next.

THIRTY
ALEXANDRIA

A vise gripped Alexandria's chest as the cabin's driveway came into view. She fidgeted with her sling, breathing out a long sigh.

In the rearview mirror, Reagan watched the woods pass by with her head on Isaac's shoulder. Leianna kept her eyes on a swivel in the driver's seat. Alexandria gave her directions, pointing to the opening in the trees.

The car stumbled over the rocky path. As they turned, her pulse quickened. In the midst of the thick trees stood the cabin, just like they last saw it, when she thought she was saying goodbye forever.

"Welcome home," she whispered.

Her heart lurched at the thought of her family being right inside. It had been eight months since she had seen them. Better that they didn't witness her futile reign, though they had likely heard about the Genean Coalition and the rebels over the radio.

She wondered how much James told them, both about her and about his time with Evangeline.

The car rolled to a stop. She opened the door and stretched out her legs, letting the familiar pain propel her to her feet. Rising light pierced her eyes through the canopy. She brought her hand up to her forehead to dim the brightness.

Isaac put a hand on her back, his other arm around Reagan's shoulders. They walked up to the door and—

A gun met them there. Adrenaline shocked her core before Elsie peeked out from behind the barrel. Her eyes lit up.

"They're here! It's Alexandria!" James's older sister shouted into the house. "With a man I've never met, but I assume he's alright."

"Some days," Alexandria replied and embraced her.

Elsie raised an eyebrow. "I'll keep an eye on him, then."

"Thanks, but I'm sure Alexandria has that covered. It's how she passes the time." He laughed as she side-eyed the both of them.

"That must be what she does when she's not being imprisoned by the queen, because that's the last thing we heard on the radio. Her parents were about to drive over there and break into the palace."

"I bet they could've done it, too," Sam said. Alexandria hugged him tightly. He had started growing a scraggly beard over the past eight months, and she had to remind herself that he wasn't a child anymore. If the Draft still existed, he would have less than a year until he was of age. A knot formed in her stomach at the thought that he had not seen Amira for so long.

After they walked through the door, she introduced Leianna, Isaac, and Reagan to the two and Mrs. Collins. She let them get settled as she went to find her parents and James on the deck.

Her father stood beside James on the grass below, showing him how to chop firewood. The blade of the axe whistled through the air. They paused at the creaking of the door.

"Alexandria?" Her father's red-rimmed eyes softened. The breath rushed from her lungs when he ran up the steps and threw his arms around her.

Her mother looked up from where she was sitting with her head in her hands. She pulled Alexandria in, pressing her face into her shoulder. "How are you here?"

It took a moment for her to respond, her tongue tied with emotion. Tears ran from her mother's face onto her blouse. The breeze chilled the ones falling down her own cheeks.

"A miracle." She sniffed, composing herself. "Speaking of which, there are a few people I'd like you to meet."

When they went inside, the crackling fireplace warmed her to the bone. She longed to curl up in front of it and forget about the world. With Evangeline in power, Natania would soon attack. That truth left her with no time to rest.

The room seemed to shrink as her father shook Isaac's hand. She had no reason to be worried, but all her senses stood on high alert. It reminded her of bringing a boy home in secondary school.

"This is Isaac," she said to fill the silence. "He was my Protector during the Campaign and is one of my guards. Well, he was, when I was the queen." The overly simplistic explanation made her cringe. Of course, they knew he was Mendoza's son, but he was so much more to her that sometimes that fact did not register.

He was also the last prince of Victori. She would do best not to forget that their time together had an expiration date.

Isaac turned to her mother, grimacing slightly. "We've met, but that was under a different name."

"I met you as Isaac, back when you were just a boy," she said. "A lot has happened since then."

His smile did not reach his eyes. "To put it lightly."

And then her mother hugged him. She watched as he closed his eyes, holding onto a moment he did not often get. Her eyes watered and she looked away.

"Thank you for saving our daughter," her mother whispered.

"I can't take credit for that." He pointed to Leianna. "She's the one you should thank."

Leianna's mouth drew into a tight smile. She clasped her hands in front of her. "I just did my job."

"Actually, you did the opposite," Alexandria said, "but I'll forever be grateful for that."

Mrs. Collins looked at Reagan from over the counter. "And who might you be?"

"Reagan." She raised her hand awkwardly and glanced at Isaac. "They found me in the woods."

The group stayed silent in anticipation for her to say more, but she stared at the ground, running her shoe over a crack in the floorboards. Elsie placed her hand on Reagan's shoulder. "Want to help me with breakfast?"

"She needs all the help she can get," James said, earning himself an elbow in the side.

Reagan shifted from one leg to the other. "I don't know how to cook."

"Never too late to learn. We'll teach you." Mrs. Collins winked and shuffled the girl into the kitchen. Isaac's smile became real as he watched them get to work.

The other three started to get comfortable, each claiming a spot to sleep when the time came. Sam had been sleeping on one couch, James on the other, but they decided James would now sleep on the floor of his mother and sister's room, and Alexandria would sleep in her parents' room. The younger ones would get the couches. Leianna and Isaac were used to unideal sleeping arrangements, if the Campaign proved anything.

Alexandria went to grab blankets from the closet, only to find that most of them were already being used. It would be a cold night. She pictured herself in front of the fire with Isaac wrapped around her, and then shook the thought out of her head.

Her memories would be nothing but a distraction. They needed to find a way to Dane and Thaertos.

Isaac leaned against the wall behind her. The last remaining blanket tumbled from its precariously balanced position in the crook of her elbow. "I thought you knew not to sneak up on me," she muttered.

"I would've announced myself, but you looked deep in thought. What's running around that brain of yours?" That familiar smirk appeared on his face as he stooped to pick up the blanket. It was difficult to ignore the reminder of him waking her up to train every morning. A part of her hoped he was thinking about it, too.

"Planning an impossible mission." She sighed and propped her shoulder next to him. "I don't know what to do next."

"Maybe you're not supposed to."

"What do you mean?"

"There are nine other people in this cabin. Nine people that can figure this out with you. You're not alone in this." He arched an eyebrow. "But you're stubborn, so you'll try and try until you realize it for yourself."

"I almost thought you had a good point until the end."

"I'm right."

Her gaze fixed over his shoulder, on her mother and Leianna talking in the living room. Leianna's face, as usual, betrayed nothing of what they were speaking about.

"You are," Alexandria said. "I just don't want anyone else to get hurt."

"It's inevitable. We're at war, Lex." The nickname softened his words only mildly.

She nodded, unable to speak with her mind racing. Her mother would have connections, even if she was no longer mayor. Leianna knew tactical strategies. James was the mastermind of their childhood pranks—he could see how all the working parts fit together. And Elsie knew her way around water, having worked with the Irvings for a while.

"The Irvings!" she all but shouted. Her lips pulled into a wide smile, and if her body didn't ache from the fight, she would've jumped. Without thinking, she kissed him on the cheek before pulling away in an instant. "You're a genius."

Shock painted the lines of his face. He shook his head and grinned. "I have no clue what that means."

She ran into the kitchen, ignoring the groaning of her muscles. Elsie looked at her from the side of her eye. "Did I hear shouting?"

"When was the last time you spoke to the Irvings? Do they still have both of their boats?"

"I saw Rose at the market before we left, but that was months ago. What are you planning?"

"I'm getting Amira out of Dane, and Isaac's getting our people out of Thaertos."

Elsie dropped a bundle of carrots on the counter. Mrs. Collins's knife clattered.

"What?" Elsie exclaimed. "You can't possibly be thinking what I think you're thinking."

"I am. We have to do this. It's the only way to stop Natania from destroying us, and to keep Evangeline from destroying everyone else."

"You want the two of us to infiltrate a country that was already our enemy, but is even more deadly to us now that Evangeline is in power."

"Not just the two of us. Leianna and James, too."

"Oh, I almost forgot. With four of us, it's completely manageable."

She pretended the sarcasm did not sting. Elsie was right, but she couldn't imagine any other choice. Even if removing the weapons was an incomprehensible task, she could not fade into obscurity while the world caved around her.

"I can help," Reagan piped up, right as Isaac crossed the threshold.

"Not this time," he said. "It's too dangerous."

"The General trained me for missions."

Alexandria held her breath, waiting for his response. His jaw twitched. "I know you're capable, but I need you to stay here and keep watch over the others. Can you do that for me?"

Reagan seemed satisfied with that answer and returned to cutting vegetables. *Good one*, Alexandria thought. He knew just the right words to say to the girl. She wished she had that ability, not solely with teenagers, but with her kingdom.

"We'll sit down and plan tomorrow once we've taken a breather. That is, if you're in." Alexandria held Elsie's stare until she spoke.

"Of course, I'm in. I'd do anything for you kids. Apparently even impossible things." Her mouth drew into a sly smile. "Who am I to argue with the queen?"

James cut in from across the counter. "Isaac, you can't take Thaertos alone."

"I'll need you to get the rebels to Kureya," he replied, running a hand over his chest, where the stitches were. "I just hope they'll trust me."

PART IV

THE PRINCE

THIRTY-ONE
ISAAC

The radio crackled, drowning the reporter's voice in a wave of static. It set Isaac's nerves on fire. He pressed his back against the couch, trying to relax, but he felt out of place among the group that had known each other for so long.

Some of them sat around the table, but Isaac, Alexandria, Reagan, and Sam ate their breakfasts in the living room. James had just walked in from his brief trip to Regia. Isla would be on her way to Kureya now, joined by two dozen of the rebels loyal to them.

"Now that you've mentioned Isla," Alexandria started as James slumped next to Sam. She gave him a dazzling smile, a hint of mischief in it. "What's up with that?"

Elsie called from the table, "Do tell, James."

"Nothing's up." He rolled his eyes, taking the plate Mrs. Collins handed him.

Isaac cleared his throat. "I'm not so sure about that."

"You were hardly conscious the entire time Alexandria was there."

"I was conscious other times."

Alexandria's eyebrows shot up. "There were other times?"

"Not like that." James tried to sound annoyed, but his smile said otherwise. "We work together. It's complicated."

"Can't be that complicated."

"You're one to talk."

Isaac swore it was Leianna who laughed behind him. James was right. *Complicated* didn't even begin to describe him and Alexandria.

The radio went silent, quieting everyone along with it. Henry tapped the machine a few times.

"It's about time this thing died," he said. "I'll run into town and get a new one this afternoon."

Alexandria tensed. He thought of reaching out to her, but he didn't know how much she wanted her family to know about them. There really wasn't anything *to* know, he supposed. The deal with Argon was a distant memory with everything that had happened over the past few days, but it changed things between them. He was no longer her Protector, but a prince in his own right.

Their plan to take down Natania would give them no time to figure it out.

"What can happen in a few hours?" Isaac asked, knowing the answer was *everything*.

She side-eyed him and returned to eating her oatmeal. An accented female voice cut through the silence, and her spoon clanked sharply against her bowl.

"Citizens of Kevelda, this is Queen Natania of Genea," the voice started.

Alexandria whispered under her breath. A chair scraped against the floor as Leianna stood. Henry turned up the volume dial. They listened without a word.

"With Evangeline's coup, we can no longer honor Queen Alexandria's partnership with the Genean Coalition. Any protection offered in the past will be eliminated. You have a choice, one that Evangeline will no doubt try to make for you."

The pause lasted an eternity. He held his breath until his lungs were on the verge of collapse.

"Kneel, or die."

His ears screamed as static burst over the radio before cutting off. The resulting quiet made him dizzy. Henry recoiled from the device, looking past him at Alexandria.

"How long until she attacks?" James asked.

Alexandria pushed her hair back from her forehead. "As long as it will take for us to get there."

"She'll never let us in."

"To her knowledge, I've done everything she has asked over the past four months. I've spilled my own people's blood for her Coalition. If I can do that, I can convince her that I'll do anything to stay in it. Even if it means killing Evangeline."

His stomach twisted into a knot at her proposal. He didn't have a problem with taking Evangeline out. It might haunt him after, but for now, he would keep them safe by whatever means necessary. Still, the memory of putting poison into her glass stuck like a spike in his brain.

Leianna crossed her arms. "That's not a possibility. As far as I'm concerned, we barely made it out of the palace alive."

"No, but I can pretend I want Natania's help. We'll make it in time for the wedding. Say we're there to show our support and get hers in return."

James sat up straighter. "What wedding?"

She gripped the cushion underneath her. *James doesn't know about Phillip*, he thought. From the pictures on the walls, he knew they had been close. What would it feel like to learn that his best friend was alive, but on the enemy side?

He didn't have to imagine James's reaction for long. Alexandria shifted forward, as if wanting to reach out to her friend. "Phillip is alive. Natania has something over him, she has to. It could be his family. It could be us. Either way, he's marrying her."

James stared at the floor, making no sound.

Anastasia moved around to the front of the couch. She set a hand on Alexandria's shoulder. "I don't know what to say."

"For now, we don't think about him. He might be useful when we're in there, or he might turn us in. I couldn't tell you."

She set her eyes on James again. "He's a variable we can't control. What we do know is that we have a way in. If we want to get Amira back and save our people, it's now or never. We've grieved him before, and if we have to do it again, we do it together. When we're home."

Her face betrayed no emotion besides determination, but it must have hurt to say those words. He used to be able to read her so well. Another thing Evangeline and Natania had taken from them.

"Will you tell the Irvings?" Anastasia asked.

Alexandria shook her head. "They don't need to know their son might be a traitor. It's better to have no closure than to have that hanging over them."

"They deserve to know," James said.

"Not right now. Not when there's nothing any of us can do." Her voice cracked and she took a breath. The tension between the two's avoidant gazes was palpable.

"If Natania knows about Evangeline, she might've increased security on Thaertos," Isaac interrupted. "I can't lead them into a death trap. I'll go alone. I might not be able to bring our people home, but at least I can stall the mining."

She clutched his hand. "Absolutely not."

"I won't risk their lives."

"And I won't risk *yours*." Despite the others in the room, her pleading stare held a silent conversation, known only to them. "If you feel you can't ask them, we'll figure it out another day. We can focus on Dane."

James's voice made him break their eye contact. "They want to take down Genea, no matter the cost. They'll do it."

"It'll be their choice," she said. "You don't know how hard it is for me to ask you to do this. All I want is for you to stay with me, even if this is a bridge we have to cross at some point."

He couldn't think of a response.

With a sigh, she unlaced their fingers. "It'll take four days to get to Dane. Let's pack up and get going. We'll plan the rest of it out on the way there."

They broke apart and began their preparations. Mrs. Collins rationed some dried fish and canned food for the next few days. He scoured the cabin for anything that could be used as a weapon, though he doubted Natania's soldiers would let the other four into Dane with them. Elsie gave him the gun, which Anastasia had acquired from one of her Argentum agents before leaving Kureya.

As he cleaned it on the kitchen table, Henry sat in the chair across from him. The man seemed friendly, with wide, emotive eyes and receding brown hair, but Isaac's muscles stiffened nonetheless. Not often did someone approach him without an ulterior motive.

"You're different from your father," the man said in a low voice, "but I need to know how different. Why did Evangeline trust you?"

He could have lied, and it likely would have been smarter to do so, but he was tired of running from the truth. "She and my father both liked to use me for their own will. They trained me to be their perfect soldier. I followed their orders for years before I realized that wasn't the person I wanted to be." His breath came short under the weight of Henry's stare. "I would never hurt Alexandria. I wish I had seen their deception earlier, but I'm done living in the past. My sole mission now is to keep your daughter alive."

"History does not always look favorably upon martyrs."

"Sir?"

"If you study the past enough, you start to see patterns. You will go to great lengths to undo what your father has done. Don't let your desire to sacrifice yourself put her in danger."

Isaac's chest tightened. The man was correct, if only about him wanting to make things right. His protecting Alexandria had nothing to do with that. It did, at one point, but now it was more. *Or is it?* He brushed aside the thought and nodded.

Henry flashed a smile. "I trust my daughter, and she trusts you. It's not easy for her to do that, not after these past few years." He turned his head to find Alexandria standing at the counter, and then faced Isaac again. "Or maybe I shouldn't be telling you this."

"Oh, I've been on the receiving end of her distrust." He laughed, though the memory made him wince. "I don't plan to do anything that will put me there again."

"Good." Henry tapped his palms twice against the table and stood.

Isaac holstered the gun and rose to see if they needed any help in the kitchen. Before he moved past, Henry took his arm. "Do you know how to fish?"

"No, I've never had the chance to learn."

"When you get back and everything settles down, Anastasia and I should take you and Alexandria out. Reagan, too." He winked. "I would offer to Captain Olivier, but she doesn't seem like the fishing type."

Isaac forced a smile. For now, they didn't have to know that he was a prince, and that he wouldn't be returning to Kevelda. He wondered briefly what made *him* seem like the type of person who likes fishing, but he didn't mind. It sounded great, actually. He had never done something like that before, not even when his mother and sister were alive.

"She certainly isn't," he said, "but I would enjoy that."

Less than an hour later, the group was ready to go. The five each carried a backpack filled with rations and extra clothes. His nerves were on fire, ready to spark into motion. He didn't know the Irvings, but he worried they might not be so willing to face treason charges by handing over their boats. Alexandria had known them her whole life, but he had had people betray him who knew him the same way, Evangeline and his father being on the top of that list.

He hugged Reagan, promising that he would be safe, that he would come back, and that Alexandria's parents would take care of her. Her green eyes glistened as she turned and went inside. She hadn't spoken much, as if acknowledging his leaving would make it permanent. *Will she like it in Victori?* He hadn't considered it before, but he had no time to think over the question now.

The cold metal chilled his skin through his jacket as he leaned against the car. Leianna positioned herself similarly, watching as the others said their goodbyes.

"Weird, isn't it?" he asked into the air.

"What?" she responded.

"Having a home to come back to."

She sighed, resting her hand on her holster. "I haven't had that in a while. Bailey's church, maybe."

"Don't get too sentimental on me." He grinned and opened the driver-side door for her.

She narrowed her eyes and threw her bag on the floor of the passenger side. As she swung into the seat, she said, "Toughen up."

He watched Alexandria hug her parents, Sam, and Mrs. Collins. Henry waved at him. Isaac nodded in response. When Alexandria came up to the car, her eyes were red. She set her backpack in the trunk and slammed it shut. Elsie took the front seat, leaving him, Alexandria, and James to squeeze into the back.

Alexandria looked out the window, gaze distant as they pulled out of the driveway and the colors of the forest began to blur. It seemed as though she forgot he was in front of her until she laced her fingers through his, closed her eyes, and rested her head against the seat.

His mind could not drive out the fear that this was the beginning of the end.

THIRTY-TWO
ALEXANDRIA

The Irvings lived in a lopsided house two blocks from the marina, close enough to walk, which was helpful since they owned no cars.

Fishing had not been a steady enterprise over the years, with weather fluctuations leading to months-long spans without any catches. They would do better at inland lakes, where the fishers did not spread their nets as frequently, but the family had settled in Kureya for generations. They were a stubborn lot. Maybe that's why Alexandria had loved Phillip so much. His family was just like her.

She pressed her lips together to avoid the frown they were determined to form. Her fingertips danced on the back of Isaac's hand. In the five hours they had been traveling, she did not let go of him.

The thought filled her with a weird kind of dread that made her heart skip a beat and her diaphragm freeze. She craved being near him, but the idea of telling him such made her pause. It would be foolish to say she didn't trust him, not after the countless times he had proven he was on her side. But falling in love again, with someone destined to leave, would destroy her.

Who said anything about love, Lex?

She could almost hear him saying it. And now she was imagining conversations with him in her head, instead of figuring out their plan to survive a kingdom that would certainly kill them. What was she thinking?

"Turn left here," she said to Leianna, a little too sharply. She winced, hoping no one else heard the anxiety in her words.

They had decided they wouldn't tell Phillip's family about him being alive, but the knowledge gnawed at her stomach. She had waited for so long to have closure. His family still awaited it. If she was them, she would want the information, but knowing he was marrying Natania wrecked her, whether or not he truly wanted it.

"Are you ready?" she asked James.

James stared out the window. "It's been three years since I've seen them. No, I'm not."

Her muscles coiled, waiting for someone to attack as Leianna parked. They would not find that kind of adversary here, but grief could be violent in its own ways.

Isaac got out of the car first, and she quickly followed. Her nerves would settle when they were on the boat, she hoped.

The rust on the house's door handle flaked onto her arm as she brushed against it. She knocked three times, hearing nothing on the other side.

When she was about to turn away, the door opened. Rose stood in the entrance, her honey-blonde hair braided over her shoulder. An infant balanced in one of her arms. He couldn't be more than a year old.

"Alexandria? What are you doing here? We heard you had been detained when Evangeline took over." Phillip's sister spit Evangeline's name with a venom that didn't match her sunny appearance.

"I need your help." She contemplated asking about the baby, but with the swath of blonde hair on his head, there was no doubt he was Rose's. Phillip wouldn't know he had a nephew. The thought punched the air out of her chest.

"Anything." Rose looked over Alexandria's shoulder, taking in the sight of the others. Lines formed on her freckled forehead. "Come in before someone sees you."

She led them into the living room, though there was really only one main room that held couches and a kitchen. Up the stairs and to the left was Phillip's bedroom. Alexandria could navigate there with her eyes closed.

"Is your mom home?" she asked, trying to break the silence.

Rose shook her head, tears welling in her eyes. "She's gone. Her health deteriorated after Phillip was drafted, and I guess it was just too much."

Alexandria stifled the sob tightening her throat. "How long?"

"Six months ago. She got to see you become the queen, though. She was proud."

Elsie wrapped her arm around Rose, careful not to startle the baby. The two had been close when they were younger, back before the Irvings lost themselves to their own sea of grief.

The idea of telling Rose about Phillip seemed even worse. But what would she tell *him* if she saw him?

"We'll be okay," Rose continued, wiping her eyes. "My husband started helping with the business. And I can tell you all about that after you tell me what you need."

"We need to borrow one of your boats," Alexandria said.

Isaac shifted next to her. "Two. We'll need two."

Dread pricked at her like the shards of glass in her back. He had decided, then.

"If it's really as important as you say it is, you can take them both. My father needs to rest for a while anyway. He won't lose out on much," Rose said.

"It is. I can't tell you everything, but we'll have them back within two weeks. If not..." She trailed off, images of her friends captured or killed searing into her mind. "Protect your family. If Evangeline comes and asks any questions, tell her we stole them. Don't put yourself in harm's way for us."

Rose nodded. "Hopefully it won't come to that. I'm sure some of our crew would go with you, if you could pay."

Alexandria bit the inside of her cheek. "It won't be easy. They might not come back."

"People are more desperate than you know." Her mouth twisted into a pitying smile. "Or you would know."

"Do you have anyone in mind?"

She told them how to find the captain, who could gather the rest of the crew. James and Elsie followed her directions, leaving Isaac, Leianna, and Alexandria to wait behind.

The baby cried, and Alexandria held him while Rose prepared a stash of supplies for them to take on their journey. She walked through the house, up and down the stairs, not daring to enter Phillip's old room.

Soon, the two returned with news that the captain, Claire, and her son Eric would meet them at the marina in an hour with everyone else who wanted to help.

Alexandria bid one last silent goodbye to the house that had been her second home long ago.

The group of rebels–*Isaac's rebels*, she thought, *there has to be a better name for them*–had stationed themselves at Isla's mother's house on the outskirts of town. From the car window, she saw the speckled flower fields, sparse remaining blooms that hadn't been picked or started to wither with the growing autumn chill.

Isaac held the grab handle with a white-knuckled fist. Panic billowed from her core and up into her throat, making it impossible for her to speak. She squeezed her eyes shut and held onto his arm as if he would be carried away by the tide.

It had been her idea for him to go. Everything they did would be for nothing if Natania could just rebuild the bombs. They needed to destroy those mines for good. Their people would have no way home without him.

There was no space to breathe in the crowded living room. Two dozen soldiers stood around the battered leather couch, tucked into corners. Each had a grim expression on their face, mouths drawn in tight lines, wrinkles between brows. Alexandria straightened her shoulders, begging her vocal cords to cooperate. Less than an hour and their end would begin.

"Thank you all for being here," she said. Their sharp gazes followed her to the center of the room, pinning her there like a map on the wall. "I know I have not been the queen you wanted, nor the queen you needed. But I am here now, and it's about time I made a stand. You aren't doing this for me, I know. You're doing it for your families, for the ones you've lost in Evangeline's war. And, I suppose, in mine." She nodded to Isaac, stepping to the side.

When he spoke, she did not recognize him. Not because he acted differently, but something in his demeanor changed. He had an assurance that settled into his bones, a strength that transcended the muscles his training built. His eyes found each person around them, as if each had meaning, as if each played a critical role in what he would say. For someone who had spent his entire life in the background, he knew how to make people feel seen.

"What I'm going to ask of you may seem impossible, and you have every right to say no," he started. "If you leave, we won't hold it against you. If you stay, then we need everything you can give. You can't back out once we're there, so think hard. We don't have a lot of time for you to make your decision, and you won't be able to say your goodbyes to those you have left."

"We've already given up everything," one of the women said.

Isaac stepped forward. "Then I hope this will give you a chance to take something back. We'll be going to Thaertos. I'll admit, I don't know how we'll do what we need to do, but I have an idea."

He explained what Alexandria had told him about the island, based on what she had gathered from the people in Bailey's church. She wished she had thought to ask them more specific questions, but her regret would not help him now. His team's first goal would be to sneak through the defenses and blend in with the workers as they lined up for their shift change.

Beyond that, their mental map of the island was worryingly blank.

"It sounds like we'll be walking in blind," a man said.

"We have no other choice."

"Why now?"

"I'm going to tear down Genea's defenses from the inside," Alexandria said. "Evangeline's ascension forced us to do this faster than any of us would like. If you don't bring our people home now, I don't know when we'll get another chance. Anyone there will be caught in the crossfire."

"She's right," Isaac said. "While I've never seen the island, we have about three days to scope it out before Alexandria gets to Dane. By then, we'll have planned our next move. I won't blame you if you stay here. Stay or go, it's up to you." The choice echoed in the silence. He let it hang for a few seconds before continuing. "This is what you've been waiting for, and it's now or never. We leave in an hour. You can take every second of it to decide, but not a moment longer. I won't take anyone who's not sure."

An hour later, the five gathered at the boats, helping Claire and Eric with their preparations. Claire did not bother with formalities; she seemed like the type to have too much pride for that, even as she smiled. Her bright blue eyes matched the sea on a winter's day, filled with wisdom Alexandria could not even begin to fathom. She wondered why the woman, who appeared to be on the tail end of her seventies, would abandon comfort and commit treason for her.

The trawlers were stocked with food for the fishermen's normal workdays, but Rose had given them as many supplies as she could to hold them over longer. While the boats were larger than most others in the marina, imagining the tight quarters below made Alexandria miss her royal ship.

Heaviness filled her chest. She pressed her hand against her heart as if the pressure would stabilize the palpitations that threatened to send her sprawling on the deck. At least the clouds dimmed the sun's light, keeping her head from aching.

The rumble of approaching cars snapped her focus to the road. She held her breath as the occupants stepped onto the loose gravel. Most of the rebels had decided to come, only three or four missing from the group.

Isla approached the boat, joining Alexandria and James where they coiled ropes. She was about to step away when Isla hugged her and whispered, "Bring him home."

"I will," Alexandria replied. "You stay safe, too. Don't let Isaac do anything foolish."

They pulled apart and shared a look of understanding before Alexandria left the two to their goodbyes.

Her body shook as the boat's engine vibrated beneath her. Their time had come.

She searched for Isaac on the deck, then started belowdecks. Before descending, she turned back to see James kissing Isla like it was the end of the world. In a way, it was. She blinked back tears and headed down the stairs.

In the cramped kitchen, she found Isaac stashing food into the cupboards.

"Your army's here," she said, attempting the levity he was so proficient in. It sounded flat coming from her mouth.

He pushed off the ground with his hands on his knees, ducking to avoid the low overhead. "Guess it's time, then."

"Guess so."

She was keenly aware of the air between them, every particle that brushed her skin. The waves lapping against the sides of the boat ticked like the seconds of a clock. They counted down to an end neither of them could foresee.

This could be the last of the two of them, of their people. Her kingdom could be dust when she returned, all memory that they had ever been there carried off by the wind. Every heartbreak and trial would wash away, but the love would, too. The parties and kisses and campfires. That's what she had to save.

He wrapped his arms around her and held her close to his chest. His heartbeat betrayed his true feelings. Underneath his nonchalant exterior, he was afraid. *We're all so scared, all the time.* Why couldn't it be easy, just for once? Why couldn't she hold him, hold *anyone*, without the fear that they would never return?

"I'm not letting go," she said. The collar of his shirt muffled her words.

He clutched the back of her jacket. "I won't argue with that."

They remained in their embrace until Claire called from above that they had to depart before nightfall. Alexandria cleared the lump from her throat and breathed a sigh that released some of the pressure from her lungs. "If either of us doesn't make it back, the agreement between Kevelda and Victori will crumble. Our people won't stand a chance."

"I'll come back. They'll have to kill me to stop me, but even then, I'll find a way."

A quiver in her voice shattered the illusion of her stoicism. "You don't know that."

He just brushed her hair behind her ear. Their situation was dire enough that even he had nothing to say.

She told herself that politics dictated her next words. That it was the logical solution to their predicament, protecting both their homeland and the other kingdom's line of succession. All of these justifications deflected the truth, but in that moment, she would do anything to secure the two of them more time.

All at once, it tumbled out. "Marry me."

Time warped as she waited for his response. It could have been an hour or less than a moment. Her limbs felt incredibly light, like she did not exist. That would have been better than whatever was happening to her now, the way her chest suddenly burned at the thought of him turning her down.

His initial wide-eyed look shifted into a dimpled smile. "Now?"

"It's the only way to protect both our kingdoms." If she hadn't rushed to give that caveat, he might have heard her heart thumping wildly against her sternum.

"You don't have to explain." The light in his expression seemed to dull a bit, pulled back into reality, and yet he took her hand. "Let's do it, then."

THIRTY-THREE
ISAAC

The sun was but a thin orange line slashing the sky and sea when Isaac pledged the rest of his life to Alexandria.

That expiration date might come sooner than he wanted, but with her standing in front of him, he couldn't think about anything besides the promise they were making. She hadn't commissioned a royal portrait like the monarchs before her, though even if she had, no artist could perfectly capture how beautiful she looked in that moment. He memorized the sight of her—skin cast a deep gold in the fading light, curls half-pinned at the back of her head, white button-down rolled to her elbows.

Claire held two sheets of paper, putting space between them with her pointer finger to keep the fresh ink from smearing. She had written up an official statement for each of them. If their missions turned deadly, this would be the sole proof of their marriage.

"Isaac," the captain said, facing him in his periphery, "do you take Alexandria to be your wife, and do you promise to honor and cherish her for as long as you both shall live?"

His throat went dry. He had imagined this, of course, in half-conscious dreams he never wanted to wake from. Those weddings took place in Bailey's church or in the palace, but he didn't regret this moment. He only wished for more than the dwindling seconds until they went their separate ways.

"I do," he said at last. He would do it over and over again. Evangeline did know him well, better than he would like to admit, and when she had made her ultimatum, they both knew who he would choose in the end.

At no point would this ever be a political arrangement to him, a simple deal between thrones. He would give Alexandria time, let her decide how their relationship would be, but he couldn't ignore the ache that threatened to tear him apart when she was near. Even if she never came to trust or forgive him, he would love her until his dying breath. Those two words would have to do for now.

She took his hand and brought him back to reality. Her chest rose and fell sharply, and he was close enough to hear her staggered breathing. Leianna, James, and Elsie were a few paces behind, with the former two serving as witnesses. With how tightly Alexandria gripped his fingers, he guessed she was trying to hide her fear from them.

Claire repeated the same declaration of intent. A small smile tugged at the corner of Alexandria's lips as she said, "I do."

The captain's eyes darted to the now-purple skyline. "Vows are not required for this to be official, but I think we can spare a moment for them, if you'd like."

He and Alexandria shared a glance. She shifted her weight and pulled her hand away. "We should get these signed."

Right. The contracts.

They balanced the papers on the railing, trading them once they had finished. He held hers steady so she could use her mobile hand to write. Leianna and James were to sign them next, but he didn't keep track as Alexandria pulled him to the far side of the boat, out of earshot from the others.

"One more minute, I promise," she cast back at Claire.

The captain didn't mind, lines deepening beside her smile before she turned to the others.

He leaned against the exterior wall of the wheelhouse, eyeing Alexandria as she paced in front of him. When she stilled, she brought her hand to her mouth, then dropped it, then looked straight through him. "I've fought so hard to push you away, and you keep coming back."

An invisible string tightened the gap between them. "I won't apologize."

"Don't. That's not what I want."

"Tell me what you want."

"I can't have what I want, not in this moment." She crossed the distance but didn't reach for him. "When we both survive this, I want you to never leave again."

"I can make that happen."

"But it's not that easy. We both have kingdoms and people to take care of."

"I promised myself I would stay by your side long before Sofie told me I was a prince. Nothing will make me break that vow. Not a throne, not a war, and certainly not my grandfather." He brushed a windblown curl behind her ear, an excuse to bridge the space. "You're not just an heir I have to protect. You're my *wife* now. No matter what your motivations are, I know mine, and I'm willing to pay any price to make this work. We'll have all the time in the world to get it right."

He thought she might pull away again. Instead, she placed her hand over the mark on his chest. Her shoulders trembled. He wished he could comfort her, but there was nothing he could do to erase the past or change what was to come.

She inhaled sharply before speaking, as if it would be the last breath she ever took. "Isaac, I vow that I will always let you in. That when the world is against us, I will still be with you. That I will trust you with my body and soul, though you deserve much more than I can give."

Her oath knocked the wind out of him. He didn't realize how much he longed to hear it until the words came from her mouth—to know that the woman he had once been ordered to deliver to her death could envision a future with him. She didn't say she loved him, or that this would have happened without the blade at their necks, but her trust was enough. He would honor it with his life.

"Alexandria, I vow that I will always be your home. No matter what happens next, whatever pain you must work through, I will be the place for you to return to. I'll never leave you." He paused and took her hand, brushing his lips against her knuckles. "The one thing I ask is that you come back to me."

Her gaze blazed a path across his face. She dragged the breath from his lungs as her scarred palm rested against his cheek. He wouldn't move, couldn't even if he wanted to. His lips burned under the trail of her cold thumb.

Eric called from the other side of the boat. Isaac pleaded with her in his mind, begging her to stay, to finish what she was about to do.

"We have to go," she said. The words were a shroud laid upon them. She drew back a step, her mouth parting when she realized his hand rested on her waist. He wasn't entirely sure when that had happened, either. His arm dropped to his side.

For a moment, she had looked like she might say something different. Or maybe his desires were playing tricks on him.

"We do," he agreed, but he did not back away. She would have to make that choice.

And, to his dismay, she did. Her staggered steps continued until a couple of meters spread between them. "Let me head down to the cabin first. I can't bear to watch you walk away again."

"What makes you think it'll be easier for me?" In fact, he thought it would be much harder for him.

The stars started to freckle the sky, and he knew that meant they needed to leave, but still he clutched onto the unseen rope that bound them together.

"We'll move at the same time, then."

They both turned, Isaac toward the marina, and Alexandria toward the door leading belowdecks. When he made it to the top of the gangway, he dared to look back. He watched her go. His heart stopped beating when she paused, but she did nothing beyond clenching and flexing her hand.

She didn't hesitate a second time before shutting the door behind her, leaving Isaac with only the hope that one day they might find each other again.

THIRTY-FOUR
ALEXANDRIA

Two nights in, Alexandria realized that Isaac and the rebels would already be scouting out Thaertos. The fear gnawing at her stomach transformed into a dread that lit a fire within her. She spent countless hours studying Amira's map. Her appetite disappeared. Leianna had to force her to stop planning and drink water.

She kept returning to her last conversation with Isaac, ruminating over what she might've done if she had been braver. *What is he doing now? Have they been captured already?* If they had been caught, she and her team would be killed as soon as they moored. She would never leave that final moment in her mind, forever regretting that she didn't kiss Isaac before sending him to his death.

Any preparations she could have made became irrelevant two days later, when they docked in Dane, and Captain Lange clamped handcuffs on her wrists tight enough that she was surprised they didn't cut her.

Leianna lunged at him. He just laughed in response, his teeth all but snapping at them. James tried to argue as Elsie and the crew were forced off the boat. Alexandria knew her words were best saved for the queen.

The radio at Lange's shoulder beeped. "Her Majesty says to leave the crew. Keep guards on the boat. Bring Alexandria and her two friends in," a staticky voice said.

He rolled his eyes and signaled to the soldiers holding them. They led the three to a similar tinted-windowed van as the first time Alexandria had been taken to the queen's office. Instead of arriving in the underground parking garage, they were shoved into a different building and moved down a flight of steep stairs that kept her struggling for balance. Lower and lower they went, and she feared they would never see the light of day again.

When they had descended ten floors, she realized that this was the bunker from the map. Three more floors and she would find the lab. The soldiers directed them down farther, however, and she lost count.

Her lungs ached by the time she was thrown into a cell. She could not catch herself with her bound hands as her legs twisted beneath her, and she crashed against the bench in the corner. Hot blood trickled from her chin, forming crimson puddles on the floor. She felt around with her tongue to make sure her teeth were still intact.

"Is she coming?" she sputtered at Lange, but he ignored her. "Tell her we need her help!" Her words echoed after the door slammed shut.

These cells seemed far more advanced than the ones under her palace. The entire room was made of a dark, rugged metal. Solid walls took the place of bars. The only space for her to see what was going on outside was the small rectangular window set into the door. Her initial idea to smash the glass with her head immediately proved impractical when she noticed crisscrossed bars over it. She cursed loudly, with no one in the room to hear.

As the adrenaline subsided, the wound on her chin began to sting. Blood dripped onto her white shirt and disappeared against the sling crossed over her chest, where the soldiers had left it after wrenching her arm free. She could not cover the cut with her hands cuffed. The tears blurring her vision made searching the room impossible. She blinked them back and dropped onto the bench. Her right thumb had likely not fully healed yet, so it would be easy to break again. But that wouldn't help in the long run, not with the lack of leverage from the cuffs and the soldiers right outside.

If Natania did not come in a few hours, then Alexandria could be desperate. There was still hope, however slight. This was a part of the plan.

She counted five-hundred and forty-six seconds before she stopped trying. The blood had ceased dribbling onto the floor. Her head felt light, but she knew the injury wasn't anything serious. It *would* be if she didn't clean it soon, however. Staving off infection would be a problem for later.

Her thoughts drifted to Amira. Was she in another cell like this one? Had she been kept in this underground hell for the past eight months? The idea made her blood boil.

She crept up to the door, straining to see into the hall. No soldiers stood in her limited field of vision. Across from her, James caught her eye through his window. He was searching, too.

Do you see anything? she mouthed, hoping he could read lips.

He shook his head. She didn't know if that was an answer to her question, or a sign that he couldn't figure out her words.

The fingers on her left hand began to tingle, and then they too lost feeling. A dull ache settled into her bones. She paced the length of the cell. At least she could keep her legs ready for whatever came next.

Time had started to unravel, an impossible tangle of seconds and hours, when the door opened. A soldier shoved her backwards. She caught herself before she could fall this time. He took the cuffs and held them, trapping her in place as Natania entered.

Alexandria forced a neutral expression onto her face. Her kingdom's greatest threat stood right in front of her, and all she could do was beg.

"I'm here because I need your help. I know I can't beat you, and I don't care. A good queen knows when to stop fighting and save her people." Her words were rushed, but she prayed it added to the act.

Natania's icy stare bore into her. The queen stepped closer, a sign that she did not fear her, though Alexandria didn't know whether to take that to heart. Natania feared no one—besides her sister, it seemed. That reminder stood at the forefront of Alexandria's mind as she prepared for her next steps.

"You're right. You can't beat me," Natania said. "I could have you executed right now. It would send a message to Evangeline."

"Evangeline doesn't care about messages, unless they're her own. You know that. That's why I came to you."

"You want your throne back. Then what? You've never been good at following my orders."

"I've lost everything. I won't be foolish enough to do it again."

Natania's eyebrow quirked up. "You would kill Evangeline and crush her rebellion for this?"

"I would do anything." She hated the way the promise tasted.

"You're weak." The queen's eyes narrowed. Alexandria's stomach dropped at the emotion in her tone. She did not respond, but Natania paid no heed. "Fortunately, your weakness is my strength."

"You'll help me, then. You'll help me take her out."

"Yes, I will kill her. It's a natural consequence of war." Her nails grazed the gash on Alexandria's chin. Pain flared hot across her skin, turning her vision red. "As for whether I will reinstate *you* in her stead, that will be determined by how convincing you are."

The queen dropped her hand and opened the door, all hope of escaping with Amira tumbling from Alexandria's grasp.

"Wait!" she shouted, and Natania glanced back at her. "Let me come to the wedding. Phillip would want me there."

Natania's lips pinched together. She eyed the soldier behind Alexandria before giving him orders. "Take her to a guest suite. Have a guard on her door at all times. I'll have a medic sent and attire delivered this evening."

Alexandria breathed a sigh of relief as she was led up the stairs. She made eye contact with James and Leianna in their cells, a silent promise that she would come back for them. It all felt too easy, the way Natania agreed to her plea. *Does she care about Phillip after all?*

~

Alexandria craned her neck toward the opening door of her suite from where she sat stiffly in front of a wooden vanity. The hinges creaked loudly, drowning out the sound of the orchestra playing in the snowy courtyard below, which entertained the guests filing into their seats. The wedding would start in an hour.

A mixture of worry and hunger set her core ablaze. She had no means of finding Amira, not with the soldier at the entrance and James and Leianna locked up. Over the past few days, she had searched every nook and cranny of her expensive prison and found no escape route.

Phillip entered, his blue vest half-buttoned. It brought out the color of his eyes. The color that held memories of the sea, of their laced hands, of his lips on hers. The pain in her chest had dulled, the sands of time smoothing down the rough edges of the wound in her heart. She wanted nothing more than for him to be happy, but she couldn't imagine Natania bringing that about.

Her breath caught. "How did you get in?"

"I've made some friends this past year." His throat bobbed as he swallowed and leaned unsteadily against the closed door.

"Shouldn't you be getting ready?" Her fingers clutched the metal comb on the vanity until the spokes indented her palm. She turned back to the mirror, noting how sickly the borrowed pastel dress made her look with the dark circles under her eyes and black stitches marring her chin.

He crossed the room with a limp. When he came closer, she noticed the paleness of his skin, yellow rimming his irises. "I can't bear watching you think I'm a traitor anymore."

"Then what are you, Phillip?"

"I'm dying."

Time stopped. She watched his mouth move but could not hear. Her head shook violently. *Let it hurt,* she thought. *Make something else hurt.*

"No, you're not. Not again. Not when I just found out you're still alive."

"Pretend you didn't. When I walk down that aisle, I'm no one to you. I died when I left the beach."

"How did it happen?" Her second question dripped with venom. "What did she do to you?" She jumped out of her chair, comb tucked into her corset. That was as close to having a weapon as she could get.

He stopped her with a hand on her shoulder. "You can't fix this. It's the wasting disease. Same as the rest of the workers on Thaertos. Natania sent me to doctors, but there was nothing they could do. No treatments helped." He wiped away the tear that trailed along her cheek. "I stayed for a cure, so I could come back to you, but there isn't one. Now, let me stay to help you."

"We have to get you out of here."

"Why? So I can die later?"

"So you can die at home. Rose has a son. She's married. Your mother…"

His arm collapsed to his side. "I can't go home. They've already grieved. I won't force them to do that again. If I stay, I can slow Natania down."

She understood his decision, because she would have made the same one in his position. It didn't ease the trembling of her shoulders as she restrained herself from reaching out to him. Her glassy-eyed reflection stared at her, looking smaller than it had moments ago.

"Why couldn't we stay children forever? We weren't supposed to end up this way."

"If we stayed the same, we would be no closer to peace."

"I'll never have peace."

"We would've been happy," he said. She tried to tune him out, but she was unsuccessful. "We would've had a good life. But you would always have run the Campaign, sooner or later, and I couldn't be the person you need. I wasn't meant for that life."

She squeezed her eyes shut.

He continued in her silence. "It's okay to let go. Please, let me go. Be happy."

She wiped away the smudges under her eyes and nodded. Her muscles strained into a false smile. If he wanted to help, she had to focus on that. Save her tears. "I need one thing. Have someone take me to Leianna and James."

He pressed his lips together. "Okay. I need one thing from you."

"And that is?"

His mouth opened and closed before he finally decided to speak. "Dance with me. One last time."

She should have said *no*. Her head screamed at her not to, but her body moved like a puppet on strings. A final dance before they parted. This was what she had craved for the past three years. Closure.

His touch rested weakly against her waist. Their movements were slow, clumsy. They returned to an embrace reminiscent of that goodbye on the beach, a swaying grasp like trying to hold water in her hand. The hourglass trickled away, taking him along with its sands. This would be the last time she would lose him.

She pressed her cheek against his chest, but she did not cry. A smile crept onto her lips. Grief had become a familiar friend, and this time, she would walk with it hand-in-hand.

As the orchestra drew its final notes, she pulled away, memorizing the glint in his eyes. "Thank you," she whispered, "for coming back to me."

He fastened his vest, fixed his hair, and walked to the door. She let herself imagine, just for a moment, what it would be like for her to be the one meeting him at the altar. That would have happened, a lifetime ago. It no longer felt like a future of her own. A new vision replaced it, the memory of the setting sun illuminating Isaac's skin, sealing their promise in golden rays.

When Phillip looked back, he said, "There's something else."

She waited for him to respond.

"Tell my family I'm not a traitor."

THIRTY-FIVE
ALEXANDRIA

Alexandria's muscles tensed as a soldier led her down into the bunker once more.

He nodded to the single guard at the door. They must have assumed the cells would hold the least amount of risk, with the wedding happening at just that moment. She bit her cheek harder when she thought about it. The metallic taste of blood warded away the memories she and Phillip shared. Though their love was not the same as it had been, he was one of her dearest friends, and Natania could never change that.

"Tobin's orders," the soldier said. The two passed without issue.

Alexandria attempted to place the name, but she came up empty. As long as she could get James and Leianna out, it didn't matter who she owed a favor to. Her mind fixated on two things: Amira and the bombs.

The soldier unlocked the first cell, letting Leianna into the corridor. Thankfully, her cuffs had been removed over the past few days. She watched the soldier with furrowed brows as he released James.

"I don't know why they're helping us," Alexandria said before her captain could ask anything. "Phillip did it."

When the soldier passed, Leianna snapped his rifle from his shoulder in the blink of an eye. The soldier simply raised his hands.

"Looks better this way," he said, though his lips drew into a grim line. "You have thirty minutes before the next shift begins."

"Where next?" Leianna asked.

"Thirteenth floor," Alexandria said. She shot a short apology to the soldier as they hurried into the hall. The guard stationed outside also surrendered quickly, handing Alexandria his rifle with Leianna's aimed at him.

This "Tobin" must have powerful connections.

She prayed the soldiers wouldn't call for backup as the three ascended the staircase. Their boots thudded against the metal, the sound echoing around them. Alexandria told herself that they could find Amira and dismantle the bombs in thirty minutes. They had to.

The fluorescent lamps flickered on automatically as they made their way down the corridor. Some sections spasmed, and the volatile light sent bolts of pain through Alexandria's skull. She tried to picture the map, but her head ached too much to think clearly.

At the end of the hall stood a set of sturdy-looking double doors. "That has to be it," she said.

Amira had not indicated where *she* would be, only the lab's location. That realization made the bunker seem impossibly large. What if they couldn't find her?

The doors were locked. She cursed under her breath. Leianna attempted to kick them open to no avail.

"Give me the pins from your hair," James demanded. She removed two and handed them over. He bent them into shape and began to pick the lock.

"You remember?"

He had learned one summer after her mother's security team started locking the windows. That was their fault, of course, after having snuck out of City Hall. His new skill meant that they could continue to do so until the excitement wore off.

"Not something I would easily forget."

Leianna surveyed the space behind them. "I'm not going to ask."

"Don't worry," James said as the lock clicked open, "the only crime I ever committed was having a good time."

Rows upon rows of black-topped tables lined the lacquered floor of the lab. The white walls hosted a collection of scuff marks, creating a marbled pattern above the baseboards. With the bunker being almost entirely metal, seeing a room that reminded her of a secondary school classroom gave her pause.

Four large cases rested on the floor at the opposite side of the room, visible over the lab stations. She approached them slowly, unsure whether they could kill her with a touch. If that were true, the scientists would be dead. Still, she kept a couple of meters between them. "I don't know what to do. We need Amira."

She studied the silver-colored latches on the front of the cases while Leianna and James explored the rest of the lab.

"How much time do we have?" Leianna asked.

James must have checked his watch, because he responded, "Twenty-five minutes."

Alexandria spun in a circle. They needed to move faster.

A dull clang sounded from somewhere in the room, followed by the grating of metal.

"In here!" shouted a muffled voice. She moved toward the sound, spotting a door in the corner.

"Amira!" James called as he ran for it.

Fortunately, the door was locked from the outside, and he didn't need to pick this one. He wasted no time in slamming it open, Amira skewing off-balance as she pushed against it. She fell into James, who wrapped his arms around her, tears sliding down his cheeks and into her hair. The sight made Alexandria want to collapse in relief, but their troubles were far from over.

She peered beyond them, seeing that Amira had been locked inside a cramped storage closet. A small bed had been set up, but otherwise, the space was empty.

"They kept you in there?" She did not recognize her own voice. Her muscles strained to keep stable, ready to jump into action—to burn this place to the ground.

Amira wiped her face. "It doesn't matter now." She inhaled, exhaled, and steeled her expression. "Grab the gloves from under that desk. James, you and I will deal with sabotaging the projectiles and remote detonation system. If we have time, we'll take the cores with us." Her eyes caught Leianna's. "Sorry, I don't know your name, but you and Alexandria need to go destroy the plans."

Leianna's gaze flicked to her watch, tracking every second. "Where?"

"They've been separated into four parts to keep any one person from stealing them and running. One part is in here. I'll take care of those. The other three are in the possession of the head developer, his assistant, and one of the scientists. Find as many as you can. It'll set them back for a few months, if not more."

Amira told them their names and where she thought their quarters might be, based on conversations she had overheard. That would have to be enough information.

Before running out of the lab, Alexandria embraced her. "If we're not back in fifteen minutes, go to the boat. You'll have to fight the guards, but you'll have more of a chance there. Leave us behind."

"I won't do that."

Alexandria looked to James, who paused before nodding. He, too, knew that Natania might keep her alive, but the others were disposable. They had not come this far for Amira to die.

Leianna held her rifle at the ready as they bolted down the stairs to the twentieth level. That was their best hope at finding some of the plans' pieces, if not all of them.

With one arm, the rifle proved unwieldy. Still, she kept it in hand, knowing that any protection was better than none.

Gunfire greeted them as they opened the staircase's exit door.

Leianna pushed her into safety. She peered through the entrance, fired twice, and ducked back inside.

Alexandria hissed through her teeth. "How many are there?"

"Four of them," her captain said, words emphasized by the bullets ricocheting off the wall.

She and the soldiers conversed through gunfire, calling and responding with piercing cries that made Alexandria's ears feel like they might bleed.

A dent appeared in the metal above her head, too close for comfort. With one last shot, Leianna motioned her forward.

The metallic scent of blood invaded her sinuses, and she swallowed down a gag. She avoided the bodies, red pools growing around them in halos. Each had a gory circle in the center of their foreheads.

"I knew I chose you for a reason." She regretted opening her mouth as soon as she did. Nausea rose in her throat at the taste of death. They might have deserved it, but she was the farthest thing from a worthy judge. There were no victors here.

This corridor had been constructed differently from the others, with textured walls that made it appear like a regular house. The white doors were chipped around the frames. A wooden sign hung from each of them, listing the names of those who lived there. Leianna kicked the first one open.

Inside, they found a simple room with minimal furnishings. Alexandria searched the desk while Leianna rifled through the armoire. Her heart raced as she dug through piles of papers. They were not organized in the slightest, just scattered within the drawers. To her dismay, most were untitled blueprints.

"Any luck?" she called to Leianna. The only response was the slamming of wood. She whipped around, finding her captain down to her elbows in the bottom of the armoire.

"I found a compartment," She withdrew a thick, folded square. "This must be it."

Alexandria ran over. "Do I just rip it?"

"Whatever you do, do it fast." She checked her watch. "Nine minutes until we have to be back upstairs."

Her fingers shook as she tore the paper into tiny pieces, hoping they would be impossible to put back together. She shoved some into the air vent, just in case.

They moved onto the next room. This time Alexandria found the plans under the mattress. She shredded them.

Leianna checked the hallway. "Six minutes. We need to go."

"One more piece. We can make it." Even while saying it, Alexandria didn't believe herself. But if Kevelda was to have the best odds of surviving, she needed to destroy them all.

They searched the third room and found nothing. The compartment was empty, and the plans did not rest under the mattress. Leianna shimmied open the vent cover, to no avail.

Alexandria swayed as she stood, leaning against the bed.

"We tried," Leianna said. "It's all we can do."

She wanted to argue, but she knew she was right. Her lungs fought for air. What if they didn't do enough? What if it was all for nothing?

Rearming herself with her rifle, she followed Leianna up the stairs. One floor. Two. Three. Four.

And then it started raining bullets.

They retreated to the previous landing, three floors from their destination. She looked down to find she had been nicked by one, blood trailing her arm. Gunbarrels blocked her view up the staircase. She counted five.

"They have higher ground." Leianna's voice shook as she dropped the rifle and lifted her hands slowly.

Her fear startled Alexandria into submission. She wanted to argue, to scream, to fight, but she mimicked her captain's actions instead.

Boots thundered against the stairs, growing louder until the sound crashed all around them. Silver uniforms clouded her vision, joined by searing pain as her arms were twisted behind her.

Before she knew it, she was thrown back into a cell.

This time, they shoved Leianna in along with her. James and Amira were already inside, the former leaning against the wall and the latter tucked into the corner of the bench. Alexandria pounded on the door with her shoulder, earning nothing but a bloodstain on her borrowed dress sleeve.

"You should have left," she snapped at James. "You should have taken her and gone home."

He didn't look at her. "We wouldn't have made it either way. The soldiers had the time wrong."

She dropped her forehead against the wall, not caring how much it hurt. Her throat constricted until her words were barely a whisper. "She's going to kill us all. It should've just been me."

Amira came up next to her. "We did our job. It'll take a few months for them to rebuild the bombs, and that's if they have all the plans."

"They don't."

"Exactly. You did well."

"Only because of you. Thank you." She rested her head on Amira's shoulder. With their hands bound, she could not hug her friend like she wanted to.

Eight months had passed without knowing if she was okay, always fearing the worst. And the worst had happened—Amira had been imprisoned, brought out solely to do the tasks the scientists thought too risky for themselves. Imagining it made her ill.

"If we make it out of here, this will look great on my application to the University of Regia." Amira let out a small chuckle. It did not lighten the dread filling the room.

"If we make it out of here, I'm hiding you somewhere safe until this all blows over. Somewhere no one can hurt you." Alexandria sighed. "Or maybe not. I'd rather keep you in sight at all times. What did she do to you here?"

"I'd rather not talk about it." Her voice drained of emotion. She wouldn't burden them with the knowledge, though Alexandria wished she would. It would be easier for both of them to carry the pain. The hope of discussing it later dimmed with every second. Natania would kill them now.

An eternity passed before the door slammed open. Natania stood in the doorway, fury painted in the furrow of her brows. Her white dress made Alexandria want to scream.

Fear seized her diaphragm when she thought of Isaac. If they had been caught, chances were he and the rebels had been, too.

She did not have to wait for her suspicions to be confirmed.

"You thought you won," Natania said, her words dripping with venom. "You didn't. My soldiers received communication about the attack on Thaertos, and it put them on alert. I should've known you would go for the bombs."

"You should've," Alexandria gritted out. "You're not as smart as you think."

Natania's mouth curled into a smile that made Alexandria's blood curdle. "It doesn't matter. The mines may be inaccessible at the moment, but we will clear them. Your friends, however, won't have another chance."

Despite the accompanying soldiers' protests, she came into the room. Her breath was warm against Alexandria's ear as she whispered, "Your prince is dead."

THIRTY-SIX
ISAAC

They had spent two days surveilling the island before acting.

Isaac feared that moving any earlier would put Alexandria and the others at risk, but as another ship docked at the makeshift port, he couldn't pass up the chance. Ten of them would go in on the inflatable raft and pose as workers. Five would station themselves in the woods, waiting to lead any escapees back to the boat. The rest would stay behind and watch for their cue to pick up the team: an explosion. One of the rebels had brought a couple of bombs that were originally created to attack Alexandria. This was a much better use for them.

The thought of her sent his pulse racing. That occurred often, but now, with her in Dane and them being married, it was impossible to know whether fear or longing spurred the reaction. He would've fought tooth and nail to make it back alive before, but now? Nothing could stop him.

Isla stuffed the explosive underneath her shirt, the outline covered by her jacket. He followed suit. Seeing her face without a smile on it unsettled him.

The salt in the air stung his eyes as they dropped into the raft and paddled toward land. He scrutinized the shoreline, squinting in the darkness, and located a spot deserted enough that they wouldn't be noticed.

His heartbeat thundered in his ears. They had to do this right. If they failed, not only would they die, but Alexandria would, too. She could be dead already if Natania didn't believe her story. He pressed his fingertips into his chest. *Stop panicking or you'll get them all killed.*

Evangeline and Mendoza had secured him desirable positions in the Argentum, but they had never put him in charge of a team. It would've cast too much light on him, visibility he couldn't afford as their pawn. He wasn't meant to be a leader, and he had no experience that would help him now. No wonder Alexandria had argued so much at the beginning of the Campaign. His decisions didn't just affect him, but everyone under his guidance.

It doesn't matter now, he reminded himself. *We're already here.*

Ten meters away from the beach, he took an oar and directed the raft toward a tangle of trees. The group jumped out, water lapping against their shins, and clambered into the forest beyond the sand. Scattered rocks and logs tugged at his pants as they made their way to the center of the island.

Hours passed in silence. When the first light of morning painted the sky in pastels, he led the team uphill until he spotted a line of workers entering through a gate. Beyond it stood a massive mountain face, sharp and unforgiving. An uneven opening marred the cliff, leading into a dimly lit tunnel. He couldn't see more than a few meters into it from where they hid.

One by one, they weaved into the line, mimicking the downturned gazes and slumped shoulders of those around them.

The woman next to Isaac whispered so softly he thought she might be speaking to herself. Her stringy hair could have been bright red, but it was caked with a dark substance. She walked with a slight limp. "Are you here to rescue us?"

He flicked his eyes up to the guards in front of them, but they didn't look back. "Yes," he said, "but I need to know everything about what we're walking into."

She inclined her head ever so slightly to the side. "That way's the barracks. In front of us is the mine. The gate has one entrance, one exit. Same goes for the mine itself."

He rolled that information around in his head. "Think people are up for some chaos?"

Only the edge of her smile was visible. "You start it, and they'll join."

That was all the hope he needed. While half his team was waiting back on the boat or in the woods, there were enough people here to outnumber the soldiers. Five or six hundred workers, he guessed, and fifty soldiers out in the open, each one armed with a rifle. He wouldn't worry about the ones he couldn't see. They didn't have the luxury of good odds either way.

His muscles braced reflexively as he approached the four soldiers at the gate. One prodded him with his gun. He winced at the jolt in his side, suppressing the urge to fight back. Every few meters, a soldier stood and watched them trudge along, weapon ready.

Dust dropped from the tunnel's ceiling in a swirling smoke that burned his throat. He coughed, joining a chorus of others who did the same.

A soldier handed him a pickaxe and ordered him to go to the western sector. He followed the woman beside him, who headed to the same destination. She told him that they had exhausted the ore deposits in the northern tunnels. Their job was to find new ones.

The other half of the workers would be sent to the eastern quadrant. He would have to get them out before he set off his explosive and blocked the exit. The space seemed to shrink when he couldn't find Isla in the mass of bodies. She must have been sent there as well.

When he reached the front of the line, a soldier directed him to an alcove in the rock wall. That would be his position for the shift. He swung the pickaxe, the impact reverberating into his torso, vibrating his teeth. He set his jaw and began chipping away at the stone.

Out of the corner of his eye, he watched the soldiers as they surveilled the others. One soldier every ten meters. About six workers in between them. Six-to-one would be great odds if the soldiers didn't have rifles on their shoulders. He calculated how quickly he would have to move to avoid anyone being hit. It wasn't the soldier he would attack that he had to worry about, but the other ones who would point their guns directly at them.

Let's see what six pickaxes can do against a rifle.

He waited until the soldier had turned his back before he drove the pickaxe in between his shoulders. Blood sprayed across his face when he pulled it out. The soldier gasped and fell. Bile rose in Isaac's throat, but he had no time to think about how many people he would have to kill today. He pulled them both into the recess, using the limp body of the soldier as a shield.

A bullet whizzed past him. He took the rifle and aimed at a soldier to his left. Before he could take the shot, a pickaxe sliced into the soldier's leg. The workers had joined the fight.

He dove out of the alcove, firing at the soldiers blocking his way to the exit. Most were preoccupied with attacks from all sides. A worker fell in front of him, blood pouring from a hole in his throat. Isaac shouted at those behind him to get out of the mine. The world swarmed around him, dirt-covered miners and lantern-lit stone blurring together.

One of the rebels picked up a rifle from a fallen soldier. She let out a guttural yell as she raced forward. Some of the workers followed her lead, dropping their pickaxes and taking on guns. The rebel cleared the way to the main tunnel, ducking and dodging as she ran. He trailed behind her, making sure everyone escaped.

This is too easy. Sure, they outnumbered the soldiers, but why hadn't any more come? Wouldn't they have heard the gunfire?

Pain erupted in his leg. The impact of the bullet set his nerves ablaze. His teeth ground together as he aimed at the soldiers ahead. Red exploded from his rebel companion's chest. She crumpled onto the floor.

And then there were nine.

Isla burst out of the eastern sector's opening, sweat and blood carving tracks through the grime on her face. Three rebels flanked her with rifles in their hands.

He fired at the shadows backlit by the sun at the mouth of the mine. It was a natural chokepoint, stemming the flow of soldiers into the cave, but also making it impossible for the miners to exit quickly.

Desperate for refuge, he hid behind a chunk of unmined rock. Every few seconds, he twisted and shot at another soldier. Each thud of a body chipped at his heart until it ached. Blood drained from his chest and his thigh in equal measure.

Isla slid across the stone, careening into the wall next to him. "They're sending in reinforcements. This is bad."

"Did you get the miners out?"

"As many that survived. I heard the gunshots too late. The soldiers started firing on us before they went to look for you. That *was* you, right?"

He clenched his jaw and nodded. "We'll set a bomb back here and one at the entrance. Cave this place in."

She took out the explosive and spun the timer to thirty seconds. "I'll set the one here, but I need you to cover me."

As he moved to the opening, leaping from one covering to the next, he only recognized three people in the fight. Dozens of bodies scattered the floor. Avoiding them was like navigating a minefield. A couple of workers dropped their pickaxes and raised their hands in surrender as the soldiers filtered in. They ran past him in his hiding place, training their guns at Isla.

He picked two of them off, but it was no use. She stood in the middle of the tunnel twenty meters down. Lantern light glinted off the bomb's casing as she held it high in the air. Her fingers spun the dial, and the earth held its breath.

She flashed him a final smile, this one painted in defiance, before an explosion engulfed her and the soldiers around her.

White spots marred his vision. He shielded his head against the shards of rock that flew at him. They scratched along his neck and hands. When he looked back, a wall of fallen rock was all that remained.

The soldiers at the mouth of the cave retreated, but those not caught in Isla's explosion turned their weapons on him.

His leg buckled as he lunged for the exit. A dark stain spread across the fabric below his knee. Bone-shattering pain exploded from the spot, forcing his muscles to give up their fight. Another jolt to his left side pushed him to the ground. Rocks lodged in the gash on his thigh as he pulled himself along with his elbows.

Blood coated his arm when he retrieved the bomb from under his shirt. The sun lit his fingertips, but he couldn't make it any farther. A rattling breath escaped his lips. He whispered for his mother before setting the timer to ten seconds, squeezing the detonator, and tossing the explosive down the tunnel.

He stared death in the face, and it pointed the muzzle of a gun back at him.

THIRTY–SEVEN
ALEXANDRIA

The soldiers had been smart to keep her hands cuffed.

A guttural cry tore from her lips, sharp blades of anguish slicing her throat. She tried to lunge at Natania but fell to her knees instead. Natania's smirk blurred. The door sealed shut, silent underneath the sound of her sobs.

She had to pull herself together. Her mind screamed at her to stop, but her chest ached. *He's dead. Isaac's dead.*

It couldn't be true. Natania was lying, she told herself. But the heaving breaths, the lack of oxygen, that was all real. Her shoulders shook. Pain echoed through her limbs as her muscles wound tighter and tighter. She curled into herself, pressing her forehead against her knees. Her face went numb.

Amira clung to her side, unable to wrap her restrained arms around her. Tears joined the bloodstains on Alexandria's dress. She started to gag, but without food in her system, nothing came up.

James explained to Amira who Isaac was, what he had meant to her. No one could know that in full. She had pushed Isaac away so many times, thinking she would lose him, but she had finally allowed herself to hope they had a chance. They had fought for each other, over and over again.

She should have never told him to go to Thaertos. That regret could kill her, if not her body, then her soul.

Grief is a terrible friend.

Time must have passed, but she didn't feel it. When she looked up, Amira was still at her side. James and Leianna spoke in conspiratorial whispers on the bench. His gaze was glassy, as if he wasn't quite present.

Isla.

Alexandria swallowed down the phlegm in her throat and moved next to him. "I'm sorry, James. I'm the reason this happened. I stretched us too thin. I—"

"Don't apologize," he said. "We both knew it would happen with what we were doing. One of us would die."

His nonchalant tone was the first indication that she shouldn't believe him. It was too practiced, like they had rehearsed it together. She had never seen that look behind his eyes. *Haunted.*

James wouldn't open up, not here. They needed to move.

"Natania knew something she shouldn't," she said. "She mentioned Isaac being a prince. That means there's a spy in Victori."

She tried not to think too much farther into Natania's words and what they might mean for her crew.

Leianna ran a hand over her jostled ponytail. "And she knows about your deal with Argon."

"We have to get out of here. We need to warn him. His people will die because of me." She struggled against her cuffs. Looking behind her, she found blood coating her wrists. Her teeth ground together.

James stood and fumbled around in his back pocket. He pulled out the pins from earlier. "I might be able to unlock the cuffs, but I'll need someone to tell me what I'm doing."

He went back-to-back with Amira, fumbling with the pins as Alexandria narrated his actions. Leianna peered out the window. Her eyes ran over the doorframe, looking for weak points. The entire room was metal, so Alexandria did not expect much, but if anyone knew how to get out, it would be her.

A minute passed, then two, before James was able to shimmy the cuffs open. Amira sighed and shook out her hands. She took the pins, and then James had to teach her how to pick a lock. With her mechanical mind, it didn't take long for her to catch on.

Once James was freed, he released the other two. Alexandria inspected the gashes lining her wrists. The graze on her upper arm throbbed, though it wasn't bleeding as furiously as before. It could have been much worse. That was one thing to be thankful for.

"I'm going to get the guards to come in here," Leianna said.

James's eyes widened. "We don't have weapons."

Leianna ignored him and rammed her shoulder against the door. The banging echoed painfully through the tight space. A soldier shouted from outside, yelling for her to quiet down. She persisted until they heard the sound of metal sliding.

When it opened, she yanked the soldier forward and pushed the door shut. Other soldiers tried to force their way inside, but James and Amira pressed their bodies against it. Alexandria threw her palm at the woman's nose before kneeing her in the stomach. The soldier doubled over, blood dripping on the floor.

Leianna took the rifle slung across her shoulder. She nodded to James and Amira, who jumped away from the entrance. Soldiers swarmed inside. Alexandria wrapped her arm around one's neck, dropping them both to the ground. Gunshots rang out, piercing her ears as the sound ricocheted across the walls. Two of the soldiers fell.

Alexandria swiped the knife from the man's side, sliding it between his ribs. Her chest heaved at the ease of which the blade pierced his skin. His eyes rolled and he slumped over. She tossed him off of her, throwing his rifle to James.

Amira struggled against a soldier, her wrists in the man's grip. Alexandria did not blink before lodging her knife between his shoulder blades. He would haunt her soon enough.

The resulting silence was broken by their ragged breaths and the groan of a soldier who had not yet died. She bent down and gripped the woman's hand, holding it for a moment before taking her weapon and giving it to Amira. James gave her brief instructions on how to shoot the rifle. It would be enough to protect her, even without practice.

They would need all the help they could get once they made it aboveground.

The walls blurred around her as they ran through the bunker. She fought with her own mind, forcing it to focus as images of Isaac's dead body shoved into her thoughts. The knife's handle dug into the sensitive scars on her palm.

Leianna shot the soldiers at the opening of the corridor. Alexandria did not look at their bodies. She kept moving, kept fighting, kept breathing. Saving Victori motivated her to stay upright, even as the world crashed down around her.

Harsh, frigid air assaulted her lungs when they staggered outside. She gasped, making the pain worse. It cleared her head for a split second, nothing more. In the rapidly dimming evening light, her sight narrowed on Leianna, who led them behind buildings and through alleys.

They ducked into the shadows of an isolated plaza. Leianna whispered, "I remember seeing this building from the ship. If I'm correct, we're heading in the right direction."

"And if you're not?" James asked.

"You don't need me to answer that." She turned to Amira. "Do you remember anything that might help us?"

Amira picked the skin at her lips. "They didn't let me outside. When they took me to Regia, they put me in a vehicle with tinted windows."

Leianna cursed, setting her mouth into a sharp line. "We'll keep moving."

Alexandria's legs groaned as she rose from the light blanket of snow and readied herself to run. Her bare shins stung in the cold.

"Wait," a girl's voice called from behind them. Leianna snapped the barrel of her rifle toward the noise.

Alexandria's heart skipped a beat. "Cassandra?"

The princess stood there with her hands raised. Her pale blue gown shimmered in the streetlights, dirt spattering the hem. "Let me help you."

"How do I know we can trust you?" Her teeth chattered as she spoke.

Cassandra's gaze fell. "I don't recognize Natania anymore. She killed my parents. Is that enough?"

"You'd become a traitor for revenge?"

"I want my sister back." There was a fire beneath her statement, desperation that flowed from her straightened spine. "But that will never happen. It's too late for her, but not for Genea. There are still good people here."

Alexandria inhaled and exhaled, weighing her options. "Come with us. Get us to the boat, and we'll figure out what to do next."

She caught Leianna's eye, and after a moment, the captain pointed her rifle at the ground.

Cassandra let out a small sigh and lowered her arms. "I know a way."

The princess led them around the city with ease. They didn't cross any soldiers, but Alexandria knew better than to let her guard down. If they weren't here, they were somewhere else. Somewhere like Victori, which had no warning.

Or Regia, which would crumble under their attack.

The docks answered that question for her. There were at least twenty soldiers, all outfitted with rifles and blades. Three stood on the deck of the trawler: two at the door to the cabins below, and the other pacing along the top of the gangway, her head on a swivel.

Leianna narrowed her eyes. "James, Amira, and I will draw their fire. You and the princess take out the ones on the boat."

Cassandra twisted her hair up and jammed it into place with a comb. She drew two long-bladed daggers from the back of her gown. James's jaw fell open. They did not have time to bask in the revelation that Cassandra was armed and potentially dangerous, but Alexandria would have serious questions later.

The two snuck around to the building on the opposite side of the pier, and then Leianna opened fire. The soldiers spun around, searching for the source. A few dropped dead before the rest hid behind crates and railings for cover. With the guns pointed elsewhere, they ran forward, ducking out of sight. The soldiers were too preoccupied to notice.

Alexandria waited for the soldier by the gangway to turn. She bolted up the plank, sliding and slicing the back of the woman's ankle. The soldier crumpled but did not lose her grip on her rifle. Alexandria squeezed her eyes shut, waiting for the shot to ring out.

Instead, the soldier shouted, a blade protruding from her wrist. Cassandra grunted and ripped the dagger from her arm, throwing it at one of the other soldiers. It hit him square in the chest.

Alexandria grappled with the fallen soldier, the woman's blood hot against her cold skin. The soldier pinned her to the deck. Alexandria slammed her forehead into her nose and launched her knee at her pierced wrist. The woman let out a low scream and rolled to the side, but not before Alexandria stabbed the blade into her shoulder. She didn't want to kill anyone else, but she would if she had to. Her and Isaac's kingdoms counted on it.

The soldier retreated, her back pressed against the railing.

"I'll let you live," Alexandria gritted out, "if you jump into the water."

Resolve flashed in the soldier's eyes. A muscle jumped in her jaw. Alexandria gripped the knife, swallowed down her nausea, and began to twist. The soldier cried out.

"Please," Alexandria whispered.

She dragged the soldier upright with the handle. Unbidden tears streamed down the woman's face. With a pained snarl, she lifted a leg over the railing and fell backwards. Alexandria watched her collide with the icy sea, waves crashing against the side of the boat. She did not wait for her to resurface.

Cassandra threw open the cabin doors, letting the crew out from underneath. The two other soldiers lay in pools of blood. Alexandria called for Claire and Eric to ready the boat. Elsie jumped into action, cutting the mooring ropes with a jagged blade.

Below on the dock, five soldiers still remained. They started to turn their weapons to the boat.

"Take cover!" Alexandria yelled. James and Amira ran out of their hiding place, firing haphazardly as they positioned themselves closer. Leianna picked off one more soldier before doing the same.

Alexandria's heart thudded against her chest. She ripped the rifle from one of the dead soldiers and dropped onto her stomach. The swaying of the boat made it difficult to aim. She balanced the rifle against the deck, pointed at a soldier below, and pulled the trigger.

The bullet hit the soldier's side. He dropped his weapon and crouched behind a crate, still visible to her. She hoped he was wounded enough not to try anything else.

James and Amira sprawled onto the boat just as Leianna took out the last soldier. Between the buildings ahead, Alexandria saw something that made her forget to breathe.

A silver mass was running straight for them.

"Leianna! Hurry!" she shouted, aiming once again. Her gun would be useless against the swarm of soldiers. She couldn't even count them all.

Leianna bolted from her shield, shooting into the distance. Bullets rained down on her. She zig-zagged, moving as quickly as she could.

Elsie called out that the lines had been cut. Claire shouted orders to the crew. Alexandria could do nothing but watch as the boat drifted away from the pier.

She's going to make it. She has to.

She shot into the army, which had come close enough that she could make out their faces. When Leianna broke into a straight run, Alexandria dropped her gun. Her fingers squeezed the railing as her captain ran up the gangway, like she could keep it steady through sheer will alone.

The unstable plank slipped under the pressure of Leianna's weight. Her jaw clenched and brows furrowed as she pushed the last few meters.

The gangway fell.

James shot out his arm, catching her outstretched hand. He and Eric dragged her onto the boat.

They all lay still until the sound of gunshots faded. Alexandria peeled herself up, chest heaving. She staggered over to where James held Leianna, who shook visibly on the deck. The sight would have made an impression if her mind wasn't so numb.

She surveyed the rest of the crew. Others had started to rise, dusting snow off their damp clothes.

All but Elsie.

James saw the blood before she did.

THIRTY–EIGHT
ALEXANDRIA

A few hours into their journey, they gave Elsie's body to the sea.

Alexandria did not want James to have to see his sister decompose. *Let him remember her as she was, not as a corpse.*

They rested her gently in an inflatable raft. Amira braided her long red hair into a crown. James held her pale hand, unmoving and unresponsive. His eyes were hollow. Both Elsie and Isla, gone. Alexandria recognized the nothingness. They had all felt it before with Phillip, and they would go through that process again. And again. And again.

Stumbling over her words, she recited a benediction, shock shattering her memory. It did not matter, in the end. Not a single one of them was really listening. Elsie would have liked it, though.

The waves dragged her body away, the fire of her hair visible into the breaking of day. It disappeared when the sun came overhead.

James stood watch until the light started to dim again. Amira rested her head against his arm, pleading with him to eat something. He disappeared belowdecks without a word.

Amira hesitated, her gaze returning to the horizon before she turned to follow. Tears stained her cheeks, but her eyes shimmered with more than sorrow. Something like longing lined her upturned brows. When she caught Alexandria looking at her, she brought a hand to her mouth.

"It's weird to see the sky. I don't know how people stayed in that bunker," she said.

It took all the strength Alexandria had left to give her a small smile. "That's why we have to make sure these weapons never exist again."

"No one should have them." Amira looked at the deck, running her shoe across it. "But I'll admit, building them felt powerful. *I* was powerful. The scientists were afraid, but I wasn't. I held in my hands the one thing that could keep Sam safe. Does that make me a bad person?"

Alexandria wrapped her arm around her shoulder. "No. It just makes you human."

She had done worse things to keep her loved ones safe. Fear had consumed her, rendered her immobile, when her people needed her most. And now, so many of them were dead.

They joined the group belowdecks, sitting at the crowded table in the kitchen. James simply stared at his food, but that was better than nothing.

She fought to keep herself together. They had lost too much to let Natania win now. Her hands shook as she set her fork down.

"We need to talk about what's next." Her voice cracked. She cleared her throat and tried again. "Cassandra, you mentioned that Natania killed your parents and took their place. That it was tradition."

James stood and left, still silent. Alexandria swallowed, taking a sip of water to relieve the tightness in her chest. Amira touched her arm before following him out.

Without the blood of battle on her, Cassandra looked far too young to be their only hope. She was just a girl. Her fingers tapped against the table in a frantic pattern. "You knew Phillip, didn't you?"

"I did. I loved him once." Perhaps the emotions of their escape lowered her guard. Otherwise, she wouldn't have admitted it.

Cassandra caught her gaze, and her fidgeting stopped. "Our first ruler after the Fall was killed by his son, my grandfather. He challenged his father to a fight. But his mother, my great-grandmother, sought to protect her husband. They fought side-by-side, but my grandfather still won. He took the throne, and in order to escape sanction, he codified the challenge."

Her expression darkened as she continued. "I guess Natania wasn't happy with the way my parents were handling the war. She challenged them. She won."

"And you could challenge her?" Alexandria asked, leaning forward. "You could take over."

Then, they could finally have peace.

"That's why she married him."

She was about to question what the girl meant before it clicked. To take the throne, Cassandra wouldn't just have to challenge Natania.

The marrow of her bones went cold, like her blood had stopped pumping. "You would have to kill him, too."

Cassandra nodded, staring at the plate before her. This sixteen-year-old girl would have to kill two people to save them all. She would have to kill Phillip.

Alexandria clutched her chest as if she could force her heart to calm. The room spun around her, leaving her grasping the edge of her seat.

Isaac. Isla. Elsie. Phillip. Too many ghosts. She would be haunted for the rest of her life.

Something shattered within her, broken pieces jutting out of her skin, pain searing her stomach. She rose, pressing her hand into the tabletop.

"Do it," she said. "No matter how much I beg when the time comes, do it anyway."

As she navigated to her quarters, she shed the last pieces of herself, the life she wanted, the dreams she held. Alexandria

Redmond died with them. Queen Alexandria of Kevelda had work to do. If she was to be the end of her line, she would secure her people's lives with her last breath.

She leaned back against the door, staring into the dark room before her.

And she wept.

~

A week later, she and Cassandra walked side-by-side into the Victorin throne room. Two future queens, ready to go into battle.

She gripped the folded piece of paper in her hand—the contract that she and Isaac had signed, that would secure their alliance even after his death. The one that had given her hope before Natania crushed it.

Argon watched them as they approached. His eyes roamed over the two, landing on where Leianna stood behind them. "Where's Isaac?" he asked.

Sofie tensed beside the throne, blood draining from her face at Isaac's absence.

"He's dead." The words sounded foreign coming from Alexandria's mouth. Too tangible, too final.

Argon's cheeks reddened. "You got him killed. I should never have trusted you." Sofie tried to intervene, but he cut her off. "We have nothing! Now, we are at war, and the throne has no heir. You have destroyed us, Alexandria, all for your kingdom. Are you happy?"

"I'm here to warn you. Natania knows of our alliance. Her army will be here soon, I don't doubt it," Alexandria replied. "And no, I am not happy. You might have just discovered your grandson's existence weeks ago, but all you care for is your legacy. I care for *him*."

"We have no more alliance. When they come, I will surrender you to them immediately."

"You'll rethink that in a moment." She clenched her jaw and unfolded the paper. Her eyes stung as she approached Sofie, but she would not let herself cry. Not yet. Argon's gaze pierced her skin as she handed the paper to the princess.

Sofie looked at her with raised brows before reading it. She held a hand over her lips, lines forming on her face in concentration.

Alexandria stepped back before the throne. She steeled her voice, proclaiming to the almost-empty room. "Victori has a living heir," she said. "Me."

Argon's mouth hung open. Sofie let out a choked laugh, dropping the paper as she chuckled and cried at once. She fumbled for it, handing it to Argon with shaking fingers.

"What did you do?" Accusation laced his question.

Alexandria did not give him time to read it.

"I married him. I am the heir to Kevelda's throne and to yours. You wanted a way out of this war?" She gestured to Cassandra, and the princess stepped forward. "It's us. Three kingdoms together as one."

The king simply stared. Sofie watched him intently. He rose from the throne, making jagged, uneven movements, before coming to a stop a few meters ahead of her.

"We will not win," he murmured.

"Then it appears we will fall either way. People died because I didn't make a choice sooner. Whether or not you make the same mistake, I will go down fighting." She dared to take another step and held out her hand. "Join us."

The air grew thick. Time stretched out between them.

And he shook her hand.

EPILOGUE

Isaac existed in a sea of darkness and light, of agony and numbness, all alternating without end.

Suddenly, stillness.

His eyes burned underneath the bright light. He tried to block it out with a hand, but still his pupils ached. Cool metal pressed into his palms as he pushed off the ground. Pain seared through his legs, and he knelt back down.

"Hello, Isaac," a man said. When his eyes adjusted, it took him a moment to place the face. *Phillip.*

Isaac clutched his side, finding the outline of a bandage through his shirt. The pressure of his touch sent a jolt through the bullet wound he knew he would find there. Memories of Thaertos flooded into his mind. Isla was dead.

"Am I the only one?" His throat scratched, dryness in his mouth making his words thick. He couldn't remember the last time he had drank anything. *How long have I been out?*

Phillip nodded as he clicked the metal door shut behind him. Isaac took the tray of food that he held out. His stomach twisted in hunger, but the thought of Isla triggering the explosion made it difficult for him to pick up the fork. He sipped the water slowly, keeping an eye on Phillip's movements.

"Why did she save me?" he asked. "She could have let me die."

Phillip leaned against the wall and coughed into his fist before responding. "If you were dead, she would lose a bargaining chip."

Natania would use him to get back at Alexandria. *Of course.* His mind raced, trying to determine if there was any way she would know about what he and Alexandria had done, uniting their two kingdoms.

He took another sip. "Always a queen's pawn."

"That makes two of us." Phillip glanced at the corners of the ceiling as if looking for something.

"Why are you here?"

"A friend of Alexandria's is a friend of mine."

You might feel differently if you knew I was her husband, he thought. "I don't mean right now. Why are you with Natania?"

"She took me out of the mines a little over a year ago. Now, here we are." The man didn't appear inclined to say more.

Isaac could only hope that Phillip was using his proximity to the queen in Alexandria's favor, but he wasn't so quick to give him the benefit of the doubt.

Still, his brain latched onto the words. Only eight months had passed since the Campaign. Why would Natania even think of searching for him if she hadn't known that Alexandria was the heir?

"Here we are," Isaac repeated under his breath.

Phillip started for the door, resting his hand on the handle. "Make sure you eat your food."

The seeping piece of meat was the last thing on Isaac's mind. He wished he had a piece of paper to write a timeline on.

If Natania knew enough about Alexandria to realize she could use Phillip to her advantage more than four months before the Campaign, then Evangeline wasn't the sole person privy to Alexandria's heritage. Mendoza could've shared that information with Natania—but Isaac only told him about Evangeline's plan to poison herself two months before they enacted it, and Evangeline would never have let his father, or anyone, find out about Alexandria before then. Keeping secrets was her specialty.

He set the tray on the floor and tried to stand again. His resulting gasp echoed across the confined space. But he couldn't sit, not with the calculations running in his head. With all his weight on one leg, he shuffled to the wall and pressed his hand against it.

Natania was the one person who could rival Evangeline as a mastermind. This entire time, they both had been playing a game with their peoples' lives. The enemy queen had discovered Alexandria when no one else in Kevelda had, when she had been a young child at the time of Alexandria's birth. A spy could have told her that information, passed it down from father to daughter...

Or his wife was more connected to Genea than they all realized.

As he stared into the metallic reflection in front of him, Isaac began to think about Alexandria's biological mother.

ACKNOWLEDGEMENTS

It's hard to believe that by the time you're reading this, I'll have started writing the last book in the *Paper Castles* trilogy. That makes me far too sentimental for sequel acknowledgements, but really, this is the beginning of the end for a series I've been thinking about for seven years.

Burned Queen would not exist without the support of my husband, family, and friends, who encouraged me (and brought me food) while I was in the depths of writing. Thank you for letting me talk *at* you about this. And mom, thanks for making me read those pesky banned books all those years ago.

There are always highs and lows in the creative process, but this book really challenged me in many ways. Thank you to my writing friends and Bookstagram community for motivating me to get this done. Though there are too many people to name, I want to give a special shout out to my beta readers—Manda, Tiara, and Amy—for pointing out things I never could've seen on my own (and fangirling at just the right moments).

Thank you to *you*, the reader, for putting up with my shenanigans for two whole books. I hope I didn't make you cry [she said, lying]. I promise your faves will be happier next time [she said, lying (???)]. Seriously, your comments and DMs gave me the courage to do this again, and I cannot wait for you to read book three.

Above all, I thank God for getting me through this year. On the days when I don't have the strength to stand, I know I can rest on Him.

ABOUT THE AUTHOR

Ellie Ember is an author who will read just about anything. From dystopian fantasy to gothic horror novels, Ellie is always looking for her next favorite book. This variety of interests doesn't end with genres; after changing her major between political science and psychology, to journalism, to communication, to anthropology, Ellie finally graduated with a Bachelor of Arts in English. She completed a thesis on the political implications of language in dystopian literature, writing double the required number of pages (*cue "Non-Stop" from *Hamilton**). In an alternate universe (from 9AM to 5PM), Ellie is a grad student pursuing a Master of Science in Library and Information Science. Yes, she writes a lot for that, too.

Ellie shares sneak peeks and mini-essays on Substack at *Ellie's Embers*. You can find her on Instagram @ellieemberwrites.